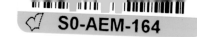

The Twisted Road of One Writer

The Birth of The Bregdan Chronicles

Book # 13 in The Bregdan Chronicles

Sequel to Horizons Unfolding

Ginny Dye

The Twisted Road Of One Writer

Copyright © 2018 by Ginny Dye

Published by Bregdan Publishing
Bellingham, WA 98229

www.BregdanChronicles.net

www.GinnyDye.com

www.BregdanPublishing.com

ISBN # 1724823779

Printed in the United States of America

Book # 13 of The Bregdan Chronicles 3

For Suess Dye – there are no adequate words to express my appreciation for the love, joy and life we share!

A Note from the Author

I never imagined I would write the book you are reading now. It was both a joy and a challenge to write, but in the end, I'm glad I did it.

I pushed aside my desire for privacy to connect with the amazing people who are my readers.

This book is for the readers of The Bregdan Chronicles. It's not a book about being a writer – it's a book about the birth of the series people all over the world have come to love.

It tells my story, but it also answers all the questions I have been asked through the years – at least as many as I remember.

I've had many requests for recipes of favorite Bregdan foods. They are included, but they're not in the format you might expect. They are actual recipes found in cookbooks from the Civil War years so they are done in true historical format. I suspect you'll have a hard time following some of them, but I also believe you'll get a kick out of trying! If you're yearning for great fried chicken and cornbread, you'll probably want to find modern renditions.

Truly, nothing gives me more joy than connecting and communicating with my readers.

This book is my gift to all of you who make my life, and my ability to write these books, possible.

Thank you from the bottom of my heart!

Sincerely,
Ginny Dye

Chapter One

The Day I Quit Writing

Some days stand out in your mind so clearly that you can remember every moment. You can remember every smell. Every thought you had. Every word that someone says. You remember that the sky was cloudless, and the day was hot and thick with humidity.

You remember it was a day that totally changed what you believed your life would be.

I had one of those days...

My story of being a writer begins the day I vowed I would never write. At least, I'm going to say it did. Of course, I imagine it started the day I was born, but this is a much more dramatic opening, so it will be more fun to start here!

A fiction writer knows the power of drama. When you have a day that totally changes your entire life, it should be given the proper credit. Back to the story...

I quit writing when I was 16.

That was the day fear swallowed my burning desire to create.

It was because of my grandfather.

*****

I'm going to warn you now that this book is not going to be a "straight line journey". Actually, I don't believe anyone's life is a straight journey. I believe we all travel many twisted roads to get to where we are right now. We experience things we don't believe are significant – only appreciating their significance years later when we're able to look back and see how each event fits into the grand puzzle of our complicated lives.

This book is not an autobiography. I'm not writing it to reveal every part of my life – just the parts that brought me to The Bregdan Chronicles. I'm not going to talk about all my relationships and mistakes – though you'll learn some of them. When I talk about my journey and where I'm living, it's just going to be me – at least until I get to the present. Things are far simpler that way!

It could be that my journey is more twisted than most, but if that's true it's what was necessary to prepare me to write. I savor and appreciate every moment now; even the ones I thought would destroy me.

I'll tell you more about my grandfather in a moment, but first I have to dive back into the years before I was 16. I've always loved to write, and I've always loved to read. I still have a vague memory of the day all the jumbled letters on a page made sense to me. I don't remember how old I was, but I do know I was reading at a college level by the time I was in the third grade.

The school librarian learned to not question what books I checked out. After many futile attempts of telling me I was too young for whatever book I had chosen, she smiled and waved me on.

The summers, when it became too dark to play ball or explore the woods near my house, were spent reading.

My mother took me to the public library every week. They had a limit of eighteen books that you could check out at one time. I would choose my eighteen books, and then hand my mother a stack of eighteen more so I would have enough to last the week.

The public librarians learned to not question my choices either, though I'm sure they didn't truly believe I was reading the books I walked out with. I'm not sure what they thought I was doing with them, but I couldn't miss the looks they exchanged with each other as they stamped my thick stack of books at the checkout. I'm sure they wondered what kind of mother would allow their daughter to check out adult books. No, they weren't erotic, just advanced beyond what the average third and fourth grader would read; at least, that's what they told me.

No matter... the books opened up worlds to me that I never knew existed. They gave me hope that my life could somehow be different.

I read.

And I wrote.

I wrote stories of worlds where people were loving and kind. I wrote about fun and laughter. I wrote about all the things I rarely experienced.

Back to the twisted road...

Once again, this book is not an autobiography. I accept that it entails revealing some of the details of my life, but only to explain how it is played out in the series that has truly captured my heart, mind and soul.

Yes, I read because I wanted my life to be different. Without going into unnecessary details, I'm just going to say that I had a traumatic childhood. My dad walked out when I was five. There was a lot of sexual, mental and emotional abuse from many different corners. The result of the abuse was that I became hard, shut off, and desperate for a love that wasn't there.

I found hope and reason to keep going through the books I read. I couldn't get enough of them because they were the only thing that made me believe life might be worth living. Surely, the writers couldn't be writing about a life that could never exist – even for someone like me.

I'll talk more about my healing from all the abuse later, but it's not necessary in this section of the twisted road.

Back to the day I was 16…

*****

To understand why I quit writing, I have to start with the story of my grandfather, Wallace Lorrimer Gaffney. He was Dandy to me.

Dandy was one of *the Gaffneys* of Gaffney, South Carolina. If you could hear my voice when I say that, you would hear the deep Southern, genteel drawl I can call on when I want. When I was sixteen, Gaffney was just a name to me. My parents had never taken me to Gaffney, but I'd heard a few stories. I've learned much more in the years since.

Gaffney, South Carolina was founded by my Great-great-great-great-great grandfather, Michael Gaffney. Captain Michael. His life could well be rich fodder for a novel, but that is not the purpose of this book so I'm going to keep this brief. Captain Michael arrived in New York City from Ireland in 1797, but left the city after Yellow Fever almost claimed his life. He eventually moved to

Charleston, SC, where malaria attempted to finish what Yellow Fever had failed to. Malaria failed, as well.

Eager to escape the low-country mosquitoes, Captain Michael moved to a little crossroads in Cherokee Indian wilderness country and decided to start a new life. His little general store grew into what is now Gaffney, S.C.

The few pages of Captain Michael's journals that I have read tell me my ancestor was quite a writer. Did my writing gift start with him? Go back further? I have no idea.

Back to Dandy... The Gaffney family was well-respected, revered, and they had high expectations for anyone who bore the Gaffney name. My grandfather was no exception. All seemed to be going as planned when he graduated from high school and entered The Citadel, a prestigious military college in Charleston, South Carolina.

He continued to fulfill the Gaffney expectations when he excelled at The Citadel. Before graduation, he was selected to be the new editor for the Gaffney newspaper. I can only imagine the excitement of this young man who was accomplishing all he had ever dreamed of. Dandy was on his way!

Until...

Until tensions in Europe exploded into World War I. Military students at The Citadel were among the first to be called into service. Instead of moving back to Gaffney and taking over the newspaper, Dandy found himself on his way to the battlefields of France.

Like so many of the young men headed into war, Dandy chose to get married before he left.

But, alas, his choice was not one the Gaffney family approved. Louise Leddingham was beautiful, feisty and strong – all wonderful qualities that were unfortunately overshadowed by the fact she was half-Cherokee. Gasp! A Gaffney heir was going to marry a half-breed? How could that be? I'm sure his family did their best to talk him out of doing this horrible thing that would bring dishonor to the family, but Dandy wouldn't let the Gaffney prejudices control his choices.

I have no idea what the wedding was like, or if anyone even attended, but he married his Louise – whom I knew as my beloved Nina – impregnated her and left for war.

This is where things got messier. In spite of how his family felt, Dandy had no choice but to send his new wife to live with his family in Gaffney until he returned from war.

Yes, I know this would be a great novel! Perhaps I'll live long enough to tell it, but for right now it's simply the story of my family, and the foundation of why I am who I am – and why I write The Bregdan Chronicles. Hang with me, and you'll understand all...

Back to Gaffney. Let's just say that the Gaffney family treated Nina horribly. They cared for her physically, especially after they found out she was pregnant with a *Gaffney* baby, but they were never kind to her.

When my mother was born, it got even worse. I sometimes wonder if Nina had any idea of what was about to happen.

My Great-Grandmother – Dandy's mother - prodded on by her family, decided a Gaffney baby would *not* be raised by a Cherokee half-breed. So... when my mother was born, they kidnapped her from Nina. I don't know the whole story of how it happened, but my writer's mind can easily fill in the details.

It did not end well.

Remember me saying Nina was feisty and strong? Let me just add that you didn't want to get in her way if she decided to do something, and you most certainly did not want to be on her bad side. I never heard the whole story of how Nina got my mother back, but she did. I wish I had been a fly on the wall!

I've seen pictures of my mother as a baby with her Gaffney relatives, but Nina is not in any of them. Bitter at how she had been treated, she refused to have anything to do with them. Who could blame her?

Dandy returned from World War I and the family moved to Charlotte, North Carolina because Nina refused to live in Gaffney any longer. Again, who could blame her?

Dandy's life was forever changed because of his family's bigotry and actions. He was a Citadel graduate and a decorated veteran, but his job as editor at the Gaffney newspaper was long gone, the economy was struggling, he had a new wife and child to support, and he couldn't return to the roots that would have opened doors for him. Not knowing what else to do, he spent his entire adult life in marketing – completely pushing aside his burning desire to write because he had a family to care for.

But Dandy never forgot his dreams. He also recognized that I had inherited his writing ability.

All I ever wanted to do was write.

I wrote endlessly. I dreamed of being a writer. I filled notebook after notebook with stories.   I amazed my teachers with my ability to use the written word.

I knew what I wanted to do.

Which leads me to the day I quit writing at age 16...

I remember that it was a hot, sunny day. I remember not realizing my dreams were about to die – smothered by an unreasonable fear.

Dandy was dying. He had been confined to bed for months. Nina had been caring for him, but he knew he was nearing the end.

I know *now* that his intention was to encourage me. I probably even knew on some level at the time, but it didn't change the outcome.

Dandy called me to his side, took my tanned hand in his white, withered one, fixed me with his glittering eyes and said, "Ginny, you have the gift that I never used. Whatever you do, don't let it go to waste like I did."

Two sentences.   Sentences uttered with burning intensity, meant to sear into my soul and fill me with passion to be a writer.

Two sentences that wrapped me in fear.

Why?

As soon as Dandy uttered those words, my brain started spinning. *What? The gift? I had the* gift*? What if I* didn't *have the gift? What if I couldn't really write the way he believed I could? What if I let him down? What if I wasted the gift like he had?* The questions rampaged through my mind and heart.

I stared back at him. Of course, I didn't speak any of the things pounding through my head. How could I tell my dying grandfather that he had just terrified me beyond all measure? I nodded mutely, managed a weak smile, and then fled from the room.

By the time I got home, I had made my decision.

I would never write again.

Yes, I know it doesn't make sense, but fear never makes sense, and I had the double whammy of all the years of abuse that had so wounded me. I just knew I couldn't face the specter of failure. I couldn't face the realization that I might not have the *gift*. I couldn't live with the knowledge that I might waste the *gift* and disappoint my grandfather. I couldn't live with discovering I wasn't good enough.

In my sixteen-year-old brain, the only way to avoid these horrible possibilities was to simply quit writing.

So I did.

Oh, I did school assignments of course, but ignored the pleas of my teachers to keep writing the stories they had grown to love. I was done.

I kept reading – diving into books more and more – but I wouldn't write. I wouldn't position myself for failure. The longer I refused to write, the larger the fear grew – until it was no longer a fear. It was *truth* to me. If I wrote, I would fail.

When I got to college, I took the required Freshman English class, but turned my academic pursuits in an entirely different direction, graduating with a degree in Outdoor/Environmental Education – which I loved! As in high school, I ignored the voices of my college professors who told me I had a special writing gift after they read my papers. So what? I just wanted to get a good grade.

I had made my decision. I would not be a writer.

You could talk me into trying just about anything else, but that topic was closed forever.

Until life brought me up short.

My twisted road took another turn...

Annie's Lemonade

2 cups sugar, 2 cup hot water, 16 cups cold water, 1-2 lemons sliced. In a large container, place sugar and hot water, and stir until sugar dissolves. Add lemon juice and cold water to fill container. Stir until well mixed. Pour lemonade over glasses of ice, squeeze slice of lemon on top of each.

Chapter Two

Once I made the decision to quit writing, I never looked back. There was too much living to do! There were too many adventures to experience.

One thing you should know about me is that I'm a wanderer at heart. I've moved 55 times (as of 2018) since I got out of school. And, yes, almost all of them were my choice. I knew there was a huge country that I passionately wanted to experience and explore.

So I did.

I've long been the renegade of my family. My two brothers and I were all born within 3 ½ years – with my brothers being almost exactly one year apart. I'm the youngest, and I have a sister nine years older than me. When it came time for me to graduate college, I was faced with the expectations my older brothers had established. Both of them had graduated with degrees in business, were hired by well-paying companies, and were well on their way to success.

Gag!

The very idea of following in their footsteps made me feel sick. I had no desire to be trapped in a *normal* existence. So, I did what any renegade does. I did my own thing.

I graduated from college, got a low paying job working for a ranch in Texas, loaded everything I owned into my

Volkswagen convertible and drove from North Carolina to Texas by myself. Let the adventures begin!

I've traveled extensively throughout 49 of the 50 states. I've crossed the country 14 times – taking 6 months... 3 months... 1 month...for a trip. If something is considered an adventure, I'm up for it!

I'm not someone who can sit at a desk in a cubicle for long hours. Wait! And now I'm a writer? Yes, but you'll understand more of that later.

I'm basically not the "Employee" type either, which explains why I've had very few jobs in my life. I much prefer owning the company and being the boss. I've done quite a bit of that. And loved it!

By the time I was 29 I had run the horsemanship program for a large ranch in Texas, led wilderness horseback trips in the coastal mountains of Oregon, worked with teenagers all over the country, and done several independent sales jobs because no matter where you live you can always make money in sales if you're good (which I was!).

I started working with high school students when I was twenty. Next to writing, teenagers are my passion. I love people in general, but teens are hands down my favorite part of the human population. I adore them! I love their energy, their passion to debate and argue anything (even if they have no idea what they're talking about), their enthusiasm for life, and their deep need to have adults understand and love them just as they are.

Put me in a room with ten 4-year-olds and I'll probably have a panic attack. What do you *do* with them!? Put me in a room with a hundred teenagers and I'm in heaven!

I've been an athlete all my life. If it has a ball involved, I love it. Especially tennis and softball.

I also adore horses. I started riding when I was twelve, and bought my first horse when I was thirteen. Her name was Sassy Saffanata Glory Be. Honest! It was her registered name when I bought her. I called her Saffanata.

I made my living for many years after college by combining my love of horses and teenagers. I've had marvelous experiences and adventures.

I was a runner. I *loved* to run. There is nothing like the feeling when you *run through the wall*, and then feel you can run forever. I've run all over America, experiencing as many trails and back country roads as I could.

I'm telling you all this so you'll understand how wrenching it was when I completely collapsed, and then didn't get out of bed for six months.

I was 29 years old.

I'm not going to bore you with the details of my illness, but it's a necessary addition to this book if you want to understand why I went against my vow to never write again.

I went from running eight miles a day, and playing tennis and softball for hours, to not being able to get out of bed. I had one of the first diagnosed cases of Epstein-Barr Virus and it was a doozy. I've battled it for the last thirty years – most of the times successfully, but sometimes not. I'll keep fighting until I've won the battle completely, but that's not what this book is about either!

The reason I'm telling you all this is because going from being massively active to not moving at all was devastating.

The only thing I could do was read. So I read. And read... and read... and read... 82 thick books and counting. Now don't get me wrong. I love to read. But there is a limit.

The day came when I thought if I had to crack the pages of one more book I was going to go out of my mind. But what was I going to do? I didn't own a television because I didn't want one. I had to do *something*.

Well... it just so happens all of this transpired at the same time in 1986 that Apple Computer came out with the very first MacPlus computer – the boxy thing that used floppy disks. I still don't know why they called them floppy disks since they were certainly not floppy, but I digress...

I had someone rig up some boards across my bed to act as a desk, plugged in my first computer, slapped in a floppy disk with instructions and learned how to use it. Then the question became, what am I going to *do* with it? This was before the days of the internet and email. My wonderful MacPlus computer was basically a sophisticated typewriter. I certainly had no use for one of *those*.

Until I did...

The day came when, faced with the prospect of reading another book or doing something on my fancy typewriter, I took a deep breath and started writing.

I really knew nothing about writing. I had taken only one required college writing course. I had certainly never studied it. All I had done was write stories until I was sixteen. And, no, I didn't keep any of them, so banish any fantasies of a collection of early stories. I destroyed them all. No one would ever have the opportunity to read them and tell me I wasn't as good as Dandy.

The one piece of advice that must have stuck from my one writing class was to "write about what you know about". I knew about teenagers and horses.

Lying in bed, typing away on that antique computer, I wrote my first book. A teen novel about horses and teenagers. 200+ pages.

I never had any intention of doing anything with it. Never planned for anyone to see it, and would have been horrified if I thought that might happen. I wrote that book to maintain my sanity while I figured out how I was going to get out of bed. At some point, I actually printed it out – perhaps just to prove to myself I did it – but I stuffed it in a manila envelope and vowed no one would ever see it.

I was also getting better. After six months, and with help from two marvelous chiropractors who became my good friends, I finally climbed out of bed and began my journey back to health.

Yes!

I put the manuscript for my first book at the bottom of a deep drawer and went back to living life. I left California and moved to Richmond, Virginia. I took over a struggling youth group for a church there and poured all my energies into the teenagers I love so much.

Until...

You'll find there are a lot of *untils* in this book, but I don't think I'm unique. All of us are living our lives, headed in a certain direction, *until...*

Until *life happens* and suddenly we have choices and decisions to make.

*****

Before I keep going with my story, I'm going to hit something head on.

I am asked all the time if the Bregdan Chronicles are Christian novels, and if I am a Christian writer.

Some people love that *Storm Clouds Rolling In* has held the #1 spot in Christian Historical Fiction for much of the last five years. Other people gnash their teeth that the books are so much about God. I also hear from readers who are quite upset that the later novels in the series don't focus on faith as much as they would like, and they think I've become too liberal. Others are thrilled.

I don't know what category you fit in, but I can tell you that I write *historical* fiction. Whether you're cheering or gnashing your teeth about my inclusion of God doesn't really matter to me. In the war-torn years of the 1860's, and the struggle of Reconstruction that followed, faith was incredibly important to people. Whether you agree with it or not, the church used differing interpretations of the Bible to support their positions – not really any different from today.

How could I possibly write about that time, and not include faith?

Many want to know about my own faith - wanting to label me with something that will make them comfortable. Do I have my own faith? Absolutely. I just hate being labeled, and I don't believe it's important enough to expound on...

Why not?

Bregdan Publishing is just one facet of what began many years before.

Fifteen years ago, I founded an organization called Together We Can Change The World. I now call it Millions For Positive Change, but its purpose is the same. I'll tell you more about it later, but regardless of its name, here is the philosophy I founded it with:

Every division of my company has been designed to have an impact on the world. What began as a mission to provide funding for charitable organizations all around the globe has turned into a movement of vast proportions that is growing explosively (including Bregdan Publishing).

There is so much division and separation in our world. People are separated by beliefs, by politics, by race, by religion... This separation and division are the cause of most of the problems in our world today. People can't work together to solve problems because they're too busy focusing on how they are different. The truth is that people have many more similarities than differences.

Millions For Positive Change *has reached beyond the divide and united Christian, Jew, Muslim, Hindu, Buddhist, New Age, Atheist, Agnostic...We embrace Black, White, Indian, Asian, Latino... We welcome a vast array of political beliefs... We welcome all sexual identities. We simply welcome PEOPLE – people who believe that by combining our gifts and hearts to make a difference, we can have a massive impact on our world.*

15 years later, that is still my philosophy. Millions For Positive Change, Bregdan Publishing, and every book I

write are the result of so many people's efforts. I want to tell you about The Bregdan Chronicles Team:

- I write the books - praying every day that each word will have an impact on the world. I include faith in most of my books because I believe almost every living being feels **some** kind of faith, as well as personally believing that life without faith is rather empty. Life in the 1800's in the U.S. meant that most people expressed their faith as Christian.

- The woman who has done every book cover is a talented graphic design artist from Pakistan who has become like a little sister to me. Iqra happens to be Muslim, and we have wonderful conversations about God's love – no matter how it's expressed.

- The woman who handles my Social Media postings is a Hindu from India. Priya is amazing and so very talented!

- I have two editors. One of them is a fabulous woman (I never asked her faith) from Oregon who is totally invested in making sure every book is perfect. Stephanie also creates what is now the three hundred page "Character Book" that enables me to keep track of everyone. I can't fathom doing what I do without her! As of the writing of this book she has two-year-old twins. I have no idea how she juggles all the areas of her life, but I am profoundly grateful!

My other editor is a new addition in 2017. Raised in the U.S., Katie married and moved to England. She is both a talented editor, and the narrator of my children's series. Her faith? I have no idea!

- My Marketing Director is a short, spunky, spiky haired, tattooed Texan (transplanted to Washington) with a heart as big as the outdoors. She is committed to helping me expose as many people as possible to The Bregdan Chronicles. She also happens to be my best friend of 39 years, and... (more on her later in the book)!

- My narrator lives here in the U.S. I've never asked her about her faith either, because I really just want to know she can bring the books to life in audio form. Tiffany loves The Bregdan Chronicles as much as I do!

Rather than put a label on my religion, I prefer to tell people I am committed to living my life from a place of love, acceptance and equality. I scour the world for people like *that*. I don't care about someone's religion. Or their past... or so many other things. I simply want to know who they ARE. I want to know if they live their life from a place of love. My great hope is that my books, my Blogs, and my life will inspire others to do the same.

Yes, when I first shared my position on religion in my Blog there were a few people who were appalled (I respect their opinion & position), but the vast majority were like the ones I'm going to share with you. These letters are proof of what I already knew - my readers are intelligent, thoughtful, caring, loving people. I feel so honored, privileged and humbled that I write books all of you are in love with. If possible, all your letters only *increased* my desire and commitment to give you nothing less than complete excellence.

Here are just a few of what I received:

I love that you are open to the world regarding your books. We all need to be more open. But I sometimes get caught up in the labels and have to work hard to remember we are all the children of a loving heavenly father (God). He made each of us different and wants us to embrace each other. So I agree with you and pray I can become more like you – open to the love of all.

*****

As I read your books I am delighted to discover your philosophy, which is complicated and so full of compassion, love, and critical thinking chances. Your books are excellent in promoting love, peace, and the equality and value of all people! You are so wise to state purposes in your writing; purposes which allow each person to think for themselves. And, I think you are very wise to have your own personal beliefs to be your own, with each person creating beliefs of their own by taking in new ideas and thoughts. I was very happy to see your written statement and your inclusion of people from all backgrounds in the production of your lovely books. Thank you for your thoughtfulness, encouragement, and great ideas!

*****

Your Bregdan books are fabulous and it is wonderful that many different backgrounds can find their own thing in each book! It shouldn't matter what they come away with. It should only matter that the book made them think!

*****

I don't care about another person's religious beliefs. And, as long as they don't try to push their beliefs down my throat, I won't push mine. I have always lived by the rule that to save friendships, either casual, social or romantic, that there are 2 major topics to avoid....religion and politics. Before my husband died, I wouldn't even tell him who I voted for or how I voted on specific issues. Funny? Maybe, But, it kept the peace. I love your books, and, historically, God was a big part of people's lives in those days, as well as today. So, just keep doing what you are doing and hurry up with the next book!

*****

As far as being Christian or religious books, I didn't find any of the books as being that way.

I think any era in history produced times when people prayed to their higher power, no matter who that may be. When times get tough we all pray and look for hope. That is my version of the law of survival, and at 83 years of age I still live that way. When someone today tells me how much better they are than someone else, my reply to them is, "Well, when you are 6 feet under, and the other person is 6 feet under, who is really going to be the best?" This is the way I live today.

*****

Please stay true to your beliefs and convictions for you are totally correct. You are touching hearts and minds all over the world, and you work hard to keep your information historically correct. Too many people don't want to read about history because it was taught in a boring way and often inaccurately. I am a newly retired elementary teacher, and I spent many years trying to dramatically act out events hopefully from primary sources. Religions vary all over the world, but most have the basic belief of a higher "being or power." The older I get, the more I believe that what's important is kindness and treating others the way we want to be treated. Random kindness is a foundation for me and that transcends all religions. I feel "labeling" is completely unnecessary. Carry on, don't doubt yourself, and keep on writing for all of us!

*****

I see the religion in the books as historical. The slaves were believers in God as a way to believe that God had a plan for them. They had to believe or they would have been buried in the grief and pain they saw every day. They sang hymns as a way to get through their day and show their joy in being a part of their God and with each other. Religion was their only path to survival. I do not view your novels as Christian but as a historical view of the times.

*****

Back to my story...
I had been in Virginia for about a year and a half before the next *until* happened.

I had just gotten involved with the youth group when a friend came to spend the weekend. We'll call her Amber because I don't want to embarrass her, though truth be known she probably takes complete credit for my career! It's probably the truth!

We had spent the night before laughing and talking. After a good night's sleep, I opened the door to my home office and stopped dead in my tracks. All I could do was stare in shock. I finally found words.

"What are you doing?" I asked quietly.

Seemingly oblivious of the dangerous light glinting in my eyes, Amber looked up with glowing excitement and said, "Why didn't you tell me you'd written a book?"

"I believe the bigger question is why you're reading it?" I struggled to control my temper. It takes a lot to get me angry, but she had succeeded. I have seldom felt so violated.

Amber had never seen me angry, so she remained totally clueless to what I was feeling.

"Ginny, this is wonderful!"

I picked my words carefully. "Let's see... You are in my office uninvited. You have rifled through private drawers, and then you opened a sealed envelope to find what you're reading. Now would probably not be the time for you to say you actually hate it, so please don't mind if I'm not giving your opinion much credit."

Something in my tone must have gotten through to her because her eyes opened wide as she carefully put the manuscript down on my desk. "Are you angry?" She was genuinely puzzled.

"Duh."

"But why?"

I shook my head in disbelief. "You really have to ask that question?"

Amber took a deep breath and then picked up the manuscript again. "Look, I realize I shouldn't have been snooping through your desk, but you should be glad I did."

I narrowed my eyes as I searched for words that wouldn't destroy her. Since I couldn't come up with any, I remained silent.

"Seriously, Ginny," Amber continued. "You needed me to find this because it really *is* good."

I shook my head in defeat. "I don't really care. Just put it back in the envelope and come have some breakfast."

"Why?" Amber persisted. "How can you not care? I had no idea you could
    write like this."

I turned and walked from the room. "I'm eating breakfast," I called over my shoulder. I thought I was having the final word, but it turns out Amber was just getting warmed up.

She started in on me again when I laid a plate of blueberry pancakes in front of her. "You need to get your book published."

"Give it up," I muttered, wondering if snatching her plate away from her would make her stop talking.

"I won't," she said defiantly. "Do you know how many people would give everything they have to write like this?"

My mind flashed back to my grandfather's insistence that I had his *gift*, but I shook my head stubbornly. "I wrote that when I was sick. I'm not doing anything with it."

"What else have you written?"

"Nothing," I said flatly.

Amber stared at me. "This is the first thing you've written?"

"Since I was 16," I admitted, wondering how I was going to stop this crazy conversation. I shoved bites of pancakes into my mouth at a faster rate. Escape seemed to be my only viable option.

Amber put down her fork and continued to stare at me. "Seriously? This is the first thing you've ever written? And it's this good?"

"What do you know?" I snapped. I was trying to stay calm, but her insistence had pushed me into fight or flight mode. Since I was sitting in my own kitchen, I decided to fight. "How would *you* know if it's any good?" Now, Amber was a good friend, but I didn't know a lot about her past.

"Do you know what I did before I became a lawyer?"

"Do I care?" I countered.

"You should," she said, her whole manner suddenly quiet and focused. "I was a middle school librarian. It was my job to choose books for the students to read."

I couldn't come up with a response.

"I *do* know what I'm talking about," Amber continued. "I don't know how in the world you could write a book like this without ever having written anything before, but when I say it's good, you should believe me."

"It doesn't matter," I finally managed.

"Why not?" Amber challenged.

"Because I'm never going to write another one."

Amber sat back in her chair and fixed her gaze on me. "Funny. You don't look that stupid," she said bluntly.

I shook my head. My appetite destroyed, I pushed back from the table and then dumped my pancakes in the trash.

Amber suddenly realized how upset I was. "Look, I don't know what happened to make you decide to not write, but it must have been huge. I'm just going to tell you that you have to get over it. Very few people have the gift you do."

I wanted to clap my hands over my ears to shut her voice out. *Ginny, you have the gift that I never used.* Nothing could drown out the echo of my grandfather's words ringing in my head. Once unleashed, they were like a tape on auto-replay. All the years of trying to shut it out had melted away in one morning. It was as if I were back in my dying grandfather's bedroom, listening to his plea.

"I'm not going to leave you alone until you send this off to a publisher," Amber continued firmly.

I glared at her and then stalked out of the kitchen. I leashed my dog and took him for a long walk, hoping she would have run out of steam by the time I returned two hours later.

No such luck. My time away seemed to have only given her the opportunity to hone her position. She started in on me with her best lawyerly arguments as soon as I entered the house.

I resisted for four months – in spite of Amber's weekly phone calls – but I finally decided to do the one thing I knew would shut her up. I would send the book to a publisher, get it rejected, and then have proof that would make her give me some peace.

I was terrified, though. What was I thinking? Did I really want to take the action that would prove I'd been right all along? That I didn't have the *gift*?

Just when I would decide to move forward something would jerk me to a stop.

I owe my decision to my dog...

Caspian was a new addition to my household. I had first seen him limping beside the road when I was on my way home from work. I pulled over to help him, but he tucked his tail between his legs and darted into the thick woods. I called and pleaded, but he never revealed himself. This went on for several days, with the same results. I finally called into the woods after another futile attempt to catch him. "Okay, this is up to you. You're going to have to come to me. I live up the road." And, yes, I was shaking my head, too, that I would say something so ridiculous. But...

It worked.

Two days later I walked out onto the porch of my 100-year-old Virginia farmhouse. A flash of movement in the bushes had my eyes wide with disbelief. We locked eyes for several minutes before he slunk out into the open. His whole being radiated terrified hope.

I could tell he was a chocolate lab, but just barely; he was skin and bones, covered with ticks, fleas and sores, and had been shot – his skinny body riddled with buckshot. I took one look at this pathetic animal and told him he was home.

It took weeks of vet treatments, baths and many bowls of food, but he finally began to look like a dog that was going to make it. His bones began to disappear, his coat took on a shine, and he became my constant shadow to show his appreciation for saving his life. He was always with me – except when I went upstairs to my office...

My home had a wide expanse of wooden stairs that led to the second floor. Caspian was terrified of them. It didn't matter what I did to build his confidence, or what wonderful tidbit of food I tempted him with, he refused to climb those stairs. He would just cower at the bottom step and shake all over whenever he got near them. Yet, when I went up to my office he was overcome with despair at being separated from me, and laid at the bottom whimpering and whining.

I had no idea what had created this fear, and I had even less of an idea how to conquer it. After two weeks of daily attempts, I finally gave up. If he didn't want to climb the stairs – so be it. But my only defense from his pitiful whining was to turn the music up any time I needed to be in my office. When I would come downstairs, Caspian would erupt with frantic joy to be reunited once again.

About a month into this pattern, I was awakened one morning by a noise. I lay in bed trying to identify what it was.

Click, click, click... Silence. Click, click, click... Silence.

It kept on for close to fifteen minutes before my curiosity finally overwhelmed my desire to stay under the warm covers. I threw aside my quilt, grabbed a robe and went out to investigate. When I identified the source of the noise, I just stood there with my mouth wide open.

I watched as Caspian carefully climbed the stairs. *Click, click, click...* He got to the top, turned around, and then started back down. *Click, click, click...*

When he got to the bottom, he turned and gazed at me as if to say, *It's really no big deal. I can do this!*

And then he did it again, and again, and again... at least 25 more times – after already having done it for 15 minutes before I came to investigate.

I watched his confidence grow with each ascent and descent of the "dreaded stairs." His tongue hung out in joy, and at the end his tail was wagging his triumph over his fears. He knew he would never again have to be separated from me because of those stairs.

I already loved him, but that day I gained an incredible respect for his courage and resilience. I was also challenged about what I was willing to do to overcome *my* fears. *Was I willing to stare my fears in the face and then take the steps to overcome it? Was I willing to feel the fear, and then do it anyway? Was I willing to attack my fears, for as long as it took to overcome them?*

Caspian broke through my wall with his courage. Fine. I would send in the manuscript.

I don't do anything without having some knowledge about doing it, so I bought a few books on how to get published, read them carefully, and then sent query letters via the postal system to three publishing companies. Once I could tell Amber I had taken steps to get published, she backed off. The wheels of publishing do not move quickly so I knew I was guaranteed peace for quite a while.

The expected failure was not something I wanted to focus on, so I shoved what I had done to the back of my mind.

I went back to building my youth group. When I had taken over the youth group for a church in Richmond, Virginia there were three kids who still had any interest in being part of it. They'd been hurt by the two previous youth directors and had no interest in going another round with a new one.

I knew I couldn't just start having meetings and expect anyone to show up, so I decided to get to know the kids I'd never met. I started making phone calls. I ate more pizza and ice cream than any human should. That's all I did for an entire summer; take kids out for pizza and ice cream. I talked and I listened. I was in heaven!

By the beginning of the school year, I had sixty kids show up at an event for the beginning of the new year. I threw my heart and soul into those kids, and into building the youth group to touch even more.

Oh, and I heard from one of the publishers, asking me to send the complete manuscript of the book. I was so immersed in what I was doing with the kids that it hardly even registered that it might be important. I made another copy of the manuscript, mailed it off, and went back to doing what I was so passionate about.

The months rolled by. My life was full of the kids and non-stop activities. 60 teenagers grew to 100... and then to 150... I added more volunteer leaders...

I was having the time of my life and didn't think for even one minute about the manuscript I had mailed out over a year earlier.

Until...

Faith's Irish Whiskey Oatmeal Cookies

(Makes 1 recipe – Double for larger group)

3/4 cup butter, 3/4 cup brown sugar,

3/4 cup granulated sugar, 2 large egg yolks,

2 tbsp. Irish whiskey, 3/4 cup flour,

1/2 tsp baking powder, 1/2 tsp baking soda,

1/2 tsp cinnamon, 1/4 tsp salt, and 1 cup rolled oats.

Cream together the butter and sugars until light. Add the egg yolks and Irish whiskey and mix well. Add the flour, baking powder, baking soda, cinnamon, and salt and mix well. Stir in the oats. Scoop out onto greased pan and bake in medium oven about 12 minutes.

Chapter Three

I was walking out the door for work when the ringing phone drew me back inside. "Hello."

"Is this Ginny?"

"Yes." My mind was preoccupied, spinning through the busy day ahead of me. I didn't recognize the voice, which told me it couldn't be an important call.

*** I'm going to change or conceal names of people and the publishing house. You'll understand why further into the book.

"This is Katrina Davis from _____ Publishing."

I paused for a moment until my racing mind revealed the name as the one that had requested my entire manuscript.

"Hello Katrina." I thought it was nice of the only company to request my book to call and reject me in person. At least I could finally tell Amber it was over. She had called at least once a week during the year to see what was happening. Her calls were the only moments of my existence when I thought about my writing.

"Ginny, everyone here at _____ Publishing loves your book. We would like to publish it."

I stared at the phone and slowly sank onto the nearest chair. "What?"

Katrina laughed. "You heard me. We love your book and want to publish it."

"I see." That's honestly all I could think of to say. My brain was too busy trying to make sense out of what I was hearing.

"There's one thing we'll need from you, though," Katrina continued.

"What's that?" I took a deep breath and forced myself to focus.

"We'll need more books because we want to turn it into a series," she said excitedly, obviously believing this was great news.

I wasn't so sure.

"More books?" I hadn't had a clue what I was doing when I wrote the first one – I just wanted to maintain sanity while I was sick. How would I do more?

"Yes, we'll want at least five more books for the series," Katrina said warmly. "Can you do that?"

How was I supposed to know? I didn't know how I did the first one! I asked the only question I could think of to ask. "How soon will you need them?"

"We would want to release a new one every six months. Can you do that?" she asked again. She was beginning to sound a little confused by my lack of enthusiasm.

I still had absolutely no idea, but I remained silent as the request spun through my mind. I thought of the eighty-plus hours I worked every week. They weren't really work because I loved being with the kids more than anything, but how would taking time to write books impact my ministry?

"Ginny?"

"I'm thinking," I said quietly, turning to stare out the window at the three hundred acre farm I lived on. I watched Angus cows amble through the fields, their glistening black bodies a perfect contrast to the lush green, as a flock of geese soared overhead. At that moment, I envied them their simple life.

"What is there to think about?" Katrina asked, giving voice to her confusion. "You're an excellent writer. We love your books, and we're giving you a chance at a great career."

I supposed she was right about the career possibility, but I suddenly realized I didn't care. My response came easily. "I'm sorry, but my answer is no."

A long silence met my announcement.

"No? What do you mean?" Katrina sounded stunned.

Saying the words out loud made all my fragmented thoughts crystallize into certainty. "It means that I have 150 teenagers whom I love, and who depend on me. I don't want to take time away from them to write books."

"But think of how many more teenagers you can reach with them," Katrina said persuasively.

"Possibly," I replied, "but my answer is the same. I'm not interested." It felt good to say the words. I was eager to get out the door because I was meeting one of my volunteer leaders for breakfast, and I didn't want to be late. "Thank you for the offer. I hope you have a great day."

There was nothing but stunned silence when I hung up.

I didn't find out until later that no one had ever turned down a publishing offer from this company before. It didn't matter to me, though. I knew I had made the right decision. My heart was light as I headed to work.

I've had people ask me if I subconsciously sabotaged their offer because I was too afraid to put my book out there. The answer is no. I honestly loved every minute of what I did. Taking time away from the teenagers that were my life would have seemed like punishment to me.

Amber, on the other hand, did not share my feelings. When I gave her the news during one of her weekly phone calls, there was a *looooonnnngggg* silence, and then an explosive, "Are you out of your ever-loving mind?"

I just laughed. "No."

"Ginny, no one turns down a publishing contract. No one."

"Well, obviously not no one," I said calmly, still confident I'd made the right decision.

"You're nuts," she said bluntly.

"But I'm a happy nut."

"You'll probably never get another chance," Amber continued.

I could see her shaking her head through the phone lines. "Then it's not meant to be. I can live with that."

And the thing was... I could. I had done what I said I would never do. I wrote.

And then I took it a step further and actually put it out there for publication.

I had overcome my fear.

I was happy about that, but firm in my decision to stay on the course I was on. The years flew by. The only writing I did was the youth newsletter I called "TidBits". I loved writing it, and the kids loved reading it – as did the parents.

My life was full. Meetings...Mission trips... wilderness camping trips... a 700 mile bicycle trip... a myriad of retreats... continuing copious amounts of pizza... Super Bowl Parties... Lock-Ins at the YMCA...hours spent one-on-one with the kids that held my heart.

No one but Amber knew I had been offered a publishing contract.

Until...

The weekend retreat that I took a small group of leaders on was just like all the rest I'd been on – full of laughter, fun and growth. On our last night there, I slept like a baby – until the dream started.

There have been many times in my life when I've dreamed of flying – simply lifting off the ground and soaring through the sky – but never quite like this. My dream was full of explosive color and the reality of my flying was more intense than ever before.

I woke with words resonating through my soul. *It is your time to fly.*

I also woke from the dream with a firm belief that I was meant to resign as youth director.

Huh?

Resign from what I loved? And do what? I had absolutely no idea, but I couldn't deny the certainty of my feelings. It was time to resign.

I can't really tell you what it was about that dream that made me know I was meant to resign – I just knew. When I know, I know...

FYI – I am known for being impulsive. If I believe I'm meant to do something, I usually just do it; and then figure out what comes next.

This was big, though. I mean, really BIG.

As I left the retreat that day, not telling anyone what I had decided, I felt nothing but sadness as I watched everyone packing the vans. What was coming next? Why was I going to say good-bye to something I loved so very much?

Thankfully, I didn't have long until I had my answer.

The drive home was about three hours. When I got to my office I called home so I could check my answering machine. I listened to the last message in stunned silence.

"Ginny, this is Katrina from _____ Publishing. I know you told me three years ago that you weren't interested in a publishing contract, but none of us can forget the book you wrote. Would you reconsider? Is it time? Please call me if you're interested in discussing this more."

Well...

I had my answer for what was to come next. But I had absolutely no clue the long, twisted road it would lead me down.

My call to Katrina led to a multi-book contract. Let me interject right here that if you're a writer looking to go with a publishing company, do NOT sign the first contract they send you! If you have an agent, they can help you. If not, you need to do your homework before you move forward!

I did my homework, and then went over the contract again. I knew I was not willing to sign the contract they had sent, so I rewrote it, adding in the changes I believed were necessary. The whole time I was wondering just who I thought I was to demand so many changes, and so much more than they had offered. Especially since I was leaving my current career, and they were all I had waiting for me. I wasn't exactly in a strong negotiating position.

Another note to writers. Most publishing companies (okay, probably all of them) will initially offer you much less than they are willing to ultimately give. It's called negotiation. Unfortunately, almost all writers are so thrilled that someone actually believes their book is worth publishing, that they just sign the first thing that comes their way, and then wonder why they can't make a living as a writer. Do NOT accept the first contract – unless you have an experienced agent that has done the negotiating for you.

And... NEVER give a publishing company the copyright to your book. You'll understand more about this later, but for now, please trust me on this.

Do I have an agent? I didn't then, and I don't now, but I'll explain all that later in the book.

Back to my first book contract. I made the changes and mailed it off. Email was not a thing 27 years ago! Which meant I would have to wait for the mail to make it across the country, and then wait for them to make a decision on my demands.

What did I do while I waited?

I agonized. I prayed. And, I shed a lot of tears. Once I had mailed it off, I was completely certain I had blown my writing career before it ever happened. I had asked for too much. I had dared to question the almighty Publisher.

I roamed the farm. I took long walks with my dog, Caspian. I sat on my porch for hours, stroking his head, trying to not freak out.

What had I been thinking? Six days of questioning turned me into a nervous wreck. I also never ventured far from my phone. Now that I had decided to do this thing called writing, had I blown it before I was out of the gate?

The CALL came on the seventh day.

"Ginny?"

"Yes," I asked nervously, glad Katrina couldn't see my crossed fingers and eyes.

"How did you know how to do that?"

I hesitated. How did I know how to do *what*? "What do you mean?"

Katrina laughed. "How did you know how to challenge all the points we were willing to change, and ask for no more than we were willing to give?"

"I did my research," I replied, relieved beyond words that she didn't sound angry. I forced myself to sound casual before I asked my next question. "How did I do?"

"We've made all the changes you requested," Katrina answered. "The contract is on its way back to you."

I sagged with relief, and then a huge smile spread across my face. Of course, I know now that I could have done far better than I did, but it began my journey of learning the publishing world and I'm grateful for all the lessons I learned along the way. "So, where do we go from here?"

"We want you to start working on the second book in the series."

"Okay," I said cheerfully, hoping from the core of my being that I could even write another book. It had been five years since I had lain in bed and written the first one.

I had no clue what I was doing then, and nothing I had done since then had made me any more prepared.

"Can I ask you a few questions for your author's biography?" Katrina asked.

"Fire away."

"Is your college degree in English?"

"No. I have a Recreation degree, with a concentration in Outdoor/Environmental Education."

I could feel Katrina hesitate as she absorbed that information. "Did you minor in English?"

"No."

"Take a lot of English courses?" She sounded almost hopeful.

I smiled. "Only the Freshman English course required for my degree."

The questioning continued. "Have you taken writing courses since then?"

"No." I was beginning to have fun.

"How many books have you written before this one?"

"None."

"None?" Katrina sounded dubious.

"None."

The pause was longer this time. "Then, how do you do it?"

"I have no idea," I admitted, hoping my honesty wasn't a mistake. What if the publisher decided I was far too flaky to take a risk on for an entire series? I couldn't really say I would have blamed them.

Katrina laughed. "It's a gift." Her voice was heavy with admiration.

I sighed. "That's what my grandfather says." At this point, there was no other possible explanation. I only hoped the *gift* would show up again before I had to deliver the next book in six months!

I never dreamed my world was about to turn completely upside down, making it almost impossible to write another word!

<u>*Annie's Ginger Molasses Cookies*</u>

One tea-cup of molasses, one half tea-cup of sugar,
one tablespoonful of butter, one tablespoon of lard,
one quart of flour, two tablespoons of ginger, one teaspoonful of
cinnamon, one teaspoonful of allspice, two tablespoons of
yeast powder. Cream butter and sugar and add molasses.
Sift yeast powder and glut together and add to butter,
sugar and molasses, then add lard and apices, etc.
and work it up well. Roll out on a board and
cut them out
and bake like you would a biscuit.

Chapter Four

It was just a few days later that the reality of what I was about to do really sank in. I had resigned my position, but had agreed to stay with the youth group through the summer to help with the transition. That meant I would have very little time for writing, but for some unknown reason I was confident I could pull it off.

What was creating so much turmoil for me was the realization of how many kids could potentially be reading my books. I had about 150 teenagers in my youth group. The first printing of my book would be 10,000 copies. I couldn't quite wrap my brain around *10,000* kids reading my book, and then the rest of the books in the series.

I was sitting outside on the farm – perched on top of a picnic table – when I came face-to-face with what was really bothering me. *Was I the type of person who should be writing books 10,000 kids would read?* I wasn't at all sure of that. The weight of the responsibility settled on my heart and soul – feeling like an anvil that kept me from breathing.

My heart pounded in my chest as I fought to control my fear. Who was I kidding to think I should be the voice to thousands of teenagers??

I remember the moment my world turned upside down. I bowed my head, closed my eyes, and prayed a simple prayer. "God, please do whatever you need to do to make me the person who should write these books."

Sigh...

That was the prayer that ushered in what I call "The Six Years of Darkness".

*****

I have to step back in time to help you understand what I mean...

I told you in the beginning that I had a traumatic childhood. What I didn't tell you before, was that at age 35, I had no memory of my childhood before I was twelve. I had brief snippets of school memories but couldn't remember one thing of my childhood within my home. I had tried for years to remember, figuring it had to be important, but it remained a blank slate. I had finally decided, just a year or two earlier, that I didn't care if I ever remembered – I was just going to live my life.

Well...

That picnic table prayer evidently removed the block that hid the memories. Within just a few days, the memory tapes within my mind started rolling. Once they started, all I wanted was for them to stop.

They didn't.

They ran for almost six years.

Somehow, I had managed through the years to staunch the memories and channel the pain into doing good things, and into loving people the best I could. I didn't realize my deep empathy came from years of heart-searing abuse. This book is not about that, but it's the only way to answer the questions so many of you ask...

"Ginny, how can you speak so directly to people in your books?"

"Ginny, where does your understanding of pain come from?"

"Ginny, why do you constantly talk about choosing hope?"

The Six Years of Darkness almost destroyed me. There were so many times I couldn't breathe. So many times I almost couldn't find a reason to keep living. So many times I knew the world would be better if I wasn't in it. So many times I was determined to do anything to simply stop the pain.

How could I be worth anything after all that had been done to me? And, if I was worth anything, why did it happen in the first place?

I won't pretend to say I can completely answer all those questions. And, I also won't tell you that 100% of my childhood abuse has been completely healed. There are scars that will remain for the rest of my life. Sometimes I hate that realization.

Other times, I know those scars are what enable me to write the way I do, and I'm able to choose gratitude.

The Six Years of Darkness brought me face-to-face with my past, and then allowed me to move beyond all that had been done to me.

I know what it's like to not have hope.

I use that knowledge to impart hope.

I know what it's like to have no reason to live.

I use that knowledge to help people find a reason to choose life.

I know what it's like to feel completely alone, and to wish just one person knew my pain.

I use that knowledge to walk into a room of teenagers and almost instantly know who is being abused, or who has been abused. I make it a point to let them know they're not alone.

I know what it's like to question why I'm still on the planet.

I also know what it's like to be certain every life is valuable beyond words, and to help people learn that for themselves.

Whatever my *Gift* is that allows me to write; it's what I choose to communicate that makes it worth using. I'm hoping that my sharing this part of my life fills you with hope and belief that you can conquer anything that has happened in *your* life; and then use it to become a better version of you.

The fact that I now write books that reach millions of people makes the Six Years of Darkness a precious gift.

*****

So, were the Six Years of Darkness nothing but stark pain and despair?

Absolutely not.

First, I fulfilled my commitment to write the first five books of my teen series. *The original books are no longer in print, but you can find the re-released one under the title, The Pepper Crest High Series, on Amazon.*

The books were astoundingly easy to write. I simply shared the stories of some of the kids I had worked with – changing enough information to protect the guilty!

I wrote about kids, horses, tennis, and hiking. Why? Because you're supposed to write about what you know about. Eighteen years of working with teenagers have given me a vast trove of story ideas I'll never run out of. I can only hope for enough years and time to write more of them.

Horses have been part of my life since I took my first riding lesson at twelve. I bought my first horse at thirteen, and then shortly afterward starting teaching beginning riding. I learned jumping, and how to ride 3-gaited and 5-gaited horses. The only thing I didn't learn when I was a kid on the East Coast was how to ride Western. I didn't care about that until...

When I graduated from college, I was offered a job running the horsemanship program for a Camp/Ranch in East Texas. 40 horses. 200+ kids a day in riding lessons through the summer. 12 high school kids that worked for me. Trail rides during the rest of the year. Even if I had never thought I would end up in Texas, the job was everything I wanted. I pushed aside my dreams of Colorado, Wyoming and Montana, and applied for the job.

When I received the call about the position of Head Wrangler, I was asked if I could teach barrel-racing.

"Absolutely," I replied with total confidence.

Yes, I did realize at the time that barrel-racing was something done in a western saddle, but that was the sum total of my knowledge.

The other thing you should know about me is that I'll almost always say, "Yes". Even if I have no idea how to do something, I believe I can figure it out. Saying *yes* puts me in the position of having to do it.

I only had one week before I had to load everything into my VW Convertible and head to Texas from North Carolina. One of the last things I did was swing by a bookstore and purchase a book on Western riding, barrel-racing and pole-bending – everything I would need to know to operate the weekly rodeo during the long Texas summers!

I studied that book cover to cover while I was on the road, and for weeks after I arrived. And, yes, I love barrel racing and pole bending!

So, when it came time to write those first five books, I knew horses would have to be part of them. Crystal, a horse I actually owned in Texas, had taken a starring role in the first book published. Horses would continue to play a key role.

Tennis? I started playing in high school and played through college. I love it!

Hiking? There is nothing I love more than being out in nature on a trail. On the beach... in the mountains... the American Plains... I don't care where I hike. I simply love to be outdoors hiking. And, please don't forget I have a degree in Outdoor/Environmental Education. All it takes for me to be happy is for me to be outdoors having fun!

*****

With the first five books in the series selling well, my publisher asked me if I would continue on with it. Gladly!

My first run-in with my publisher came when I wrote the requested sixth book. It dealt with the very difficult subject of sexual abuse – something I knew beyond a shadow of a doubt needed to be communicated in a way that teens could find freedom.

My publisher refused to publish it because they said it was too raw and painful.

Raw and painful? You bet the subject of sexual abuse is raw and painful, but millions of kids are crying out for it – especially twenty-five years ago.

I made the second of two decisions that day to not compromise my beliefs for my career. The first decision was to turn down the writing contract offered me almost five years earlier. My second decision was to not continue with a series if I wouldn't have the freedom to write what I knew my readers needed to hear.

You might think that was a wrong decision because it silenced my voice to the teenagers reading my books, but I was already chafing under the publisher's control of what I did. I thought their decision was wrong then, and I think it was wrong now. I had to follow my heart.

My publisher was a little stunned when I made my announcement, but they already knew I was a renegade. I made it easier by already having another idea for them.

I had learned through years of working with teens that they are first going to listen to each other – before they listen to adults. I've had so many adults tell me that's not a good thing.

I laugh and answer, "Whether it's a good thing or not is not relevant. It's true. If you want to reach kids, do it in a way they can hear."

That's what I did when I put together *Teens Talk About Dating*. What a complete joy that book was. First, I got in a room with sixty of my old youth group kids and had them anonymously write down all the questions they had in regard to dating.

Whew! Just the questions were eye-opening.

I took those questions to high schools and college campuses all across the country so the students could anonymously answer them. I was in classes with the students during the day, and also spent many nights (until 2:00 AM) in dorm lounges waiting for students to finish their answers.

Wow!

When I say I "put this book together", that's exactly what I mean. My name is on it, but I didn't write it. The teens and young adults I had the privilege of spending time with did. All I did was edit it. I didn't really do much of that because I wanted them to answer in their own voices. I gave clarification where needed, but I changed very little. It was too powerful exactly the way it was!

It was received so well that my publisher was eager to do the next Teens Talk book. I met with them for lunch during a promo tour that included radio interviews and book store signings.

"Are you ready to do the next book in the Teens Talk Series?" they asked eagerly.

"Absolutely," I replied. I could hardly wait to get back on the road and meet with more amazing young people.

"What will you do it on?"

"Teens Talk About Sex."

Stunned silence and blank stares met my announcement.

Finally, the president of the company found his voice. "I'm afraid that won't happen, Ginny."

I took a deep breath. "Why not?" I asked, though I already knew the answer.

"We can't publish a book about sex for teenagers – especially one that has the word Sex on the cover."

I shook my head, determined to do battle. "It's exactly what should follow a book about dating," I argued.

"Whether you like it or not, these kids are having sex. The least we can do is give them a book that will help them more carefully examine their beliefs and actions – in a way they can hear it. They've already asked me for it."

No matter what I said, they would not give in.

Neither would I. To me, it was a blatant show of disrespect to my readers to not give them what they desperately needed. I wasn't going to come up with another topic, when I knew the one they really needed would never be addressed. Once again, I chafed under the constraints of a publisher.

And, once again, I made a decision to not compromise my beliefs. "I'm not doing another book, then," I said quietly.

They attempted to change my mind, but I believe they knew it was futile even while they were trying over dessert.

It was the second time I had walked away from potential books, but I knew I was making the right choice. My integrity and my respect for my readers is far more important to me than a career and money.

However, it did leave me with a dilemma. If I wasn't willing to write either series for them, what was I going to do?

I had absolutely no idea, so I started exploring different options – other than writing. I was willing to use my *Gift*, but I was not willing to compromise my beliefs, so it seemed I was at an impasse.

Until...

<u>*Annie's Quick Corn Bread for a Busy Day*</u>

Two eggs, one pint of corn meal, half pint of sour milk,

one teaspoonful of soda – beat eggs very lightly –

one tablespoonful of melted lard or butter,

mix all together, well stirred.

Bake in an ordinary pan.

Chapter Five

I'm not sure how much time passed as I dealt with the disappointment of my failed writing career. Coming in the midst of the Six Years of Darkness made it an especially difficult blow to absorb. And, yes, it restarted all the questions about why I was alive, and what purpose could I possibly have in the world.

I had overcome my fears. I had taken the leap and done what I said I would never do – become a writer. And now it had all come to a screeching halt.

The Darkness intensified as I struggled to understand what was next.

Until...

Until the phone rang again.

"Ginny, this is Katrina."

"Hello Katrina." I was surprised to hear from my publisher again. I figured they had decided dealing with their renegade author was not worth their time and trouble. I waited to hear what she had to say.

"Are you interested in historical fiction?" Katrina asked.

"If you're asking if I like it, the answer is yes," I said carefully. I had no idea where this conversation was going.

"Would you like to write it for us?"

I held the phone away from my ear for a few moments and just stared at it. I was not at all certain I had heard Katrina correctly. "What did you ask me?"

I could hear the smile in Katrina's voice when she answered. "I asked if you would be interested in writing historical fiction for us. We recognize your gift as a writer. We're looking for a way to continue working with you."

In a flash, I was fourteen again. I had just returned home from the library with my first Eugenia Price novel about life in the South. Little did I know her books would spark a love for historical fiction that would never die. I've read everything she's ever written, and without ever meeting her face-to-face, she became an inspiration and a mentor for me.

Once I'd read all of Eugenia's books, I devoured as much historical fiction as I could find. I hated the boredom of history in school, but I loved learning history from within the pages of a novel.

But *me* write historical fiction?

The whole idea was far-fetched and ludicrous. It also ignited an excited possibility within me.

Remember what I said earlier about saying, "Yes", and then figuring out how I was going to do whatever I had just agreed to?

"Yes," I said firmly.

"That's great!" Katrina said excitedly. "What are you going to write about?"

I was back to staring at the phone again. Of course, I had absolutely no idea because the concept of writing historical fiction had never crossed my mind until that very moment. But, don't forget I'm a fiction writer. I'm quite gifted at making up things on the spot!

"Katrina, there are so many topics and eras I'm fascinated with. Let me think about it for a little while and get back to you," I stated calmly. "It won't be long."

Right...

I did a little dance around my house when I got off the phone. Perhaps my writing career wasn't over yet! Once the euphoria had passed, I was left with deciding what in the world I was going to write about. I only had all of time to choose from!

*****

It took me a little while to decide what I would write about, so I'm going to use the break to tell you more about my writing.

It truly is just a *Gift*. I have no idea how I do it, and I could never teach someone else to write. I meant it when I said I never took a class. I don't read books about writing. I don't read books about characters, or dialogue, or *anything*. I'm not saying these aren't good things, or that it might not help me be even better, but it's not something I do.

I just write.

And it comes.

I can do rudimentary editing, but I've learned to never edit my own writing. I'll do a read-through each morning of what I wrote the day before and make a few changes, but you pretty much get what comes out the first time I put it down.

Final editing comes from my team. 99% of it is grammatical or spelling corrections. I can edit someone else's work (if I have to), but I've learned that when I read my own work, I see what was in my head in the first place – even if it's not really there. Every writer needs new eyes.

Let me tell you a little story here to make my point.

Several years ago, a friend of mine had just finished a book that was due to be released in a few days. I wanted to be helpful, so I offered to edit it for her.

"Oh, it doesn't need editing, Ginny," she said confidently. "I've gone over it several times. It's perfect. I'm 100% certain."

I'm glad she couldn't see my eyes roll on the other end of the phone. "Then I should be able to go through it very quickly," I said cheerfully. "I'm just telling you it's not a good idea to release a new book that hasn't been seen by anyone's eyes but your own. You only have one chance to make a good first impression."

She very reluctantly agreed. I could tell she was offended by the idea that her editing might not have created a perfect book, but I also thought too much of her work and her life to not make sure it actually was. She was probably also looking forward to hearing me say she had been right all along; that nothing needed to be changed.

It took me only ten minutes of reading to send her the first email. I copied and pasted the three paragraphs on the first ten pages that had spelling and grammar errors.

"Would you like me to continue?" I asked when I followed up with a phone call, once more glad she couldn't see my smile.

She was mortified and humbled, and also very grateful. When her book was released, it communicated her professionalism and commitment to excellence.

*** *Now, please take note of this. I no longer edit or review books. I'm quite sure there are amazing books out there, but I just don't have time to do it. I hope my getting* *new books to you is far more important than editing or reviewing yours. There is not time to do all of it well, so I choose to focus on what I believe my purpose is, and also on the thing that gives me the most joy!*

I'm quite sure there are errors in my books, but not because I've tried to edit them myself. They've gone through two other sets of eyes. My editor and proofreader go through them carefully, working hard to make them perfect, but it's incredibly hard to make 500+ pages perfect. Once they have done their magic, I take a week and read every word out loud, trying my best to capture mistakes or things I believe can be better communicated.

We'll keep trying our best, and I ask you to be patient if you find mistakes. Let me know. I'll correct them quickly!

*****

I'll never forget two instances that magnified, not my ability, but my limited knowledge of writing. You'll understand this sentence in a minute.

One of my closest friends from college is an English professor. One year, when I was visiting North Carolina, she asked me to speak to her class about writing. Being in a room of college freshmen sounded fun, so I agreed. I assumed I would be talking about how I got started as a writer.

Instead...

Bobbie stepped to the front of her class and wrote a sentence. She then turned to me, handed me the marker, and asked me to diagram what she had written. (I just had to look online to make sure that is even the correct word!)

I looked at her, shook my head and laughed. "Sorry. I have no idea how to do that." I know I learned that in class at some point in my education, but it definitely didn't stick in my memory.

Bobbie stared at me in complete disbelief, and then asked one of her students do the deed.

When she finally called me forward to speak – though she was probably terrified of what I would say at that point – I started my talk with the obvious. "I'm happy to tell you that you don't have to know how to diagram a sentence to be a successful writer!"

The class laughed, and I rolled in to the rest of what I said that day.

My knowledge of grammar, vocabulary and spelling comes from decades of *reading* everything I can get my hands on. Remember me telling you I was reading at a college level in the third grade? Everything I read evidently stuck!

*****

Several years later, I was asked to speak to a high school English class in Washington State. Hang out with high school students? I was in!

I'm a very casual person so I showed up dressed the way I dress – in jeans and a denim shirt. I did add earrings to give it a little class! When the teacher called me to the front, I glanced at the podium and then walked over to her desk, sat down on top of it and crossed my legs. I'm a firm believer in comfort, and I hate looking down on people as I speak.

I could tell by the look on the student's faces that they weren't sure how to take me. I rolled into stories about writing, about the adventures I'd had during my research, and about how much fun it was to tell stories for a living. I perched on the desk... I jumped up and roamed around the room... I sat down at empty desks and chatted with the students around me.

We laughed. We talked. I answered questions.

I was in my element.

I never said a word about proper writing technique.

When I finished talking, the teacher asked if anyone had another question or comment before I left. Several students raised their hands, but the first comment was my favorite.

"I think you've convinced me to be a writer. I love to write, but I thought all writers were serious, conservative, and not much fun. You're crazy!"

I laughed along with everyone else. It was one of the best compliments I've ever received!

*****

Here's another story... I've told you about my grandfather's gift of writing. I truly had no idea if anyone else in the family had it – other than the few pages of Captain Michael Gaffney's journal that I'd read.

Until...

Just a few years ago, I was going through boxes that had been pulled from my brother's attic – boxes of pictures and letters my mother had stored there before she passed away.

I was stunned when I found a letter from my great-grandfather, Paul Gaffney – written to his wife. As I read it, I felt like I was in some kind of alternate universe.

The writing was mine.

The same tone... the same rhythm... the same feel. It was as if I were reading something I had written – except that it was written in the early 1900's! Completely bizarre, and even more evidence I have a *Gift* that has been passed down through generations.

Does it go back further? I have no idea, but my guess is yes. The knowledge makes me even more determined to use my gift well.

What I discovered while writing *Carried Forward By Hope* made me realize even more, but that's for later in this book.

*****

Since I was still trying to decide how to answer my publisher's question in regard to what historical period I would write about, I'll answer another question I'm asked all the time.

If you are a writer, be warned – you're not going to like my answer.

I normally release two to three 500+ page historical novels a year. I'm often asked, "How fast do you write, Ginny?"

I'll start to answer that question by telling you a story. Twenty-four years ago, when I was just getting started, I attended my one and only writer's conference. I think they are wonderful things for many writers – it's just not *my* thing. I simply want to write.

Anyway, I was in a session with about twenty other writers – all very serious, focused and professional – but none of them had been published yet. I strolled in with my jeans and noticed the eyebrows raising, but I ignored it and took my seat.

At some point in the session, the instructor asked how many pages a day we all wrote. I didn't realize I was in trouble until four or five people had given their answers.

"I usually write 1 -2 pages a day," one particularly well-groomed woman said, her eyes flashing with purpose.

"On a good day, I'll get one or two pages," another person revealed. "I want to make sure I think through every word I write."

I know my eyes were growing wider as they spoke, but no one noticed. There seemed to be some sort of unspoken agreement that lesser pages revealed more commitment.

"On an average, I'll write at least a page," another revealed, "but I'll spend many hours on the page I wrote the day before to make sure it's perfect before I keep going."

When it came time for me to answer, I had not yet learned that it's best to lie whenever I'm asked that question. It's taking a lot of courage to tell all my readers the truth!

"Well, on a good day, I'll get 15 to 20 pages written," I said honestly.

I swear you would have thought I had just cursed and taken the Lord's name in vain. Horrified eyes skewered me as their faces filled with disdain.

Only one lady had the nerve, though, to say what the others were thinking. "Well, they must not be very good!" she said haughtily.

Remember me saying I'm a renegade? Challenge me, and I'll usually give it right back to you – but I'll do it with a smile to keep you off guard, and unsure if you should be offended.

"That might be," I said cheerfully, "but I have three books published, and an ongoing contract with my publisher. How about you?" I asked with a warm smile.

You're right – I couldn't resist!

The look on her face was worth it, and no one else in the room dared speak up after that. I did, however, learn to avoid the question in the future. Now that I'm a successful author, I figure I can tell the truth, and let people figure out for themselves how they want to feel about it.

Here's the thing... I don't think I'm a better writer than other people because I write fast. I simply believe God understands that I have no patience. I mean, honestly, if it took me all day long to write one or two pages, I just wouldn't bother. I would die of either frustration or boredom before I ever got anything finished.

Once I've written it, I read it the next morning, change maybe one or two percent of what I wrote the day before, and then keep going. I won't look at it again until it's been returned by my editors for the final out loud read-through.

I met a writer one day who told me he had re-read and re-edited a 2000 word article he had written over one hundred times before he submitted it.

I'm glad if it works for him, but I would be out of my mind!

Writing fast works for me. It keeps me loving to write. I see no reason to change it.

I pray I become a better writer with every book I write, but I have to do it the way that makes me happy and that makes sense for me.

It's the *research* that takes the most time, but I'll dig into that later...

*****

Okay, I've rambled long enough. After two weeks of pondering what I was going to write about, I knew I had to give my publisher an answer. The problem was, I still had no idea what it was.

Until...

Opal's Biscuits

Mix half a pound of sugar with one pound of flour, half a tea-spoonful baking powder, and rub in four ounces of butter; make into a dough with warm milk, roll out, cut them out, and bake immediately in a quick oven.

Chapter Six

It was a beautiful spring day in Richmond, Virginia, but I was distracted as I made my way downtown to meet a friend for lunch. My thoughts were completely filled with the decision I knew I had to make. I'd spent three weeks pondering how to respond to my publisher. I had no answers, but questions clogged my mind.

What did I care enough to write about?

What would hold my attention as I did the research?

What was I passionate about?

That was the big question for me. If I'm passionate about something, nothing can stop me from accomplishing my goal, but if I'm not completely passionate, I'm easily bored.

A message from Katrina the day before – asking when I would have an answer – had intensified the pressure, but certainly not provided what she was looking for.

I had no idea as I made my way down Monument Avenue, almost not seeing all the Civil War statues that line it because I'd seen them every day for years, that *this* was going to be the day my life changed.

I had no idea I would find my answer because the pizza restaurant wasn't open yet!

My distraction had resulted in me showing up for lunch an hour early – and one hour before the restaurant opened.

It was a beautiful day so I decided to go for a walk. As I strolled along the treed streets of Richmond, I saw a sign indicating there was a re-enactment happening that day for the Chimborazo Hospital. I had no idea what that even was, but I decided since I had time to kill, and because I had heard the site offered a fabulous view of the James River, that I would go up the hill to discover what it was all about.

Little did I know how much it would change my life.

When I arrived on the bluff overlooking the James River, I saw several large tents that had been set up to represent the hospital wards where tens of thousands of Confederate soldiers were taken care of during the Civil War.

Fluffy white clouds flowed across the sky, casting dark shadows on the glistening waters of the James River gliding past below me. I smiled as two kayakers took on the rapids, admiring their grace and evident skill.

After watching for several minutes, I turned around to look at the tents. I could hear voices coming from inside one of them, so I went inside.

I was delighted to see a young woman dressed in 1860's clothing, and a circle of twenty to thirty second graders sitting around her on the ground, listening with rapt attention.

I listened along with them, enjoying learning more about what had happened at the hospital, but also horrified by the hardships and suffering that had been endured there.

When the young lady finished speaking, she asked if anyone had questions. I waited to see if any of the children would respond. When they remained silent, I raised my hand.

"Yes?" the young woman asked pleasantly.

I asked what I thought was an innocent question. "Are there any of the documents left from the original hospital?" I love original documents because they haven't been doctored yet!

She appeared exasperated, gave me a look that clearly said she doubted my intelligence, and snapped, "Well, no, of course not. They were all burned when the Yankees came down here and set fire to Richmond!"

Well, I didn't know a lot about the Civil War at that point, but I knew *that* wasn't true.

I pondered whether to challenge her because I didn't want to cause embarrassment, and then looked again at the group of 2nd graders clustered around her – listening... believing they were hearing the truth.

I raised my hand again. I could tell she didn't want to acknowledge me, but she did. "Yes?"

I spoke calmly. "Isn't it true that the Confederates set fire to Richmond?"

Her eyes flashed with anger as she snapped, "Well! They wouldn't have done it if those damn Yankees hadn't been here!"

THAT was the moment I decided to write about the Civil War.

In spite of the fact that I lived in the capitol of the Confederacy, I had never considered writing about the Civil War. That had been done. By a *lot* of writers. I'd read many of the books, myself. Why would I want to tackle something that didn't need tackling?

I got my answer that day.

As I looked at all those impressionable children who were being poisoned with ignorant bias, I knew I had to write books that would tell the truth.

I walked back down the hill, found a pay phone, and called my publisher.

"Hello Katrina. I'm writing about the Civil War."

To her credit, she didn't question me or remind me that Gone With The Wind, Cold Mountain, and John Jakes' books – among a myriad of others – had already been written. She certainly had more confidence in me at that point than I did, but I knew I had identified my passion. Each book has only deepened that passion as I have discovered the truth about so many things.

"The Civil War it is," Katrina said cheerfully. "When should we expect the first book? A year?"

My walking away from all my other books had put a crimp in my finances at that point. Also, I had learned just how fast I could write. Factoring research into it, I took a huge leap of faith (or insanity – the jury is still out on that one!) "I'll have it to you in six months," I said confidently, praying I could actually pull it off.

"I see…" Katrina said slowly.

I could feel her preparing to tell me it should be a year. "I can do it, Katrina."

Katrina sighed, but relented. "Okay." I could tell she didn't believe I could pull it off, but she'd also learned to not argue with me.

"Another thing," I said. "I don't want to write under my name."

"What?" Katrina was clearly startled. "You've already developed a following for your name. It makes no sense to not use it."

"I have a following of teenagers," I reminded her. "I'm writing for adults now. I want to do it under a pen name."

"Why?"

I smiled. "If I ever develop enough of a following to be famous, I don't want to be."

"You don't want to be famous?" Katrina was clearly skeptical.

"I assure you I don't," I said firmly. "I want to write books, and I want to live my life. I don't want to be recognized."

"I see..." Katrina said again. "What name do you want to write under?"

I had already given it a lot of thought. Without having written the first one, my gut told me historical fiction would be my future. "Virginia Gaffney."

"I assume there is a story behind that?"

"Yes." I told Katrina the story of my grandfather, Wallace Lorrimer Gaffney. "My legal first name is Virginia. I want to use Gaffney as my last name so my writing will be a tribute to him."

"We'll do it your way," Katrina agreed reluctantly. "Make sure the first book is a good one."

*****

By now, I know you're scratching your head. Who am I? *Ginny Dye? Virginia Gaffney?*

Both, actually.

You'll have to keep reading to understand the whole story, but *The Bregdan Chronicles* began their life as the *Richmond Chronicles* – written by Virginia Gaffney.

It's a convoluted story (remember the Twisted Road?), but it will make sense in time.

*****

Once I'd decided what I was going to write about, it was time to dig into the research. I was astounded to discover how much I loved it.

Trust me, things were quite different back then. The internet wasn't a thing; at least, not a thing I knew anything about. I did all my research the old-fashioned way. I checked out every book from the library I could get my hands on, and had books delivered from both the North and South via interlibrary loan.

I spent countless hours in the archives of the Virginia Historical Society in Richmond.

I have no idea how many dimes I fed the copier so I could take home pages of the archived materials I found. I lost track of how many hours I spent writing the contents of books by hand because they were too old to put on the copier.

I was relentless in exploring and understanding the truth.

The day came when I knew it was time to stop researching, and time to start writing. Gathering all my information, I worked to put together an outline for the book. The very act of doing it brought home the truth that I had absolutely no idea what I was attempting to pull off!

Writing 200-page teen novels, drawing from my own experiences, was one thing. I'd never even written an outline! A 500-page novel with complex plot lines and many more characters was another thing, altogether.

I plowed on, finally coming up with what I supposed was an outline.

It was time to write.

I printed out my outline, put it beside my computer, and sat down to write.

I stared at the screen.

Then, I stared at it some more.

Three days later I was still staring at a completely blank screen, and I was in a state of terror.

What had I done? I couldn't write a 500-page historical novel! I had said yes, but this time it was going to come back to haunt me. I couldn't do it.

It was really just that simple.

I couldn't do it.

Except, I'd made a promise. More importantly, the research I'd done had created a story in my head that was begging to be told. It didn't change the truth, however, that I had absolutely no clue how to do it. I found myself wishing for a degree in English, the experience of countless English classes, or that I had at least paid a little more attention at the one writer's conference I'd been to.

The sick feeling in the pit of my stomach threatened to consume me.

At my wit's end, I did the only thing I could think of. I lowered my head to my desk and prayed. "God, what am I going to do?!"

Now, this next part you may have a little difficulty swallowing, but I'm just telling you what happened.

Have you seen the movie, The Field of Dreams? If not, you should. Anyway, one of the iconic lines is, *If you build it, he will come.*   In the movie, it's referring to building a baseball field for deceased players to return to.

Now that I have you totally confused, there really is a point to this...

As I sat there with my head lowered to my desk, I heard a voice. *If you write it, it will come.*

I bolted straight up and stared around my office, relieved to find I was alone, but shaken. "What?" I stammered.

The voice came again. *If you write it, it will come.*

Was the voice real? Was it just in my head? I don't really know. I just know it reverberated through my entire being with truth.

If you write it, it will come.

I sat there for a few minutes, trying to absorb what I'd heard, and then decided I had nothing to lose. Nobody was there to witness me losing my mind. I put my fingers on the keyboard and started moving them.

Six weeks later, I had six hundred pages.

The first book of The Richmond Chronicles, *Under The Southern Moon* was done.

Yes, it's the one you know now as *Storm Clouds Rolling In.*

If you write it, it will come...

I've been doing this same thing for the last twelve books. I fully anticipate doing it for every book that follows!

You see, I believe writing The Bregdan Chronicles is a main missions in my life. I believe writing them is so much bigger than I am. It astounds me every day that I have the privilege of creating these books. When I'm shaken by the responsibility, and doubt I have what it takes, I hear the voice...

If you write it, it will come.

*****

When I finished the first book, I knew I had found one of the huge purposes of my life. What a joy!

Purpose. So many people struggle to define their purpose. Purpose is the *why* – why you're here. It's knowing what your special calling in life is. Your purpose is what makes you unique – the special gifts and abilities you were born with, and can contribute to the world.

Young or old – it can be tough to know what your purpose is, yet it may be the most important thing you discover about yourself. I believe your lasting happiness depends on it. Knowing your purpose will fuel your efforts and give you the drive to keep pressing on, no matter the challenges you face.

Some people think you can't know your purpose when you're young, or they think if they're older that it's too late for it to make any difference. Nonsense! It's never too early or too late to live the best life you can live. It's never too early or late to live with the feeling you're fulfilling your destiny.

Here's a thought to wrap your brain around: **Everyone dies, but not everyone really lives.**

Too many people flounder through life – waiting, hoping that the moment will come when their purpose becomes clear. In the meantime, they're simply going through the motions of living, never experiencing the exciting spark of aliveness that comes from knowing your purpose.

What about you? Do you know why you're here? Do you wake up every day, excited about your life? If you don't, you're not alone, but I believe you can change that. Finding your purpose is a process requiring self-reflection and patience. It seems unfair that you don't just *know* why you are here, but life is not always fair (surprise, surprise!).

Here's the first thing I want you to do... whether you do it is totally up to you!

Pull out a sheet of paper and write, "How I Want to Be Remembered." Then add columns: Friends; Spouse; Children; Co-Workers; Community; the World. If you go to church, belong to a team, or another special group, add them in.

Now...List all the qualities, deeds and characteristics you would like to be remembered for. If you're still breathing it's not too late...

When you've done that, go back. Find the pattern that shows you your highest values. Discover what drives you. Determine your purpose.

People ask me, "Once I determine my purpose, does that mean I quit whatever I'm doing to pursue that?"

Maybe.

Maybe not.

I never tell people what I think they should do. Each person has to make their decisions about how they live their life. The important thing is to spend enough time with yourself to learn your purpose, and then make your decisions around that knowledge.

It's also important to realize that your Purpose can change. Your purpose at 60 might not be the same purpose at 25. And it may change again at 75... or at *any* age. Don't stick yourself in a box. Life changes... *you* change... your PURPOSE changes...

But whether or not it changes, I believe all of us should be able to wake up every day with the excitement of PURPOSE.

*****

Of course, I still didn't know if my publisher thought I had found my purpose. What if they hated the first book?

Chapter Seven

I will admit I was on pins and needles while I waited to see how my publisher would respond to *Storm Clouds Rolling In*. I had given it my best, but I knew they might think it was awful.

The call came a few weeks after I mailed it off.

"We love it!" Katrina said enthusiastically as soon as I picked up the phone.

I sagged against my desk with relief. "Of course you do," I responded calmly.

Katrina laughed. "You've been driving yourself crazy waiting for this phone call, haven't you?"

What can I say? She knew me well! My laugh was answer enough.

"Start work on the next one, Ginny. The *Richmond Chronicles* are going to do great!"

Just like that, I was off into the adventure of research and writing Book # 2. Writing it brought so many things into clarity for me. As the black characters in my series came to life, I realized my books were going to communicate not just the truth of the Civil War, but also my hatred for prejudice and racism.

Most of my childhood, I wondered if I was adopted because I was so different from everyone else in my family.

One of the few memories I have of my childhood was Ruth. In the vernacular of the 1960's, she was our maid.

In reality, she was a huge part of my salvation from the abuse of my childhood.

I can still see her clearly in my mind. Ruth was tall, slender, and a beautiful caramel-colored woman. Her eyes, though, are what I will always remember most. Dark brown, they were the kindest, most loving eyes I had ever seen. I'm sure she was aware of the trauma I endured so she did the only thing she had the power to do – she loved me.

She held me on her lap. She brushed my hair. She let me work with her in the kitchen. And she taught me how to iron. One day she arrived with a six-year-old size ironing board. I was delighted beyond words to stand by her side, ironing with her as I imitated what she did. We started with handkerchiefs, moved to napkins, and eventually graduated to pants and shirts.

I loved ironing because I was doing it with Ruth! I never spared a thought as to what color she was, or the fact that her life as a maid, made possible by a long bus ride from the other side of Charlotte, must have been very difficult.

I loved her.

She loved me.

That was all I cared about. I don't remember how long she was our maid, or why she left. That's another one of those things I've blocked out. I'm sure I was heart-broken, though, the day I was told she wouldn't be coming back. It was another arrow into an already wounded soul.

Ruth came to my high school graduation. My heart filled with so much joy when I saw her come into the building. I ran into her arms, once more the little girl who had found a safe haven with a woman who embraced me with her huge heart.

I wasn't aware enough at eighteen to make sure I got her contact information. I've never seen her again, but I sure wish I could!

*****

Racism was not part of my reality when I was growing up in an all-white neighborhood in Charlotte, NC. I went to an all-white elementary school, and then moved on to Smith Junior High, which had always been white.

I was in the seventh grade when the first black students arrived at my school in 1968. There were only a few, and I know now that it was just a token effort by the school system to comply with new laws. I didn't know anything about the Civil Rights Movement or how schools were being desegregated to follow the law. I didn't know that it was actually 1954 when the Supreme Court ruled in Brown vs. Board of Education that "separate educational facilities are inherently unequal", and thus unconstitutional. The decision mandated that schools be integrated, but in reality, very little happened following that ruling. It took years for momentum from the civil rights movement to create enough political pressure for truly meaningful integration to take place in classrooms across the country.

I just knew that one day there was a black girl in my gym class. Her name was Cheryl. I know there were other black students, but I don't remember them. I remember Cheryl.

Cheryl was quiet. She was also tall. As tall as I was. I hit six feet tall when I was just fourteen. It was fun to have another girl to look eye-to-eye with.

Sports filled my life. I had just started horseback riding, but I also spent hours playing softball, basketball and soccer. I ran track, but only because they figured someone six feet tall could handle the hurdles. Oh, I could jump them, but I've never been all that fast, so they sent me on my way after a little while. I was happy to have more hours to play softball and basketball.

Cheryl was an athlete, too. We played on the same teams and we also competed. I respected her and admired her. I also loved her quiet ways and her beautiful smile. It wasn't long before we were fast friends.

Once again, I didn't care, or even particularly notice, what color she was. Cheryl was my friend.

Fast forward two years. Racial tensions had reached a frightening height in Charlotte. 1971 was like a powder keg, with far too many people eager to light the match that would ignite it. For three years, Charlotte was like a battlefield. The headlines were a blur of fights and riots at area high schools. The mass fights were so frequent that police stood outside schools with tear gas and masks, ready to break up the next riot.

I was still in junior high when the worst fights happened at the high school I would attend – the one both my brothers already attended. The three of us were all born closely together, so I followed them in school, with a grade between each of us.

Neither of them felt about black people the way I did. Prejudice and racism ran strong in my family back then.

I can remember the day I had to make my decision with crystal clarity.   I was in my Algebra class when the principal opened the door and beckoned for my teacher to join him.   She instructed us to keep working on whatever problem we were on, and then went out into the hall.   Several minutes later, she walked back in with a serious expression.   My gut tightened when her eyes settled on me.

I knew something bad had happened.

My teacher, Mrs. Paules, beckoned me out into the hall and then quietly explained that one of my brothers had been seriously hurt during a riot that morning at his high school.   He had been taken to the hospital, and a neighbor was on her way to pick me up so I could join my family there.

I will never forget the rage that filled me. Rage at the kids who had done this to my brother.

Rage at *all* black people.

Just like that, I went from loving feelings about Ruth and Cheryl, to being filled with hate and rage. My mind raced as I planned how I would avenge my brother.

Mrs. Paules correctly interpreted the look on my face. She took both my hands in hers and forced me to gaze into her expressive brown eyes.   "Ginny, you have a choice to make. Hate is not the answer."

I wrenched my gaze away from hers, determined to feel what I was feeling, but when I did, I locked eyes with Cheryl over her shoulder. My friend was watching me with a scared, sorrowful expression on her face – somehow knowing what was going on. As I looked at her, I didn't see a black person. I saw my friend.

My friend.

I made my choice in that moment.

I would not hate.

I would never hate.

Let's be honest here. I hated that my brother got hurt and I'm happy to report he recovered fully. I also hate he chose to be involved in the riot. If he had not been the one hurt, I know he would have inflicted as much damage as possible.

There was enough hate in the world already. It didn't need mine. The world needed me to do something different.

I would never hate.

The riots and violence continued for two more years. I hated all aspects of it but it didn't alter my decision.

I made my choice and I've lived it ever since.

*****

Other things happened in my life to cement my hatred of prejudice and racism of any kind.

When I was fifteen, a group called The New Directions came to my church. I'm sure my mouth was hanging open when they walked up to the front of the sanctuary – a completely interracial group of high school and college students. You could tell they were all great friends, and could they ever sing!

As the months passed, I became very close to some of the black members. I went to see them sing every chance I got, and because many of them stayed with a family that had become like a second family to me, I was able to develop real relationships.

One of the relationships I built was with the niece of one of the members. She was several years younger than me, and I became a big sister to her. Lots of letters and phone calls deepened our friendship.

When I was a senior in high school, I would often borrow my mother's car and drive the two hours to her house, spending the weekend with her and her family before I came home again. On one of my trips back to Charlotte, I stopped by my father's house to drop something off.

We were sitting out on the porch talking when he asked me how my weekend went.

"Great!" I said cheerfully. "Diedre and I had a great time!" As soon as the words were out of my mouth, I saw his eyes and mouth harden, and the lines on his face tighten.

"Diedre?" He spoke the name as if it was something vile.

I nodded, suddenly afraid of what was coming. Because I didn't live with my father, he didn't know much about my life. I didn't know much about his either, but I'd heard enough to know how he felt about black people.

"That sounds like a black name," my father said with gritted teeth.

I met his eyes evenly. "It is."

His eyes flared with anger. "Are you telling me that you stayed at a n*****r's house this whole weekend?"

I tensed but wasn't going to back down. "Her name is Diedre, and she's my friend."

His eyes burned hotter as he snapped the next question. "What did you do while you were there?"

"I played basketball." I figured that was a safe enough answer. I was wrong.

"You played basketball with n***** boys? Don't you know what you were inviting them to do to you?"

I was now as angry as he was. My thoughts shot back to the fun-filled games, loud with laughter and joking. I had many friends in Diedre's neighborhood, and no one had ever been anything more than friendly and welcoming. "I was inviting them to play basketball," I snapped. "They're my friends."

My father tensed with rage. "My daughter will not be friends with n*****s," he growled. "I forbid you to ever go there again."

I managed to hide the laugh that wanted to escape. When had my father ever told me what to do? I'd practically raised myself all my life. My only response was to look at him.

"You give me your word that you'll never go there again, or you can kiss college good-bye, young lady."

His threat got my attention. I had just been accepted at my first choice of colleges (chosen because the tennis courts were behind the freshman dorm!) and didn't want to throw that away. I calculated quickly. I was already pretty much on my own. Once I started college I would be two hours farther away, and only thirty minutes from Diedre.

"I promise," I said quietly.

I'm not necessarily proud of the fact that I lied, but I would do it again. At eighteen, I was all too aware of just how violent racism could be. I also had observed the blatant racism in my family. I refused to become like them, but I wouldn't help anyone by throwing away my chance to go to college, so I lied.

And then I kept living my life – building my community of friends – both white and black.

*****

When I was in college I ended up dating a guy who had been my best friend for a couple years. And, yes, he was black.

One of our favorite things to do was go out to a lake about thirty minutes from campus. There was a rope swing that provided hours of fun.

It was late one spring afternoon when we were headed out to the rope swing. We were laughing and talking, bouncing to whatever music was blaring on the radio of my yellow VW Convertible when we rounded the curve and fell into a shocked silence.

A large, charred cross stood in the yard of one of the houses.

We were both furious and terrified at evidence of the Ku Klux Klan at work.

We also never returned to the lake. We were smart enough to know that in the late 70's our interracial relationship would not be well accepted by the bigoted people who had burned a cross in that black family's yard.

My sheltered life on a college campus came crashing into stark reality that day. We continued dating for a while longer, but we had a new awareness of the dangers.

I graduated in 1979 and moved to East Texas to run the horsemanship program for a ranch. About a month later I was stunned to read a newspaper article about an entire black family that had been found hung in a local salt mine. Their "sin" had been to move into a white county.

I was sickened and horrified – and once again made to face the reality of what so many people in our country face on a daily basis. A reality I was protected from simply because I was born with white skin.

I could go on and on with stories, but I believe I've made my point; and hopefully given you an understanding of just why I'm so passionate about eliminating prejudice and racism in our country, and in our world. It's not just Black and White. It's also Latino... and Asian... and Native American... It's about prejudice toward women... and gays... and transgenders... and any other group of people who find themselves the target of ignorance and hatred.

I will always add my voice to the call for equality.

*****

Doing the research for Book # 2 was as much a joy as doing it for *Under The Southern Moon/Storm Clouds Rolling In*, but I was continually amazed to discover how clueless I was about so many things.

While I didn't enjoy history the way it was taught in school, I was an excellent student so I can truly say I learned it. Well, at least the version I was taught. The more research I did, and the more I learned, the more I realized how much of a disservice our education system does to history – at least in regard to the Civil War.

If you're from the South, you're taught Civil War history one way.

If you're from the North, you're taught Civil War history another way.

If you're from another part of the country, you get another version.

Here's the kicker, though...

None of them are true!

I think it should be a crime for people to use textbooks to push their own agenda. The truth, taught well, should be the litmus test for education. Let students take the *facts* and come to their own conclusions. Unfortunately, that is rarely done.

The result is what happened with the young lady in the tent at the Chimborazo Hospital Re-enactment.

The result is the ignorance that continues to inflame bigotry and prejudice in our country.

The result is the fear that people live with because too many schools teach a curriculum that is meant to put forth their agenda.

It breaks my heart.

It also makes me furious, and it makes me determined to fight back with every ounce of my being.

How?

By telling the truth in my books.

I love how many people contact me to tell me they have researched the things I write about – astounded at how accurate I am. I love that they're double-checking. It's only when people question the things they are taught, and find out what is really true, that we stand a chance of not being taken by people with agendas.

My favorite reviews and letters are the ones I get from people who want to let me know that The Bregdan Chronicles changed how they view people and life. They admit they've had to confront their prejudices, and they're committed to changing them within themselves and within their families.

My heart sings and I do a happy dance in my office every time I read one of those!

Here is my promise to all of you. I will never write something I don't know is the truth. I told you earlier that I write really fast. It's not the writing that takes so much time; it's the research. It takes hundreds of hours to research each book. I dig deep to learn, and then understand, the truth.

I've been accused of having an agenda. I don't.

I've been accused of being too Christian.

I've been accused of being a horrible liberal feminist.

None of it bothers me.

Just because you don't like the history I write about doesn't mean I have an agenda.

Just because you don't like the truth of something doesn't mean I have an agenda.

Just because you do, or don't, want a certain type of person or a certain situation to exist in one of my books, doesn't mean I have an agenda.

It means I'm not going to change what I write because someone might not like it.

It means I let history carry every book.

I research like crazy, and then I let what happened in that time dictate the lives and actions of my characters, so I can bring it to light.

It's tremendous fun. It's also tremendously challenging, but I wouldn't change what I have the privilege of doing for anything!

You know, I used to think I wanted to be a history teacher. I longed to teach history the way it should be taught – with stories that made people real. That made the times they lived in real.

I realize that in writing The Bregdan Chronicles, I'm kind of the ultimate history teacher! And, I can reach far more people than I ever would in a classroom.

******

The challenges of facing the Six Years of Darkness continued, but I could forget the flashbacks and the night terrors when I was researching and writing.

My work gave me a sense of purpose that sustained me through all the years that I often doubted I had any purpose at all.

In many ways, writing these books kept me alive. It was so exciting when I delivered # 2 to my publisher. It was *Carry Me Home* in The Richmond Chronicles. All of you know it as *On To Richmond* in The Bregdan Chronicles.

It's the same book!

*****

Richmond, Virginia was my home. I thought it always would be.

Until...

Annie's Chicken and Dumplings

Cut a fowl into pieces to serve and cook in water to cover until the bones will come out easily. Before taking them out drop dumplings in, cover closely and cook ten minutes without lifting the cover. The liquid should be boiling rapidly when the dough is put in and kept boiling until the end. For the dumplings, sift two cups of flour twice with half a level teaspoon of salt and four level teaspoons of baking powder. Mix with about seven —eights cup of milk, turn out on a well-floured board and pat out half an inch thick. Cut into small cakes. If this soft dough is put into the kettle in spoonful's the time of cooking will be doubled.

Annie's Chicken and Dumplings

The bones and meat will keep the dough from s

ettling into the liquid and becoming soggy

Arrange the meat in the center, with dumplings

around the edge and a sprig of parsley between each.

Thicken the liquid and season with salt and pepper

as needed and a rounding tablespoon of butter.

Chapter Eight

With # 2 behind me, it was time to tackle # 3. Other than knowing I would be covering the second year of the Civil War, I didn't know what the book would hold. People often ask me how far in advance I plan the plots and outlines of my books.

The short answer? I don't.

The longer answer? I want the lives of the characters in The Bregdan Chronicles as close to real life as I can make them. With that in mind, none of us have the option of making choices and decisions about our lives based on what we know will happen. Oh, we can have goals and plans (trust me, I have tons of them!), but none of us has the luxury of knowing exactly what will happen in our lives.

One accident can change our life in a Nano-second. One illness can alter what we're capable of. Someone else's actions can take away the opportunities we thought were ours. One storm can destroy our home. A business going under can remove the job security we thought we had.

You get the idea... I know you've had things like this impact you many times in your own life.

The Bregdan Family is no different. I don't even think about what will be in the next book of The Bregdan Chronicles until I've finished the one I'm working on. Besides the fact that it's truer to real life, it's also far more fun that way! I never know what's going to happen in everyone's life until I've done the research.

I can't tell you how many times my eyes have widened with disbelief when I discovered something. Or how many times my mind spun with how a character's life would change because of what I had learned.

Research is just *fun*. It takes me in directions I never thought I would go. It sends me on journeys of discovery that make me shake my head. It has given me a deep appreciation for people who have made sure history is protected through historical societies, and for those non-fiction writers who are determined to share the truth of what has happened in our past. It has given me such vast respect for the women who fought back against the stereotypes society tried to strap on them. It has given me such appreciation for the men full of integrity who made choices to move our country forward.

And, yes, it has also filled me with anger and disdain for poor choices that destroyed so many lives and made life unbearably difficult for millions more.

Every book has made me more determined to reveal the truth. Why? Because when the truth is hidden in shadows of greed and personal agenda we don't know what we're fighting. When the light of truth reveals the reality of our past, suddenly we look at attitudes and actions with new eyes and a deeper understanding. We develop new passion to right the wrongs that have been done, and also set in place the standards that will keep it from happening again.

At least, that's what it's done for me. I pray that every person who reads my books comes away with the same conviction and passion.

Writing # 3 was especially life-changing for me.

You know # 3 as *Spring Will Come*. It first was published as *Tender Rebel* under The Richmond Chronicles.

One of the challenges of writing this book is to talk about the books in the series without revealing plot lines that will diminish your reading enjoyment if you haven't gotten to a particular book yet.

Having said that, Robert's transformation was amazing to write about. As I watched it come to life beneath my fingers on the keyboard, I was constantly reminded that *anyone* can change. It's so easy sometimes to put people in a box because of their actions and attitudes. The problem with that is that boxes can be broken out of. They can be torn apart, or they can melt away beneath love and compassion.

We all do a great disservice to people when we believe they can't change.

I believe the greater challenge, and the superior way to live, is to believe people *can* change. If you can truly believe that, then it changes how you deal with people. You don't see them as a hopeless case – you see them as someone who needs an opportunity to be different. What an incredible joy it is when you can be the person who opens their eyes to an alternate way of seeing the world – an alternate way of being.

My experience shows me that it doesn't happen with ridicule and disdain. It doesn't happen with angry name-calling, or with believing they're a hopeless case.

Robert's transformation in *Spring Will Come* was made possible by a love and compassion he did not deserve.

The people who extended that love and compassion were the real heroes in this book.

Every book I've written has made me a better person. It has challenged me to be more than who I was when I started it. *Spring Will Come* was no exception. It sparked in me a desire to give people a love and compassion they don't deserve every day of my life.

Does that mean I look the other way when I see something being done that I believe is wrong? Definitely not. I fight for what I believe in. I always have, and I always will. But I believe you can fight from a place of hatred and disdain, or you can fight from a place that offers grace and compassion to the people you're fighting against.

If you're rolling your eyes, and you have no concept of what I'm attempting to communicate, take just a little while and think about it.

Think about times in your life when you changed your opinion about something.

Think about times in your life when you became a different person who was committed to doing different things.

What happened in your life to change you?

How can you use your answers to enable you to spark change in others?

*****

Writing *Spring Will Come* was often a surreal experience. I've told you already about the voice I heard in my office... *If you write it, it will come.*

While there are many times I feel completely inadequate to write what I'm writing about, I am 100% committed to preparing myself to write on a daily basis. I'm an early riser. Most mornings you'll find me up by 5:00 AM. It's my favorite part of the day because the world is so quiet.

The vast majority of the time I'll go outside and slip into my hot tub. As I watch a new day come to life, and I listen as the hoot of owls gives way to the song of birds singing to the dawn, I pray. I ask to be a vessel. I ask that my own ignorance and fears will not get in the way of my writing powerful books. I sit quietly, letting the beauty of nature fill me.

Only then, will I go to my office and write.

I write, I close my computer down, and I call it a day. The next morning, I read back over what I've written. There have been so many times when I truly don't remember writing what I'm reading. Now, that may seem a little "woo woo" (or out there) for some of you, but it also happens to be the truth. There are moments my eyes will grow wide as I absorb the power of what I wrote. When I don't remember writing it, that's when I know it's *really* good!

I had so many of those moments when I was writing *Spring Will Come*. Smiles... goosebumps... tears.

Those experiences have taught me the most powerful time of my day is not when I'm writing – it's when I'm sitting in my hot tub... or on top of my mountain... or simply leaning against a tree in the forest. Any power in my writing comes from my commitment to *listen*. Am I listening to God? To the Universe? To a Higher Power?

I give you permission (not that you need it, of course!) to call it anything you want. I simply know my most important job is to get quiet. And to *listen*. It's when I listen the most that my writing is most powerful.

I feel so strongly about listening that I'm including something I wrote several years ago...

*****

Every now and again I will get a comment that I know I should share the answer with everyone. This was one of those...

Hi Ginny, I have read all 8 of your Bregdan Chronicles and always find myself amazed at how much I emotionally grow as I read each book. I was raised in the Deep South and have experienced many extreme opinions regarding the Civil War era, although I quickly learned to keep my thoughts to myself. For example, as a young child, I was spanked once for what I was thinking. Through the Bregdan Chronicles, I finally found validation in the beliefs I've held quiet and dear to my heart for many years. Finally!!! I'm enjoying your Bursts of Hope videos, but I'm finding that my many years of frustration are exasperated by watching them. I have pondered for years.... What am I passionate about? Honestly, I don't know! I've pondered this for many years - all my adult years! Who am I??? If nothing stood in my way, what would I do? Who would I be? Where would I go? I am always there for others... loving, serving, giving, uplifting, sacrificing my wishes for whatever is needed by another. I give 110%. I have developed an innate ability to know what others need, but

I don't know what I need. I don't know who I am. I don't know what I could/would be passionate about. I will continue to watch your Bursts of Hope videos and maybe, just maybe, I will be inspired and will finally KNOW who am I? What is MY passion? Where I can find joy for myself in life? And then, I hope your inspiration will give me the motivation I need to follow my dreams, whatever they may be. Thanks for listening........

This was my response to her powerful communication in the Blog I wrote after receiving it...

*****

This will not be a short answer, because the question is simply too important. For me, personally, I believe it may be more important than anything I have ever shared with you, and I believe you're going to need it for every day that will unfold before you for the rest of your life. How's that for a lead-in?

Doing it is the most important part of my day.

Doing it is the only thing that has taken me through really challenging times in my life.

Doing it is the only thing that allows me to put into practice all I've learned through the years.

Doing it gives me what I need to face whatever each day brings.

What is it??

Let's dive right in because I'm so excited to tell you!

I have spent the last 30+ years working with people. Teenagers and Adults. Everyone struggles with the same things.

How to find direction.

How to find purpose.

How to know what to do with their life.

How to make the right decisions.

How to find the answers to the questions they have for their life.

You read books. You attend seminars. You look for teachers. But too few people (in fact, *most* people) don't do the ONE thing that will give you what you're looking for. Now, don't misunderstand me. Books are great. I read all the time. Seminars are wonderful. I attend many of them. Teachers are great – I hope I'm one of them... but still, MOST people don't do the ONE thing that will give you what you're looking for.

The ONE THING?

One word...

LISTEN.

People don't listen. And I don't mean listening to other people. I'm talking about listening to YOURSELF. Listening to a higher power. Listening to the Universe. No matter what your faith or belief system, you simply don't listen.

You are failing to give yourself the greatest gift you possibly could.

How can you? From the minute you get up your world is full of activity and noise. You turn on the radio, stereo or television. You're uncomfortable with too much silence.

And then you fill every minute of your day with activity. Working. Talking. Texting. School. Responsibilities. Fun. Every minute is crammed with some kind of noise or activity, and then you fall into bed (many of you even watching television then!) so that you can get up the next morning and do it all over again.

And yet your head spins with the questions of how to find direction, purpose and answers. How exactly do you think the answers are supposed to filter through all the noise and activity?

It's a lot like trying to bash through a concrete wall in order to get into a building. There's a door right there, but you don't step back long enough to see it – you just keep bashing against the concrete, wondering why you can't get to your destination.

I watch people bash against that wall every day. When I suggest they should get QUIET and listen for the answer, they look at me as if they feel sorry for my very naïve and simplistic way of them getting what they need. I mean, after all, they just got back from four days of a seminar that had them listening to great speakers for twelve hours. Or, they just finished reading an entire series of books on their problem. It's clear to them that they just haven't connected with the right person or book that can give them the direction they need.

Wrong!

What's *clear* is that you can have all the information in the world, but if you don't get *quiet* for long enough to LISTEN for your answer, you will never find what you're looking for.

And please know I'm not talking about turning off the TV for five minutes, and then turning it back on to fill the void when you don't hear a booming voice that gives your answer. It's not like that.

You have to make listening a priority. You have to make QUIET a priority in your life. Well, no of course, you don't *have* to (it's a choice), but if you want to quit floundering and being frustrated, I suggest it is something you *decide* to do.

The time I spend in quiet, just listening, are the most treasured and valuable moments of my day. Claiming those times is my highest priority because I know I cannot be who and what I want to be in the world if I don't have those times. I know I can't give what I'm meant to give without time to be quiet and listen. I know I can't come up with answers. And I definitely know I can't live the life I dream of living.

I know everyone has to design those times for themselves, but I'm going to share with you what they look like for me – hoping that will help you develop your own Blueprint for Listening.

When I wake up in the morning I fix a cup of hot chocolate (yes, I'm a chocolate addict, but because you've heard me talk so much about health, you need to know I make them with organic almond milk, organic cocoa, organic cinnamon, and organic stevia as my sweetener!) Then, after time in the hot tub, I head for my office. I do *not* turn on my computer. Instead, I sit down at my desk and pull out my journal. I have huge ring bound notebooks full of journaling throughout my life.

And then I just sit there quietly. Sometimes I sing a little. Sometimes I pray. Other times I just close my eyes and let the silence embrace me. Yes, I'm just like everyone. Sometimes my spinning thoughts are louder than the silence, but that's when I turn to my journal. The only way to quiet those spinning thoughts is for me to write them down. There's no format. This is *my* journal. I just write. I pour out all the things that are inside me.

And then, if I have problems I'm dealing with, or questions I need answers to, I just keep writing. Somehow, the answers come pouring out. If I get stuck, I just put my pen down, close my eyes, and let silence wrap around me again.

I LISTEN.

I'm not saying you're listening for a voice, though I would certainly never say you might not hear one. I'm listening for answers within. Whether your faith systems believe those answers come from a higher power or your own self; if you listen long enough and carefully enough, you will discover you have the answers.

Think about it this way... When you buy a fancy piece of electronics, doesn't it come with a User Manual? The person who created it knows you need the right information to know how to use it. Right? Well, don't you think whoever or whatever created your life, knows that you need the right information to know how to use it, and live it in the best way possible?

It's *not* about what someone else may have written or created to tell you how to live your life – though they can certainly have value.

It's about what was created INSIDE of you from the very beginning.

YOU have the answers for your life.

YOU are the one who knows what your purpose is.

You just have to listen long enough to discover what it is.

Now, granted, I have learned how to listen because I've made it a priority for a long time. Don't think you can just decide to trot downstairs one morning with a cup of hot chocolate, pull out a notebook, start writing, and come up with all your answers.

You have to learn how to listen. You have to commit to choosing *Quiet* over frenetic noise and activity. People put such a premium value on doing. I've learned my best doing comes when I first put my focus on *being*.

You have to learn how to hear what your heart, spirit and mind are telling you. And, folks, there is only one way to do that. You have to make it a priority.

You have to choose to LISTEN on a daily basis.

Perhaps you'll need a small devotional or guide type book to jumpstart your heart and mind. That's cool, but don't turn your

Listening time into reading time, because then all you're doing is listening to someone else, not to YOU.

Perhaps you don't need a journal at all. Sit in your hot tub. Go out on a trail. Climb a mountain. Sit in your backyard, or on your porch. Find the only quiet place in your busy home, even if it's a closet. Put in earplugs if that's what's necessary. You'll find what you need if you truly want to.

People come to me for advice all the time. I rarely give it. Who am I to know the answers for someone else's life, and besides that, as long as I'm the one giving the answers they can either blame me if I'm wrong, or they can blow me off because I don't know what I'm talking about anyway. It's an easy out that I don't give people.

When people come to me for advice, I usually just ask questions.

I want them to look inside themselves for their answers. I want them to think. I usually send them away with questions, tell them to get quiet, pull out a notebook and start writing the things that come to them.

Writing them is also a great way to remember the powerful epiphanies you have!

I even take my notebook on my mountain in a hip pack because I can have some of the greatest ideas and revelations in the world, but if I don't write them down I'm probably not going to remember them when I return home! Some people might blame that on old age; I prefer to believe my mind is simply too full of powerful thoughts and information to hold it all!

But seriously, I cannot possibly know what's right for someone else's life. I have a challenging enough time knowing how to live mine.

And why would you want someone else to tell you how to live your life anyway?

It's *your* life! You are the only person who can possibly know what's right for you.

A good book, seminar or teacher should ask you questions. They should open your mind to possibilities that you explore when you get QUIET and LISTEN. They should tell stories that make you think deeply – applying what works for YOUR life and tossing out the rest.

I spent 20+ years working with teenagers. I saw this so very often. So many people think we have to teach teenagers what they are to know, think and believe. They have to prepare them for the future with the right information. I disagree. It's not that I didn't teach. It's not that there wasn't information I thought they needed to know, but it was not my job to program their lives for the future. It was *their* job.

What was especially intriguing was to work with kids that had spent their entire lives having that done. They would talk about what they believed.

Then I would ask them why. Usually they would stare at me. "Why what?"

"Why do you believe that?" They'd go back to staring, probably wondering if there was something wrong with me, or if it was a trick question.

Their answers eventually revolved around someone told me, or I read it in a book or on the Internet, or heard it on television.

"Okay, so do you believe it's true?"

"Yes," they would reply.

And I'd go right back to my question, "Why?"

Folks, do you seriously believe that just because someone writes a book, or tells you in a seminar, or posts it on the Internet, or teaches it on television, that it's true?

WHY?? When I was working on the research for The Bregdan Chronicles, I did a ton of research on slavery. What I discovered was that both sides sincerely believed they were right.

The abolitionists in the North who wanted the slaves free completely believed it was wrong. Everything they had been taught, heard and read, told them slavery was wrong.

On the other hand, slave owners in the South had been taught that slavery was right, that it was ordained by God, and that whether they liked it or not, it was their responsibility to have slaves because blacks couldn't take care of themselves.

I believe that's total nonsense, and this southerner is glad slavery was abolished. The point, though, is that these people were taught completely different things, but because someone in authority told them what to believe, they believed it! I need to tell you something... They couldn't both be right!

I don't believe either side truly took the time to understand why they believed it. I don't believe they took the time to understand why the other side believed what they did. I don't believe anyone got quiet long enough to listen for their own beliefs and for the ways to make things right in the world. Why do I believe that?

Because if it had happened the way I just suggested, I don't believe close to one million men would have been slaughtered or injured in the Civil War!

The same scenario has been repeated throughout all of history. So that's the big picture, but it always comes back to the individual little picture. YOU.

How can you possibly find directions and answers if you don't listen?

How can you possibly know if they're the right answers for your life if you don't listen?

How can you possibly have the confidence in your decisions if you're not listening??

Okay, I already know what some of you are thinking.

I don't have time to listen.

Ginny, every minute of my day is already full.

I'm totally stressed with all the things I have to do.

I couldn't possibly...

Yeah. Yeah. Yeah. Been there. Done that. Heard that. It's not that I don't have empathy for your busy life. I just know that you of all people should choose to get QUIET and LISTEN.

Knock something out of your schedule. Get up early. *Make* time for yourself.

There's something else I do when I really need direction and answers. I walk away from my life and find quiet. The magic comes from walking away from the noise, activity, and demands long enough to find what I need.

So you have to decide how to walk away from *your* life. And I mean *really* away. If you decide to go for a long walk, do it where you don't know anyone that you're going to need to talk to. If you decide to go to a nearby park, choose a bench that is as far away from people as possible. Claim your quiet. Claim your chance to listen. If you have to lock your doors, turn off every phone, and unplug every appliance, do it.

The gift you are giving yourself is beyond measure...

Can you tell I'm a little passionate about this?

*****

Readers sometimes ask me why I write about fear so much. I also receive countless letters from readers to thank me for helping them overcome their fears. That's the key. *That* is the reason I write about fear so much!

It all began, however, because of my own battles with fear.

I've told you about my grandfather telling me I had the *gift*, and how the fear that I *didn't* have the *gift* made me stop writing.

Fear is a funny thing. Very few people are afraid of *everything*. Most people, though, have fears that paralyze them in different areas of their life. I was no exception. There was very little I was afraid of. I've always been a dare-devil and there is very little I won't try.

I've rock-climbed. Jumped motorcycles over hills. Bungee jumped. Sky dived. Ridden bucking horses. Done long wilderness trips – solo and with others. Spoken before groups of hundreds and thousands of people. I could go on...

Brave, right?

Well... I could be "brave" about all those things because I didn't believe they reflected who I was in any major way. I didn't do them because I was brave. I did them because they were fun! I love outdoor adventures. I love speaking. What's brave about doing the thing I love?

What I *wouldn't* do was write. It was the one thing in my life that I was convinced would destroy me if I ever found out I truly couldn't do it. I didn't believe I could live with myself if I failed. I believed that not doing it protected me from failure.

Wrong.

I failed, simply because I wouldn't try.

I failed, because I let my fear wrap its tentacles around my heart and squeeze the life and breath from me.

I learned true courage when I chose to face the possibility of failure. I learned true courage when I did the thing I most cared about – the thing I'd been running from for almost twenty years.

It breaks my heart when I see how many people are living their life the same way I lived mine for so long. My goal, when I focus on overcoming fear in The Bregdan Chronicles, is that I will inspire people to move beyond whatever fears are holding them back in their own life.

Nothing gives me more joy than the letters I receive from readers that inform me they have conquered their own fears because of something they read in one of the books. That's when I get up and do a Happy Dance around my office.

I dance because another prisoner has been freed from the bondage of fear.

Writing historical fiction gives me the opportunity to write about fear over and over. Change in our world only happens when people are willing to face their fears and do the things other people aren't willing to. There have been so many amazingly courageous people who have led the way in our country to make powerful changes, but I guarantee every single one of them had to battle fear.

The battle never really stops, though the battlefield often changes.

I had to overcome my fears to write the book you're reading right now. Writing about fictional characters is one thing. Revealing my own life is quite another because I cherish my privacy. I spent hours wondering if anyone would ever want to even read it. I wondered if people would think I was writing it only to stroke my own ego. The fears plagued my thoughts for months before I finally committed to doing it.

My commitment came when I realized that all the lessons I've learned in order to reach this time in my life should be shared. I have no problem sharing them in Blogs, but putting them into book format was entirely different to me. Yet, I couldn't deny they should be shared as a way to encourage, inspire and motivate people into action in their own lives.

I chose to move beyond my fear...

Whatever you are afraid of – what thing will you most regret not doing when you get to the end of your life?

That is probably the thing you need to move heaven and earth to make happen!

*****

It was August of 1996 when I knew it was time to make a change.

I've told you already that I'm a wanderer at heart. I've traveled extensively through the United States, crossing it from the East to West thirteen times, so far. I've explored 49 of the 50 states. Alaska has remained beyond my reach, to date, but I know I will spend several months there soon!

I've loved something about every single place I've lived, but none of them were able to hold me. I was famous for saying, "This place is great! Next..."

Back to August 1996. I was thirty-nine years old and was researching *Spring Will Come.* I had been invited out to have a meeting with my publisher. I decided to blend a face-to-face meeting with the woman who was my editor at the time. We'd become close friends over the phone. Since she lived only a few hours from my publisher I decided to rent a car and drive up to see her in Seattle, Washington.

She surprised me during the visit by taking me out to the San Juan Islands off the coast of Washington State. I knew Oregon well, and had spent a little time in Washington, but didn't know anything about the San Juan Islands.

There are actually 172 of the San Juan Islands (more if you count the Gulf Islands of British Columbia, Canada), but only four of them in the United States are accessible via the ferry system.

I'm quite sure my mouth never completely closed as we loaded onto the ferry and then crossed the glistening waters of the Puget Sound. We threaded our way through several lush, green, mountainous islands, the air alive with the sound of seagulls and cormorants, before we pulled up to the Orcas Island ferry landing – overseen by the beautiful and stately Orcas Hotel. Besides the fact that it has great lodging, it also serves the best cinnamon rolls on the planet!

I sucked in my breath as we pulled off the ferry and began to traverse the roads of Orcas Island. I knew within five minutes that I would come back to this island to live.

I have never felt such a strong pull to a place in my life. It was as if all my moves, to date, had been leading me to this place.

As I wandered the streets of the quaint little town of Eastsound, sat out on a deck to eat lunch while seals cavorted in the waters below me, and then drove to the top of Mt. Constitution to gaze out on incomparable beauty, I knew I would return.

Soon.

It took almost one year before my truck pulled out of Richmond, Virginia, hauling a pop-up camper that would be home for 2 ½ months, and headed west toward Washington State.

However, I'm getting ahead of myself. There was a lot of living, and writing, to be done in that year.

I finished up *Spring Will Come*, and then turned my time and attention to book # 4. *Dark Chaos*, known also as *Magnolia Dreams*, was the last book of what was known as The Richmond Chronicles, under my pen name, Virginia Gaffney.

The research took me in a direction I had never envisioned, and gave me a deeper clarity of the reasons for my passion.

Janie's Southern Style Apple Pie

For four pies, half a pound of butter, quarter pound
of lard, half dinner teaspoon of salt, work four cups
flour and the above ingredients with a fork,
then mix with ice water and mix it so it will just stick
together. Then ready for use. Roll out thin
and cut out eight pieces to measure the same
as the pie pans. Place one pastry on the bottom
of each pan. Pare and quarter apples.
Put a layer of apples in pie dish, sprinkle
with sugar and add a little lemon peel cut up fine
and a little lemon juice if you have it, a few cloves and the rest
of the apples, sugar and so on. Put on an upper crust
and bake. Pies may be buttered when taken from oven.

Chapter Nine

Research for *Dark Chaos* was illuminating, as well as deeply disturbing on a personal level.

My research took me to both Norfolk and Hampton, Virginia to learn more about contraband camps. I already had an appointment to do research in the archives at Hampton University, but first I would have lunch with Effie, the head of the Black Historical Society in Norfolk.

Effie was a complete delight. She looked like a petite fairy as I gazed down at her from my lofty six feet. Her ebony skin glowed, and her bright eyes snapped with life and intelligence. I liked her on sight.

During our conversation to arrange the luncheon, she asked me if I would bring the books I'd written so far. Before we ordered our lunch, I placed copies of the first three books in The Richmond Chronicles on the table. She looked at them strangely but didn't say anything. I shook if off and began to ply her with questions.

We had a fascinating hour of conversation before she turned her eyes to the books again. "Your name is Ginny Dye. Where did Virginia Gaffney come from?"

I smiled and launched into the story of how my great-great-great-great-great grandfather, Captain Michael Gaffney, had founded Gaffney, SC. I could tell by her avid expression that she was intrigued by my revelation, so I elaborated on the story; explaining how Captain Michael had come from Ireland when he was twenty-five, eventually finding his way to an undeveloped crossroad that would become Gaffney, SC.

Then I rolled into the story of my grandfather, explaining how I had decided to use his last name as a tribute to him.

Somewhere in the telling of the stories, Effie's face had taken on an odd expression. I stopped abruptly, leaned forward on my elbows, and peered into her eyes. "What? Effie, what are you thinking?"

Effie paused, and then smiled sweetly. "Ginny, one of my very best friends has the last name of Gaffney. She told me *her* family founded Gaffney, SC."

"Cool!" I said enthusiastically. "We must be related."

Effie never lost her smile as she gazed at me. "Yeah, honey, and she's black."

I'm sure my reaction wasn't what Effie expected. I was *thrilled* to discover there was a black side to the Gaffney family – until it dawned on me what that actually meant. I sobered when I realized that it had to mean one of two things. One, Captain Michael had owned slaves who had taken the family name after Emancipation, or two, Captain Michael had fathered children through his slaves.

Either way, my Great-great-great-great-great grandfather had owned slaves.

My stomach turned as I absorbed the truth. I was an author committed to revealing and abolishing prejudice and racism, who also had a heritage of slave owners.

Effie correctly interpreted all the emotions racing across my face. "What your relative did almost 150 years ago has no bearing on you, Ginny. You're doing everything you can to make it right."

Her words helped marginally, but when I walked out of the restaurant that day, I felt a heavy weight in my heart.

What happened next blew me away...

When I got to Hampton University, a black university in Hampton, Virginia founded in 1868 by black and white leaders of the American Missionary Association after the Civil War to provide education to freedman, it was obvious there was a conference of some type going on. I asked for directions to the historical archives, noticing that most people roaming around Harvey Library had on nametags.

When I got on the elevator to head to the archives on the third floor, I was joined by two young black men who made me feel diminutive. When you're six feet tall, that's hard to do. But these guys were huge! They towered above me in height and both of them outweighed me by at least one hundred pounds. What really got my attention, though, was what was on their nametags.

They were both *Gaffney's*!

I longed to introduce myself to them, but was stupidly held back by being the only white face I had seen since arriving on campus. It was a good taste of being a minority, something I had not experienced much in my life. No one was anything but kind to me, but the expressions on their face clearly indicated they wondered what I was doing there. I have regretted not talking to those two young men ever since that day. I hate lost opportunities – especially when it's because of my lack of action based on fear.

I swallowed all the questions I had, left the elevator at the Peabody Reading Room, and spent the next hours absorbed in research.

When I returned home later that evening, I called my mother, eager to share what I had learned. Regardless of what it revealed about my ancestor, I was still thrilled to realize there was a black side to the Gaffney family. I wanted to know more.

My mother was not so thrilled. In fact, she was appalled.

I can write this story now because my mom passed away. She knew that someday I would write the story about the things I learned, but she begged me to not do it while she was still alive. I honored her request. Little did she know what I would discover years later when I was writing # 7 (*Carried Forward By Hope*), but you'll have to wait to learn that.

Back to the story...

My mom was appalled. She was also virulently adamant that Captain Michael did not own slaves.

"Mom," I answered, "of course he did. He was a wealthy land owner in the 1800's before the Civil War. He owned slaves."

"No, he *didn't*," she hissed angrily.

Seriously, she hissed. It was another lesson in the depth of ignorance and racism held by my entire family. I held the phone away from my head for a moment, and then made a decision. "I'll be at the house to pick you up tomorrow morning," I said firmly. "Be ready at 10:00 AM." Before my mother could utter another word, I hung up.

I had to wake up very early the next morning to shower, eat, and make the five-hour drive to Charlotte, NC, but I was on a quest. I absolutely had to know the truth.

My mom was ready, but obviously confused when I pulled into the driveway of my childhood home the next morning. "What are you doing here?"

"*We* are going to Gaffney, SC," I announced.

"And just why would I do that?" my mother demanded.

"Because even though you don't think so, you want to know the truth as much as I do," I said calmly. "And, I can't get into the archives without Gaffney on my ID. I need your driver's license." *That was true at the time. I don't know about now.*

She opened her mouth to argue, but closed it quickly because she knew it wouldn't do any good. She knew once I made up my mind about something, it was going to happen. She got her purse and slid into the passenger seat of my car.

I knew what I would find when I got to the archives of the Gaffney Family at Limestone College, but I didn't expect to find it so quickly. My mother, having the drive time to rethink her decision to accompany me, had refused to get out of the car when we arrived, so I was on my own, using her ID for entry. It was for the best.

The 1850 census, taken before Captain Michael's death in 1854 revealed that he owned forty slaves at the time of the census. 46% of households in South Carolina owned slaves, but a much smaller percentage of them owned more than a few. By any count, Captain Michael was a wealthy man.

Whatever. I couldn't have cared less about his wealth.

All I could focus on was that my ancestor was a slave owner. I had known it, but seeing it in print somehow made it more real – and more deplorable. My mind filled with all I had learned about the institution of slavery in order to write the first three books of The Richmond Chronicles. My stomach turned as I clenched my teeth and forced myself to focus. I had come here to learn everything I could about my heritage. I wasn't ready to leave.

I took a deep breath, turned the page and looked down. What I saw there turned my blood to ice. I closed the book, squeezed my eyes shut as I tried to control my breathing, stood up and walked out of the library.

I wasn't ready to acknowledge or face what I had read on that next page. It would be almost twenty years before I could...

*****

I returned home to Richmond to finalize preparations for the move I had decided to make the year before. The pull of Orcas Island, Washington had not diminished. If anything, the draw had increased to the point I could hardly wait to step foot on "my island" again. I'm not quite sure how one afternoon so completely cemented that small piece of land in the Puget Sound in my heart, but I wasn't fighting it.

It had taken me a year to save money, get rid of almost everything I owned, and be ready to move. Perhaps the most shocking thing I did – at least, it was shocking to my friends – was open my house and tell them they could come get whatever books they wanted. I wasn't taking them with me this time.

Now, you have to understand that I had 5000 books. Yep. 5000. Books I had saved since childhood, and thousands I had bought over the years. I'd moved them across the country five to six times. I was done. I refused to move them again. I knew each book that walked out the door would take a piece of my heart, but it was time to let go. Somehow, I knew this move was different from all the other ones.

I was going to take three months to travel across the country, stay on Orcas Island for a year or so, and then move on to the next adventure. Now that I knew I could make my living writing, I could live anywhere! My wandering heart responded with great enthusiasm to all the adventures waiting.

If you had asked me, I would have told you I had no intention of staying on Orcas Island, or in the Pacific Northwest. I had bought a brand-new pop-up camper, and a new Toyota 4 x 4 to pull it. That's why I was getting rid of so much. If it wouldn't fit in the back of my truck, it wasn't coming.

My friends responded with delight, descending on my home, and then walking out again as quickly as they could with boxes and bags of books. I know each one of them looked nervously over their shoulder before they got in their vehicles to drive away. They told me later they fully expected me to come charging out of the house to reclaim the books – certain I would never give up my collection.

They were wrong.

I was starting a new season of my life.

The only books I took with me were the ones comprising my research library. It wasn't huge at that point, because I had to rely heavily on library books, but something had happened a few months earlier to grow it substantially.

A new neighbor learned I was an historical novelist. He was thrilled because he owned a bookstore with an emphasis on historical books. Of course, we had many long, fascinating conversations.

He called me one day with news; the plumbing in his bookstore had failed, causing flooding in his basement. Many books had been damaged. Thought not sellable, they were still readable. He knew of my financial limitations, so he asked me if I would like to go through them – buying them at a reduced price if I was interested.

How could I not at least check it out?

When I walked out of his store several hours later, I had two huge boxes of books on Civil War history. They had been priced to sell for a total of $2000. He let me have all of them for $50!

After I hugged him and kissed his cheek, I drove off a very happy woman. Those were the books that accompanied me on my trip across the country.

I couldn't have known, when I pulled out of the driveway in July 1997, just how much of a new life I was beginning. I was about to do something that would throw my existence into complete turmoil.

Something I had previously decided I would never do.

*****

My trip across the country was full of adventures. I rafted down the New River in West Virginia, played in clear swimming holes in Kentucky, bungee-jumped in Wisconsin, played many rounds of golf in Illinois, did a lot of hiking, and ate a lot of tacos on Taco Tuesday nights.

I also worked on *Dark Chaos*.

I had left home with a large screen tent that served as my office when I was on the road. I'd set up my camper and then erect my screen tent. I put up my folding table, ran an extension cord to my MacPlus laptop, surrounded myself with the research books I hadn't gotten rid of, as well as the reams of paper gathered from copiers in historical archives, and I wrote.

I loved my life on the road.

When I got to Minnesota, I knew I needed to take a week or so to really focus on writing if I was going to finish the book by deadline time. But, *Minnesota* in the summer? By a lake? The hordes of mosquitoes were terrifying. Minnesota is known for hummingbird-sized mosquitoes. It's not much of an exaggeration! All I knew is that no matter where I was, the buzz of flying, blood-thirsty creatures filled my ears.

I was only safe in my camper and my writing tent – but only because I went in every morning and sprayed like crazy – eliminating all the mosquitoes that seem to have just melted through the fine screen netting guaranteed to keep them out. The company clearly didn't understand Minnesota mosquitoes! They obviously had the ability to morph from hummingbird size to gnat size on a whim.

I wasn't even safe in the shower. Oh, as long as a hard stream of water was beating down on me, the mosquitoes stayed at bay. Let me step out from under the water, however, and within seconds they were landing on me – feasting on me. There is something highly dissatisfying about taking a long, hot shower, and then coating yourself with bug spray moments later. It was disgusting, but I wasn't willing to be their feasting ground.

I knew I was stuck for a while, though. There wasn't anywhere I could go at that time of year to escape the mosquitoes (unless I wanted to go to the Southwest – which wasn't really on the way to Washington), and I was running out of time on my deadline. I sat in my screen tent, stuffed in earplugs to attempt to drown out the army of mosquitoes battling to reach me, and I wrote.

And wrote... and wrote...

I also thought. I thought a lot – not even the hordes of mosquitoes able to distract me for long.

I had been hiding something in my life for several years. A few of my friends had finally been let in on my secret a few months earlier, but I had made the firm decision to never reveal it to my publishing company because I knew what would happen. I wasn't just afraid of what *might* happen – I *knew* what would happen.

After days of writing and thinking, I also knew I could no longer live a lie.

Yet, to reveal my secret would end my career. Writing was my life. Now that I had finally embraced it, was I willing to give it up? Now that I was using my *Gift*, was I going to throw it all away?

There were also practical sides to the dilemma. What was I going to do if I walked away from my career? I was in the middle of a huge move; based on the reality of regular advances and royalty payments. They weren't big, but they were enough to support me. How would I handle financial realities?

I also loved being known as a writer. Yes, I'll admit it was fun to see people's eyes widen when they learned I was the author of nine books – soon to be ten. While the Gaffney pen name protected me from the general public, my friends knew how I made my living. I had resigned from the position I loved as a youth director in order to write books. What was I going to do if that suddenly disappeared?

The struggle was relentless. The questions pounded in my head, even while I was writing what I already knew, deep in my heart, would be my last book for my publishing company.

I'll never forget the day the struggle ended. It was a typical hot, muggy Minnesota day. I left the protection of my screen tent, hopped on my bike, and drove to the payphone located next to the general store in the state park I was camped in.

By the time I got off the phone with my publisher, my career was over.

Well... put on hold for 16 years.

May's Pan of Rolls –

Scald one pint of milk and add one rounding tablespoon of

lard. Mix in one quart of sifted flour, one quarter cup of

sugar, a saltspoon of salt and one-half yeast cake dissolved in

one half cup of lukewarm water. Cover and let rise overnight.

In the morning roll half an inch thick cut into rounds, spread

a little soft butter on one half of each, fold over and press

together. Let rise till light and bake in a quick oven.

Rolls may be raised lighter than a loaf of bread because the

rising is checked as soon as they are put into the oven.

Chapter Ten

Book #4, *Dark Chaos* (known then as *Magnolia Dreams*), was published in January of the next year because the advertising and promotion had already been done. But a few days later, *Dark Chaos* and every book I'd written, was taken out of print.

What I'd known would happen – happened.

What was my secret?

Let me answer that question by sharing a Blog post that I wrote in 2017, shortly after I released *Walking Into The Unknown*.

*****

I've only gotten a small number of messages like this since I released # 10 (*Walking Into The Unknown*), but I've decided it's time to respond. Not because I'm angry or upset with their position, but simply because it gives me a door to reveal… Well, just keep reading…

I received this message a few days ago.

Dear Ginny. I just finished your latest book. I have read the whole series and I must say I was very involved in all of your characters. I want to tell you that this is the last book I will read in the series. I have found that the liberal agenda you are pushing in this book is very disappointing. It is so apparent that you are intent on bringing out all social liberal issues which I tolerated until the homosexual was introduced. That caused me to come to the conclusion that you are not an author who is uplifting the soul but is interested in social, unChristian motives.

Hmmmm... Let me share another true story with you:

About 12 years ago I was talking to a woman who worked for me in one of my Internet companies that I started. Christy (I've changed her name), whom I liked tremendously was on a *negative* tirade about gay people. Gay people this... gay people that...

I listened for a while, and then asked, "Do you know any gay people you like?"

"No," she snapped angrily.

I waited a moment, and then replied quietly, "That's too bad, Christy, because I thought we were pretty good friends."

Yes, the silence was very long – perhaps as long as the one you are feeling right now as you read this.

Yes, I am Gay.

If you don't have a problem with gay people, you aren't going to care at all.

If you do, then I'm going to ask you to take some deep breaths as I challenge you to consider your position.

Christy and I continued to talk that day. I told her I was more than willing to answer any questions she had. She struggled with it for many months – until I had a retreat in the mountains of North Carolina for all the people who worked for me. I arrived with my partner, whom Christy immediately liked. We shared a meal together – not talking about the fact that we were gay – just eating and talking about life.

The next morning Christy came walking up to me, tears streaming down her face. She begged me to forgive her and told me she simply hadn't understood – that she didn't realize we are simply people like everyone else. She loved *me*, so how could she hate gay people? The moment those words came out of her mouth I knew telling her the truth had been worth it.

What I didn't tell you was that during the months Christy was struggling, she was telling me and anyone else that would listen, that I shouldn't be running my company, and that my lifestyle was going to destroy it. Yes, it hurt deeply. She was confused when she saw the company continue to grow and do amazing things in the world because it simply didn't fit with her belief system. Many people asked why I didn't fire her when she said all these things...

Oh, I'm honest enough to say I thought about it, but in the end I knew it wasn't the answer. I chose *love*. Anger and hatred have never changed anything.

When she met my partner and me, the reality didn't fit with how she viewed gay people. She had the choice to continue to hate my lifestyle, or to accept that perhaps she had been wrong.

She asked me later why I had never told anyone I was gay before. *You might be wondering the same thing...*

I told her that I didn't reveal it because I don't think it should matter at all. My friends all know I'm gay – that was enough for me. My being gay is such a tiny facet of who I am as a person. My being gay wasn't going to change how I ran my company. It wasn't going to change the fact that my company was in existence to make the world a better place. It wasn't going to change how I love people, or accept people, or how I challenge them. I only told her that one day because we were talking one on one about how she hated gay people – with her not realizing I was one of the people she was talking about. It was at that moment when I felt the need to share it with her.

You can't help change things if you choose to hide.

So why am I telling my readers now? Because I can't help change things if you don't know I'm gay.

I've been a gay woman since I began writing the Bregdan Chronicles – what began as the Richmond Chronicles.

It's a gay woman who walked away from her career for almost 16 years because she refused to live with anything less than integrity.

It's a gay woman who has a precious, deep faith that is the foundation for every book I write.

It's a gay woman who has a passion for historical accuracy, and who believes history can teach us how to live our lives now.

It's a gay woman who wrote The Bregdan Principle.

It's a gay woman who does Bregdan Gatherings around the country because I love and respect ALL my readers.

It's a gay woman who longs to make a difference in the world with every word I write.

I didn't include a gay woman in the Bregdan Chronicles because I have an *agenda*.

I included her because there were certainly gay people in the 1800's. We didn't just suddenly spring into existence. I included her because they were treated horribly, and the truth needed to be told – just as I've told the truth about slavery and now the Native American population.

I included her because about 5% of all people are gay (the statistics vary, but I chose a lower number). Since 5% of 321 Million (the U.S. population) is over 1,650,000, that's an extreme number who are being told by certain individuals that they're horrible people, and who are wondering how they will be stigmatized today.

That breaks my heart! We have come a long way in this country, but we still have such a long way to go. The message I received from the reader above reminds me how far we still have to come.

I read a book about 25 years ago that made the following statement: *If everyone who is Gay woke up purple tomorrow, homophobia would disappear overnight.*

That is so true. I can so easily imagine 5% of everyone you will see today being purple. You would spend the day saying "*He's* gay? *That* person is gay? *She's* gay?? I had no idea!" By the end of the day you would realize you're surrounded by wonderful people who just happen to love someone of the same sex. Heartbreakingly, many of them are hiding because of their fear of bigotry and prejudice. You have no idea how many people around you are hiding because of fear.

Be careful who you hate, it might be someone you love!

I could go into a long, doctrinal discourse of why I don't believe God condemns homosexuality, but then I would never reach an end to this book. It's enough to say that I believe the hatred and bigotry toward gays that is expressed around the world makes God weep. There are certainly many countries where gays are embraced and accepted, but there are too many places where they still are not.

America has come a long way, but not far enough.

At my last Bregdan Gathering, the readers who were there had the privilege of meeting my beautiful, talented, amazing wife. Like me, she is an author. Like me, she longs for what she writes to make a difference. Like me, she loves and cares for people. Like me, she believes life is meant to be lived as a grand adventure. I am blessed beyond words to have her to share my life with! Our friendship and marriage extend almost 40 years. What a journey it's been!

Will some people stop reading my books because I included a gay woman in The Bregdan Chronicles? Probably.

Will some people stop reading my books because I am a gay Woman – a Lesbian? Probably.

I can live with either of those scenarios, though my greatest hope is that by revealing the fact that one of your favorite authors is gay, you will accept the challenge to re-examine your beliefs!

*****

I knew my publisher would never publish a lesbian writer if they discovered the truth. I made it easy for both of us by walking away.

If you're still reading, you're wondering just what I did when I walked away from my career.

Honestly?

I cried.

Buckets of tears poured from me as I grappled with the loss of what I loved more than anything.

Well, not more than *anything*. What meant more to me than *anything* was my integrity. What meant more to me than anything was the freedom to live my life as the person I am, not ever having to wonder what I would do if someone found out.

I've never regretted my decision, but that doesn't mean I didn't grieve it.

I've never regretted my decision, but that doesn't mean I didn't go through difficult times as I fought to recreate my life.

So, yes, I landed on Orcas Island with nothing but the money in my savings account. It was not an impressive amount, but the sheer joy of being in Paradise overrode my concerns. I already knew Orcas Island was beautiful, but I had no idea just how beautiful until I began to explore the nooks and crannies of my new home.

I lived in my camper in Moran State Park for two weeks while I waited for the house I had rented to come available. I hiked around Mountain Lake. I swam in both Mountain Lake and Cascade Lake. I explored more of the trails. I met lots of new people – all of them who welcomed me with open arms.

Coming from the very conservative South landing on liberal, open-hearted, loving Orcas Island even more amazing.

When I moved into my new home, walked out on the deck overlooking the breathtaking view of the Puget Sound, and then looked up to see two eagles swooping and soaring over my house, I knew I was indeed *home*.

Remember my intention to only stay on the island for a year, and then continue traveling? Right. Within two weeks I knew I would never leave the Pacific Northwest. My heart is completely at home here with the towering fir trees, the glistening waters, the majestic mountains, the misty rainy days, and the incomparable beauty of our summers. My heart soars every time I see an eagle fly overhead, an orca whale breech the waters, or salmon fight their way upstream.

I was thrilled to discover a world with no ticks, few mosquitoes, no humidity, and no hurricanes. I truly don't mind the rainy days because they're perfect for writing and curling up with a book in front of the fire to read. By the time summer ends here, I can hardly wait for a cold, rainy day to eat a steaming bowl of chili while I watch the Seattle Seahawks football game. As I finalize this book, I am counting down the days to my first bowl of chili!

What do I love most?

The people.

Sure, we have our share of small-minded, bigoted people, but it's a very small number compared with most of the rest of the country. The people in my life value inclusion and acceptance. They choose love. The people in my life value education and learning. They value the splendor of nature and know we must do whatever is necessary to protect it. The women are strong and resilient, and determined to live life on their own terms. They challenge me, stretch me, and thrill me.

I'm going to go ahead and answer a question I've been asked many times.

Ginny, do you mostly just hang out with other gay people?

It's a fair question, and my answer is certainly not the answer for all gay people.

My answer? No.

I love *people*. Gays make up 5-10% of the population. That means there are a whole lot of people who are *not* gay. I don't consider a person's sexuality when I meet them. I want to know who they are – not who they sleep with! I have far more straight friends than I do gay friends, simply because there are more of them in the world.

Do you hate men, Ginny?

Seriously? Yet, I know there are people who believe lesbians hate men. Not me, and not my gay friends. Just because we don't want to partner with men doesn't mean we don't value and desire their friendships. Some of my closest friends are men. I love them.

*****

Okay, time to return to living life now that I had ditched my career as a writer. Just because I no longer had a publisher didn't mean I quit writing; it just meant I quit making money.

I can hear your thoughts... Why didn't I just get another publishing company who wouldn't care if I was gay? Why didn't I get an agent?

Those are fair questions. I suppose the entire answer is that I was burnt out on the whole "publishing house" scenario. If I hadn't come out of the closet I probably would have continued writing The Richmond Chronicles because I so loved the story. However, once I made my decision I realized how tired I was of having so many aspects of my writing controlled.

There are parts of the first four books of The Richmond Chronicles that were removed by the editorial team before they were published because they thought they were too intense. (Yes, of course, I put them back in later in The Bregdan Chronicles.)

I was tired of fighting to write the books I knew I was meant to write. I was tired of walking away from series because to do anything less would compromise my beliefs and my integrity.

I hated not controlling when books were released, or how they were marketed. Many writers don't want anything to do with that part of the business. I'm not one of them.

I loved to write, but I didn't love the publishing world. I had done what I said I would never do. I had used my *Gift*.

Writing without a publisher wasn't really a viable option at that time. Knowing the truth of that I was ready to turn my attention to something else. I also had a big goal that drove me forward. I dreamed of the day I would be financially secure enough to write whatever I wanted, without any publishing company able to control the end product. I had no idea what that would take, but I was determined to make it happen.

I just had to figure out how.

My whole life had changed...

*****

One of the letters I received in the last few years talked about change. Parts of it said:

I have to tell you how you and your characters, their stories of life, death, trials and the good and bad outcomes, not only helped me see life differently, but made me realize the world changes, and sometimes we have to change with it, like it or not.

I was in the midst of a very deep depression, which I know now happens very often in people my age when they are forced into change. I started seeing a counselor, someone to talk to that would listen. I would sometimes discuss your books with my counselor, explaining to her the parallels in my life, and that of Carrie and friends.

As I have read these wonderful books, I have cried, smiled and celebrated with the characters. I identify with how they have changed, what it took for them to see and make the changes in their lives that were necessary for them to move on and into another phase of their lives.

The lessons I have taken away from these characters, I have applied to my life. Bringing me back to the real world, pulling me out of a depression that pulled me down so low; I was having thoughts I never would have imagined myself thinking.

I have learned a great deal about our country and the ugliness of wars. I was never a History student, but between your amazing research, writing of these books, the characters, the profound affects all have had on my life, how I have handled this drastic change in my life, and my ability to move on into another phase with a bit more clarity and thankfulness, I have you to thank.

Of course, I cried when I read it! Wow! Nothing gives me more joy than knowing my books are making a difference! I've had so many comment on how much I talk about change, and then ask me why. I'm happy to answer that question...

The vast majority of people avoid change. They fear change. They do everything they can to keep things the same in their life because they believe it will make them more comfortable. They want to know what to expect from each day... from each week... from each month... from each year.

My thoughts about that? YUCK!

Personally, I can't stand it when things stay the same for too long. I have always thrived on change and adventure. Let me give you some examples:

- I'm six feet tall. I have been since I was fourteen. Everyone expected me to play basketball in high school. Both my brothers were stars. Everyone was excited that I would soon be joining the "Dye Legacy", but I decided I was tired of doing things that my brothers were doing so I refused to play basketball. After playing in junior high, I was ready for a change! I played tennis and trained horses instead. I'm so glad I did!

- When it came time for me to go to college, it was fully expected I would go to the University of North Carolina at Chapel Hill. It was simply what was *done* in my family. Not me! My two brothers were already there. Once again, I figured it was time there was a change. There was no way I would follow them and be on the same campus. I chose another college and loved every minute of it!

- When I graduated, it was expected I would get a good-paying job just like my brothers had in the two years before me. NOT. I took a job making $8000 a year on a ranch in Texas because I wanted to explore the country and have wonderful adventures. No one was pleased with the changes I forced on the family - except me, of course!

- I've moved 55 times since I got out of college - relishing in each new experience. Sure, some of them were scary, but I never said change isn't scary. It can be. But it is always SO worth the fear and uncertainty!

I could go on and on, but I think you have the picture...
There are many kinds of changes. The letter I received made me think of one of my favorite quotes:

If you don't like something change it; if you can't change it, change the way you think about it. ~Mary Engelbreit

So many times we're forced into a change we don't want. Okay. That's called life. The sad thing is that too many people let that reality cause depression or bitterness. They resent the change so they lose themselves in the resentment. How can that possibly create a good outcome? They have done nothing but mire themselves in depression or bitterness.

If you can't change it, change the way you think about it...

Ahh... this truth is so powerful. Most of us have no idea how powerful our minds are. If you don't like something **change the way you think about it.** It's so simple. Now, don't confuse simple with easy. I'm not saying it's easy. It requires work and persistence to change how our minds operate, but it is so very possible!

If you have a situation in your life right now that you can't change - I invite YOU to change.

Change how you think about it.

Change how you feel about it.

Change how you live with it.

Choose to change and make the most of what life has handed you.

The other situation that comes to mind is people who plod along in their nice, safe life - totally afraid to change. They believe it's nice and safe, but I've talked to so many of these people. Their lives are also boring and predictable, and absolutely *not* the life they thought they would be living when they once dreamed of their future. But... their fear of change keeps them from striking out in a different direction.

How sad...

I mean that. People tell me all the time that I've had such an incredible life... that I've done such interesting things... that I've seen more of the country than they could ever hope to... that I have been incredibly blessed.

Hmm... Let's stop on that last statement. *I have been incredibly blessed.* While I believe that's true, and I am so grateful for my life, their statement comes close to being an excuse for why *they* haven't had the same kind of life. It must just be because they haven't been *blessed* like me.

Nonsense!

Change is a CHOICE.

Moving in different directions is a CHOICE.

Taking risks to create a new life is a CHOICE.

You can either curse change, or cheer it...

The question you must ask yourself is what kind of choices you are making every day.

I have a truth I have been living by for a very long time.

The Choices I Make Today Will Determine The Rest of My Life.

I believe that totally. The Choices I Make Today Will Determine The Rest of My Life.

I would also add... The *CHANGES* I Make Today Will Determine The Rest of My Life.

So then, of course, the question becomes...

What choices are you making today?

What Changes are you making today?

Go ahead.

CHANGE.

Live life full out.

Take risks you never thought you would take.

Embrace the change and view it as a blessing.

CHANGE how you think about it!!

<u>Opal's Fried Chicken</u>

Cut the chicken up, separating every joint, and
wash clean. Dry. Salt and pepper, it and roll
into flour well.

Have your fat very hot and drop the pieces into it
and let them cook brown. The chicken is done
when the fork passes easily in the skillet; t
hen take a tablespoon of dry flour and brown
it in the fat, stirring it around, then pour
water in and stir
till the gravy is as thin as soup.

<u>Chapter Eleven</u>

One of my basic philosophies of life is *Nothing is Ever Wasted*.

No time in my life is a waste. No mistake is a waste. Nothing I create that doesn't seem to have a purpose is a waste. No experience is a waste. No relationship is a waste.

They may be painful. They may not be pleasant. But they are never a waste, because I have learned something from every single moment of my life.

By the time I got on Orcas Island, the Six Years of Darkness were slowly grinding to an end. The flashbacks were mostly gone, though there were still things that would occasionally trigger them. The dogged hopelessness that could strike me at any moment had been beaten by daily decisions of determined hope.

While I wish with all my heart that the years of abuse had never happened (and I wish the same thing for every survivor I talk to), they were also not a waste. Every year of my life shows me the lessons and blessings of the fact that I survived. That I choose love and hope. That I can reach out to other people because I have walked their path.

I didn't just survive. I THRIVE.

The scars remain, but most often they are simply a reminder of how far I've come.

I choose gratitude.

*****

Even though I knew I was going to run out of money before I ran out of time, I decided to savor Orcas Island for a while. I would need a job of some sort eventually, but not right away.

I was done with the publishing world, but I set up an office in my new home and kept writing. I didn't write any more on the Richmond Chronicles, though. I was sure that season was over. I was sorry my readers wouldn't get the final year of the Civil War, but there was nothing I could do about that.

One morning I woke up with a dream swirling through my head. I'm sure I dream all the time (I'm told everyone does), but I don't usually remember them. I wake up, believe I've had a dreamless night, and dive into my day. Not this time...

This dream was so vivid. I could close my eyes and see the dream come to life in bright, vibrant colors. I still can! I laid in bed, watched a new day unfold over the Puget Sound with the sun glimmering off orange and purple clouds, and then walked down to my office and wrote the book, *Dream Dragon*.

It was so much fun to write. By the time the sun was setting, casting its lingering glows on the mountains across from my home, I was done.

I'd never written a story like it before. It's not exactly a children's story, but it's in a children's book format. The lessons in the book are both incredible simple, and quite complex – depending upon the stage of life you're in when you're reading it, or having it read to you.

I didn't write it to do anything with it. I wrote it because I had to honor the beauty of my dream. I put it away, much as I had done with my first teen novel years before, and went on with my life. Occasionally, I would share it with someone who needed it.

One of my joys while living on Orcas Island was the high school girls' basketball team. They went from an almost winless season the year before, to making it to the state championship the first year I lived on the island. I attended almost every game, and was with them in Spokane, Washington for the championship games.

The second day, they had a particularly rough game that they lost. They were crushed, but because of how the tournament was run they had a chance to win a wild card in the finals if they won their game the next day. Their confidence was shattered, however. They wondered what in the world they were doing at the *state* championships.

I wrote them a story that night, and then read it to them the next day before their game.

Born To Fly.

It's the story of Quest the eagle, and how he overcame his fear of flying after a particularly terrible crash during a vicious thunderstorm.

They listened intently and then went out to play.

They won.

No, I don't believe my story made them win, but I know it helped them gather the confidence to go out there and utilize the talents they had exhibited all year. I was so proud of them. They didn't win the championship, but they returned to the island with their heads held high.

As with *Dream Dragon,* I shared *Born To Fly* with people who needed it.

More stories followed during those years. They eventually became the *Fly To Your Dreams Series.*

Little Heart was next.

My great hope for people is that they can discover the Greatest Love of All. I wrote *Little Heart* for them.

Again, I had no intention of doing anything with it, except to give it to the people in my life whom I knew needed to hear the message.

My last one in that series is called *The Miracle of Chinese Bamboo.*

I wrote it for the people building my company at the time. More on that in a minute...

I loved writing this story so much because it challenges people to move beyond their fears and the limitations they put on themselves – to believe their dreams can come true.

Yes, I eventually put all of them into print and on Kindle. You can get all of them on Amazon. Just put the title of the book, and then my name in the Search box.

I published them almost eighteen years after I wrote them. Remember what I said about *nothing is ever wasted*?

It's true.

Nothing is ever wasted!

I've been too busy writing The Bregdan Chronicles to do much marketing for the Fly To Your Dreams Series, but the time will come because I know the power these little books have to change lives!

*****

I adored living on Orcas Island, but it's not really the place to live unless you have recurring income or a solid job. Since I had none, I sadly said good-bye to my beloved island after two years and moved to Bellingham, WA, on the mainland. I got a marketing job and made a living; returning as often as I could.

But things were about to change again...

What I perceived as being the tragedy of losing my career turned out to be one of my greatest blessings. I won't go through all the events of the sixteen years that passed before I returned to my true love, but they were full of adventures, risks, mistakes and glorious victories.

What I will tell you is that when I walked away from my writing career the only thing I knew about computers was how to write books on them, save them to a floppy disk, and mail it off to my publishers.

The world was changing rapidly, but little (if anything) was changing as fast as technology. I remember how proud I was the day I purchased a used 520K tower computer for $100, and entered the world of the internet through my dial up service. I thought I was really hot stuff when I got an email address.

I was at a conference in Las Vegas for a company I worked with when I had what I called my *Epiphany*.

I don't remember what they were talking about on stage, but I know it had nothing to do with the vision I saw so clearly in my head.

I've always had a passion for non-profit organizations, as well as a deep empathy for what they go through to raise money to fund their missions. It's an ongoing struggle that ends in going under for far too many of them. When I was a youth director, constantly coming up with fundraisers to generate income for events and mission trips, I would have dropped to the floor and kissed the feet of anyone who would have walked in and told me they had a way I could generate ongoing income that wouldn't take time away with the kids.

Of course, no one ever did that.

Back to my epiphany... Sitting there in Las Vegas, I envisioned an online shopping mall where people could buy things and automatically have a percentage of their purchase go to the non-profit organization of their choice. Wow! My mind spun with the possibilities.

Yes, I know there are many options to do that now, but please remember this was twenty years ago. No one was doing it.

Right on the heels of my mind spinning with possibilities came the brutal reality that I was out of my mind. *I* was going to develop an internet company for online shopping that would automatically funnel money to thousands of worthy non-profit organizations?

Right...

The only thing I knew how to do on a computer was send an email. I didn't even know what the word *coding* meant. I was beyond clueless.

Yet, I couldn't erase the epiphany from my mind.

Without going into how I did it (because that would be another book), my vision became a reality.

The right people came into my life.

I was relentless in my quest for knowledge and understanding.

I learned early on that all I needed was a clear vision. Once I had that, I would find the people who could make it happen.

I taught the people around me that I didn't need to know *how* something worked because I wasn't going to understand a word they said. I just needed to know *if* they could do it. We all learned how to work together, though I know there were times my Tech Team simply shook their head with disbelief over my ignorance.

My job was to envision the final product. I did. And it happened.

Along the way I learned a tremendous amount.

That was the beginning of my internet companies, and the road that would eventually lead me to where I am right now.

*****

The road was not without twists and turns, disappointments and pain. I'm going to share one of the twists with you because it created another one of the core philosophies of my life – one I hope will encourage you as much as it does me.

My company went through several transformations. The first version was created with the help of a man that I loved like a brother. I envisioned everything, formed a team of one hundred people that shared my vision, and gathered hundreds of non-profit organizations eager for our help.

Peter (I've changed his name) had the job of creating the technology to make it happen.

We made the perfect team. We spent hours on the phone talking, laughing, dreaming and celebrating our successes. I loved him.

My company grew rapidly.

One of the things about Internet companies and the power of the phone, is that you can build tight relationships with people you've never laid eyes on. I had several people on my management team I'd never met face-to-face, though we'd been working together for close to two years. I decided to change that.

I rented a wonderful home on the Long Beach Peninsula of Washington, made flight arrangements for everyone, and went on a shopping spree. My firm condition for their attendance was that no one bring their computer. I wanted a true "family retreat", not a work event. I loaded my truck with food and beach toys. The whole time, I tried to ignore a funny feeling in my gut. At the last moment, I threw in my laptop.

Everyone was coming to the Management Team Retreat, except for Peter. He had decided that taking the time to come to Washington would not work for him at that moment. Other things happened that had red flags flying in my mind and heart, but I kept trying to ignore them. Finally, I could no longer pretend I didn't have reason for concern.

On the way to pick up Gary, one of my Management Team, from the airport, I made the difficult phone call that confirmed what I already knew in my gut. Peter was stealing the company.

You see, I had not yet learned the hard lesson that you *never* give up access to the data for an Internet company.

Without your data and your coding, you can lose everything you've so carefully created. I was still naïve.

I learned my lesson that day.

I cried on the way to the airport, but then swallowed my tears, met Gary with a smile and chatted all the way to the beach. I had decided to not ruin everyone's first night. This was the first time we were all going to meet each other and I was determined to have fun before I revealed the truth of what had happened.

The evening was amazing. We stayed in a hotel before we drove the final ninety miles to the house I had rented. We hugged, laughed, talked, ate pizza and played pool. When the night wound down and we retired to our rooms I couldn't sleep, however. Not much keeps me awake, but the reality of what had just happened spun relentlessly through my head.

What was I going to tell them?

A check on my computer revealed I no longer had access to our systems. How was I going to tell them that everything we had worked for was gone?

I tossed and turned for hours before I gave in and got up. I jumped into my truck, drove to the coast, and stepped out onto the sand just as dawn was kissing the night sky. I was desperate for the freedom I find on the beach. I was crying so hard while I walked that I was barely aware of the crashing waves or the screeching gulls wheeling out to welcome the new day.

That's when I saw the first sand dollar through my tears.

I have a love affair with sand dollars, so I reached down to pick it up. Once I confirmed it was not live, I put it in my pocket and kept walking and crying.

I truly had no idea what we were going to do. All I could see was that I had failed. I had failed all the people who worked for me. I had failed the non-profits counting on our company. I had failed whatever power had given me the epiphany in the first place.

The sense of failure threatened to choke me as I walked down the beach, grateful it was deserted.

That's when I saw the second sand dollar.

Absentmindedly, I scooped it up and put it in my pocket with the other one. A few steps later I spied another one, glistening as the water from a wave receded. I picked that one up, too.

Suddenly, I was on a mission to pick up as many sand dollars as I could find. Since I had found the first three at the water's edge, I continued to walk there, my eyes glued on the sand. I picked up two more, hardly even aware I had finally stopped crying.

I still had no idea what I was going to do about my company, but the thrill of the hunt was at least a distraction.

The problem was that the tide was coming in. Every time I bent my head to search the water line, a wave pushed me back, forcing me farther up the beach. Strolling through the surf in January was not tops on my list of fun things. I clenched my teeth with frustration as the waves approached, walked away from the frothy water, and kept looking.

I found another one!

I added it to my collection, and then turned back to the water line as the wave receded – back to where I had discovered the first ones.

Another wave pushed in, forcing me farther up the beach again, away from where I knew the sand dollars were.

I found another one!

This game continued for a while. I kept returning to the water line, refusing to acknowledge that the incoming tide was going to win. Each time the victorious surf pushed me up the beach, with me clenching my teeth all the way.

Every time I found a sand dollar.

Finally, when my pockets were too full to hold even one more sand dollar, I stopped and turned to face the ocean. With the hunt over, tears filled my eyes again as the reality of my situation came crashing back in – harder than the waves crashing into the shore.

You still don't get it, do you?

By now, you know I believe I hear voices (whether real or in my head), so this shouldn't be a surprise to you.

"Huh?" I spoke out loud, staring out at the waters, admiring the white tops of the waves that were catching the first rays of the sun.

You still don't get it, do you?

"Obviously not," I muttered. The moment the words left my mouth, though, I suddenly got it. I turned and stared back down the beach. The whole time I had believed the incoming waves were knocking me off course. They weren't.

They were redirecting my path.

My heart pounded as the truth roared through my entire being.

My path was being redirected.

Just like that, the fear disappeared; replaced by a burning determination. I patted the sand dollars bulging in my pockets, returned to my truck, and drove back to the hotel. I arrived just as my team was emerging from their hotel rooms.

Two hours later, after a hasty breakfast, I sat them down in the living room of our vacation rental house and told them what had happened. The expressions on their faces echoed the fears and concerns that had coursed through me from the moment I had discovered the truth.

"What are we going to do?" one of them stammered.

Thanks to my early morning beach walk, I was ready. "We're going to build a new company," I said calmly. "Our path is being redirected."

Looking back on that time, it was truly miraculous. We had never all been together in one place. Now here we all were, united as a team, and ready to do the impossible.

We did the impossible.

When we left that house four days later we had designed a company that was far superior to the one stolen from us. When we relaunched two months later, our online shopping mall had gone from a couple hundred products to 1400 stores with *millions* of products, and technology and programs to support it that were lightyears beyond what we'd started with.

We did what countless people told us was impossible, in an amount of time that was inconceivable to experienced tech people – including my own! All of us learned a lesson in just what was possible.

Peter? Once he had stolen the systems, he attempted to steal my team of one hundred people, believing they would come with him since he had the power. What he didn't calculate into his plan was that every one of those one hundred people weren't in it for the money. We had a passion to make a difference for non-profit organizations, and we were determined to do it from a place of integrity. Sure, we all wanted to make money, but it wasn't our driving force.

Every single one of my team told Peter they weren't interested in working with him. He tried to make it work for a couple months on his own, but with no team, and no relationship with the non-profits my team had brought on board, he finally had to give up. He offered to sell the systems back to me.

I declined.

Two weeks later we opened our brand-new shopping mall.

The power of that experience has never left me. Every time I run into a difficult challenge... every time I hit something that seems insurmountable... every time I have a failure... I remember the words on the beach that day.

You're not being knocked off course. Your path is being redirected.

Now, instead of clenching my teeth with frustration, I start looking for the next path. I know it's there, and I know the waves and challenges are pushing me toward it. All I have to do is find it.

I always do!

I also still have every one of those sand dollars!

*****

Those years were full of so many lessons and experiences.

It all began under the umbrella of a company I named Together We Can Change The World, Inc. It has morphed some, and is now known as Millions For Positive Change.

Bregdan Publishing is one piece of the entire puzzle that still has so many pieces waiting to be added to it. The next years are going to be full of so many amazing things as I continue to push toward the initial vision that started all this.

Did I write anything else besides the four books of the *Fly To Your Dreams Series* during those years? Oh yeah...

I wrote countless scripts for videos that I made. I wrote more marketing material and training manuals than I care to remember. I wrote emails to the more than 160,000 people that were part of one of the companies. My job was to inspire and motivate. I loved doing it all.

I started a series of stories that eventually claimed the name Someone Believes In You, though I have also used them to create the Kick Ass Woman videos now on YouTube. I love learning, and then writing, the stories of people who have accomplished great things or overcome intense challenges. Every one of them inspires and motivates me.

I had written about one hundred of them, but I was barely scratching the surface, so I added two more people to the Someone Believes In You team. One of them happens to now be my wife! As of this writing, there are close to eight hundred stories.

I have to share one of them that challenged me to pursue excellence in everything I do.

*****

Debbi was only 19 years old when she reached a cross-road in her life. She was married to a well-known Economist and Futurist, and had quit work to play the role of a conventional wife. She hadn't expected her decision to deal such a hard blow to her self-esteem. No one seemed to think she had anything to offer – including herself.

One night, at a party, things reached a head. People were falling all over themselves to talk to her husband – they were treating her like she was an absolute zero, walking away from her in most conversations. Until the party host approached her... She *tried* to talk to him, answering his barrage of questions. She *tried* to appear sophisticated, urbane and clever – failing miserably at her attempt to be something she wasn't.

Her host finally asked, "What do you intend to *do* with your life?

Debbi was a nervous wreck at this point. She blurted out, "Well, I'm mostly trying to get orientated."

Her host looked at her with disgust. "The word is oriented," he snapped. "There is no such word as *orientated*. Why don't you learn to use the English language?" He spat out his words and walked away.

Well, you can imagine. . . Debbi was crushed. She cried all the way home. But somewhere, in the middle of all the tears, she made a decision. She would never, never, NEVER let something like that happen again. She was done living in someone else's shadow. She would find something of her own.

As she pondered what she was going to do she thought back to the old boat motor that had accumulated dust in her family's basement when she was growing up – her parents and 5 girls in a 2-bedroom, 1 bathroom home. Her father was going to buy a boat for that motor *someday.* He never did, and to Debbi that motor became a symbol of putting off dreams until it's too late to achieve them.

Debbi had watched her father die with his dreams unfulfilled. She didn't want the same thing to happen to her. She would do *something.*

But what?

The only thing Debbi was really good at was making cookies. She had been baking and experimenting with recipes since she was 13. She'd add more butter, use less flour, or try different kinds of chocolate. She'd finally hit on a recipe that she believed was ideal. Her cookies were soft, buttery and crammed with chocolate chips.

She realized she had to use her gifts so. . . Debbi decided to open a cookie store. Every single person in her life told her it wouldn't work. No one believed in her.

It didn't matter. On August 18, 1977, when Debbi was 20, she opened her first store. No one came. By noon she was desperate. She stared at the empty store and decided if she was going to go out of business, she would at least do it in style.

Debbi loaded up a tray of cookies and went out in to her shopping arcade, trying to give away cookies. No one would take them. She figured she had nothing to lose at this point, so she headed out to the street. She begged, pleaded and wheedled until people finally took her samples. She smiled as their faces lit up.

She went back to the store and sold cookies to the people who had followed her wanting more. By the end of the day she had sold $50 worth. The next day she sold $75 worth.

The rest is Cookie History. . .

Debbi Fields is now the owner of over 600 stores – with sales in the multi-millions. She is also the mother of 5. She did indeed find something of her own!

You will face obstacles. You'll face people who don't believe in your dreams. So what? It's YOUR life. It will become what YOU decide to make it.

Debbi Fields shared this in a speech she gave: *"Whatever you do in your life, you have to be absolutely passionate about it."*

Debbi was passionate about cookies. Passionate about excellence. Passionate about living with no regrets.

Take some time to think about what you're passionate about. Make a list. It might be long. It might be short. What are you MOST passionate about? What will create the greatest joy and success in your life if you decide to do it? What will you most regret if you *don't* do it?

Right now – TODAY – you have gifts that can make a difference in how you live your life. How will you use them? What will you do? It's up to you.

*****

Debbie's story inspires me to do everything I do with excellence.

What will I do with the 800+ stories? I'm not sure, though I've used hundreds of them in different ways already.

The one thing I'm quite certain of, however, is that *nothing is ever wasted*!

My life during the sixteen years outside publishing was full and rich. There was so much fulfillment. I thought I was doing what I would do for the rest of my life.

Until...

<u>Opal's Southern Cornbread</u>

Mix two cups of white cornmeal, a rounding of tablespoon of

sugar, and a level teaspoon of salt, then pour enough hot milk or

milk and water to moisten the meal well,

but not to make it of a soft consistency.

Let stand until cool, then add three well beaten eggs and spread

on a buttered shallow pan about half an inch thick.

Bake in a quick oven cut in squares, split and butter while hot.

Chapter Twelve

There were many twists on the road that led to my growing restlessness... that led to me making a radical change.

The first one put me in bed for two months. Though it was common for me to crash for a few days at a time, due to the Epstein-Barr Virus I was still battling, I was always back up and at it fairly quickly. My passion drove me. It almost drove me into the ground.

By January of 2007, it was common for me to work 100+ hours a week. From the moment I opened the floodgates to my newest company, My Power Mall, it had been like running from an avalanche. My Power Mall was an online shopping mall – but this one was open to people all over the world, not just non-profits. It allowed members to shop online, but also generated income for them. The growth far surpassed even my lofty expectations.

My initial plan was to just grow it in the United States for the first year, and then slowly expand out internationally. The reality of the internet created an entirely different scenario. Just two weeks after we opened the company for membership, I had another Management Team retreat on Orcas Island.

I was puzzled by my Webmaster huddled in a corner with four others on the team, scribbling away on something. As soon as I called the first meeting, I looked at him. "What's on that board?"

He smiled and turned it around for me to read.

I stared at it for several moments and then looked back at him. "I don't understand."

"These are the fifty countries we have My Power Mall members in," he answered.

I opened my mouth, but nothing came out. Probably because there was nothing available in my brain cells to respond to that revelation. I finally managed a weak, "Excuse me?" I walked closer to gaze at the board, stunned at the vast reach of our new membership.

Just like that, I went from planning growth expansion to trying to figure out how in the world to pay people in Zimbabwe! And soon, 220+ countries around the world as people poured – reaching 160,000 members in less than six months.

Trust me; it created many sleepless nights. Finding a payment processor... coding our system to handle payments in 220 countries... figuring out how to help support people all around the world.

Sleeping did not really figure into the equation.

Until I crashed.

I had just adopted a six-week-old puppy (my beloved Bogey), and now I couldn't move or even think. My company was growing explosively, and my brain cells wouldn't operate because I was so sick. Thankfully, I had the most amazing people in the world to handle things, but it was hard on everyone.

Without going into long details that would probably just bore you, I had burned out every gland in my body.

I was no longer able to produce hormones. No Estrogen. No Progesterone. No Thyroid. No Adrenal.

Dr. Wendy Ellis to the rescue! I discovered Wendy after a friend gave me a book that sent me in her direction. There was no way I could haul my body the two hours to her office in Seattle, but I did manage to haul myself into a car for an extensive blood test and hormone imbalance test in Bellingham.

When Wendy called me two weeks later with the results, she was blunt. "You're a mess, Ginny. Not only have you blown out every gland in your body with your ridiculous work schedule, you also have the worst gluten intolerance of any of my patients."

"I see," I said weakly. My mind was focused on just one thing. "How do I fix it?"

It didn't take Wendy long to discover I want every fact I can find before I make a decision regarding my health, but once I do, I'm a bottom-line kind of woman. Just tell me what has to be done. If my research supports it, I'll do anything.

Wendy had the answers. Bio-identical hormones. Natural Thyroid tablets. No bread or gluten of any kind.

Whoa! Hold on... Back up... *WHAT* did you say? No bread? No pizza? No cookies? No cereal? No burritos? Give me a break!

"Just exactly how am I supposed to eat?" I demanded. I decided to not tell Wendy that my dietary mainstay was grilled cheese sandwiches. They were easy to make, delicious and filling. I used organic whole wheat bread and organic cheese. Surely, they were good for you.

Wendy was sympathetic, but firm. "You're supposed to eat in a way that won't kill you."

From my position in bed, I couldn't really argue with her. It's been eleven years since gluten has passed my lips. At least on purpose. There have been a handful of times, when eating out, that I have been served something with gluten in it, despite my instructions. I pay the price for about a week. Not fun.

It's certainly easier now because there are so many more options, but in the beginning, it was very difficult. But... certainly not more difficult than being sick, weak and bedridden.

Within a few weeks of beginning Wendy's regiment, I was back on my feet. It took a month or so to balance things out, but I knew I was going to be alright; *if* I made some other changes. My new doctor had also been blunt about the fact that my work schedule was going to destroy me.

"No one is meant to work 100 hours a week, Ginny. You may think you can get away with it, but you'll pay the price in the long run."

Yeah... yeah... Once I was back on my feet, I was once again running from the avalanche of growth; only now I was also trying to catch up on everything that hadn't been done while I was sick. How exactly was I supposed to back off? The stress of not getting things done that absolutely had to be done would only create unending pressure.

I pressed on for another year, but was becoming more disillusioned by the number of hours I worked. I had no time for anything else. Friends faded away as they realized I would never be available. The few times I tried to meet with someone, a phone call would send me scurrying back to my office so I could get online with my development team in India over some new system crisis.

I made time almost every day for exercise, but that was it. My life was spent at my desk; on the phone, and in front of my computer screen. In spite of the joy of what we were accomplishing, and all the good that was being done around the world, it was a lonely existence. I didn't even have pizza to make it easier!

I was also being brought face-to-face with something I didn't want to recognize. There are few people better at starting companies than I am. When I catch the vision for something, I'm gifted at sharing it, bringing people on board, and then overcoming any and all obstacles to bring it to reality.

However...

I am terrible at running what I build. And, I hate doing it. Trust me, honest evaluation of self is a good thing!

The dreaming, creating and building are what I love. I was no longer doing that. Oh, we were still growing, but we'd settled down into the nitty-gritty of daily operations. Because I hated it, I did it poorly, but was too stubborn to see what was happening.

Combine that with the fact that while an online mall was a cutting edge, pioneering venture four years earlier, it was now being done by companies with far more resources than we had.

To make a long story short, the day came when we were forced to accept the truth. It was time to close the doors on My Power Mall. It broke my heart, but I couldn't ignore the facts staring me in the face. I will always feel badly because if I had run it better, things may have turned out differently. Or not. I'll never really know.

When My Power Mall ceased to exist, I had absolutely no idea what I would do next. I was certain, however, that I needed to take some time off. I was done with hundred-hour weeks. I remember sleeping a lot the first month, and then I spent the summer landscaping my yard, swimming a mile each day, and watching hundreds of hours of episodes of McLeod's Daughters on Netflix.

It was great for the summer, but inactivity is not part of my personality, so I was soon chafing at the bit, wondering what would come next.

I had no intention of starting another company, but that's exactly what I did. There is little I am more passionate about than inspiring and motivating people to be their best self. Six months after I closed My Power Mall, I launched The Ultimate Life Company with a close friend and some of the management team from my previous business.

We created a faculty of 100+ of the most powerful, influential speakers and leaders within the personal development field, and I also created a large number of my own webinars. Our goal was to accumulate a vast library of materials and webinars that the average person could afford.

We accomplished our goal, but once again we couldn't find a way to make it financially viable.

A year later we closed the doors. I'll always be proud of what we accomplished, and once again not one second of that endeavor was wasted.

Fifteen years after walking away from my writing career, I was once again wondering where the next twist in the road would take me.

That's when the email showed up in my Inbox.

*****

I get a ton of emails and have ended up on a lot of mailing lists that I no longer care about. Rather than go through and unsubscribe from all of them, I'll usually just peruse the list and then do a mass delete of those that don't interest me. I had done just that thing, and had my finger poised over the Delete button, when something caught my eye.

Sell your books through Kindle.

Hmmm... what was Kindle? I was curious enough to ignore the Delete button and click on that email. What I read piqued my interest enough to make me attend the online webinar that night.

I was astonished at what I discovered. I'm glad no one was in my office that night because I doubt my mouth ever closed, and I know my eyes never changed from wide with amazement and wonder. I suspect I looked remarkably like a blowfish.

Once the webinar finished, I spent hours doing more research; discovering just what Amazon was doing in the world of digital publishing. By the time I finally shut down my computer early the next morning, a whole new existence had opened up for me. While I had been busy building internet companies, the world of publishing had undergone a radical transformation.

I knew it was offering me what I had never stopped dreaming about – the ability to return to writing books.

I would become my own publisher!

Suddenly, the fifteen years that had passed made perfect sense. Remember what I keep saying about *nothing is ever wasted*? This is another perfect example. I already knew everything needed to accomplish what was being talked about, and I knew I could conquer any new technology or software that came my way. I may have turned my nose up in the beginning about understanding and learning the technology behind my companies, but through the years I had absorbed massive amounts of knowledge and experience.

*****

Let's talk about Self-Publishing for a little while because it's a question I'm often asked – even by non-writers.

Ginny, how hard is it to publish your books?

Doesn't self-publishing mean your books aren't good enough for a traditional publishing company?

Why wouldn't I want a publishing company to handle all the details for me?

Ginny, I just want to write – I don't want to do all the other things.

The list of reasons to self-publish is quite long but let me start by painting a simple scenario for you. At one point, you could write a fabulous book, get a publisher to take you on as a client, and then sit back while they turned your book into a best-seller.

At least, that's what people think. The reality is that while, yes, publishers are always looking for good books, and they did the best they could to make them a success, very few books become best-sellers. Most of them just fade away into back storerooms, and then disappear altogether. The publisher's job is to get the books they want for as little of an advance as possible because they want to diminish their risk. The author, if they accept the advance offer, hopes the royalty payments from their best-selling books will make all their work worthwhile. Unfortunately, they usually end up with nothing except disappointment. Best-seller status seldom happens, and they join the ranks of "Starving Artist".

I know it happens because it happened to me, and scores I have talked to.

Fast forward to today, 2018. The traditional publishing world has changed but, in my opinion, not for the better. They still are looking for great books to publish, but their criteria have changed. It's not enough to just write a great book. You also have to be able to market it, and what they really want to know is that you already have a horde of hungry readers eager to read your book.

That may be possible if you're a celebrity, a sports star, or royalty with a huge following, but for the vast majority of writers, you have nothing of the sort. Your book is either ignored, or it's picked up by a small publisher that doesn't have the resources to do anything to give your book exposure. There are certainly stories you hear about a new writer who writes a blockbuster bestseller that defies all the odds, but they are a tiny percent of the books that are written.

If you can get a publisher to take your book, they usually will print a small run for you, and they'll even include it in their catalogue, but it's up to you to market it and promote it. It's up to you to sell it. If you prove it can be done, and that your book is worthy, they are likely to work harder to promote it, but you have still done the vast amount of the work.

So, let's see... You write the book. You promote it and sell it. And the publisher gets 90 – 95% of the royalties for printing it and including it in their catalogue.

Along the way, they've taken control of what actually ends up being in your book, and they also have control of your cover, no matter what you think of the final product.

Oh, and to add to it, most of the publishers persuade writers to give them the copyright to their books; which means if they ever decide to take it out of production, or if you want to do something different, it is no longer your book. It technically belongs to them.

Does that seem fair to you?

It doesn't to me, either – which is why I walked away from the publishing world fifteen years earlier.

Here I was fifteen years later, staring down at the answer I had dreamed of for so long.

I realize there are people who believe Amazon has made it difficult for small bookstores to exist and thrive. You struggle with the massive impact Amazon has on the world.

I understand, but isn't it similar to railroads taking the back seat when passenger airplanes became available and affordable? The world changes. It always has and it always will.

On the flip side of the Amazon coin, they have opened the doors for authors to be heard that would never have been heard before. You have to market your books, but no one can tell you that what you wrote isn't worthy of being published. The public gets to decide.

As far as I'm concerned, the power of that far outweighs any negative aspects of the new digital publishing world. Amazon led the way, but the number of digital platforms for writers expands on a daily basis.

*****

My mind spun with the possibilities as I absorbed what I'd learned. I would have the full control I had always dreamed of. Building my internet companies had taught me massive amounts about internet marketing – though I would discover I still had much to learn!

I could design the covers myself.

I was the only one who would determine what ultimately ended up between the covers of my books.

I could release them as fast as I wanted to, and follow the schedule that would work best with my life.

I would have access to all my readers through marketing and social media avenues.

I already had an Auto-responder system that would allow me to send out newsletters very easily, and communicate with readers who wrote back.

But the best part??

Because I had kept the copyrights of all my books – starting 20 years earlier – I had full control of everything I had ever written. Which meant that I could bring The Richmond Chronicles back to life!

When that truth fully penetrated my mind, I jumped up and did a wild dance around my office. It was time for me to return to my first love – writing.

I could make all my books available via e-books through Kindle.

I could also make them all available through paperback by going through Create Space, the print division of Amazon.

I wouldn't have to mail or distribute them.

All I had to do was market. Amazon would do everything else. Wow!

I was determined to give it my best.

If you're a writer yourself, I encourage you to self-publish – for all the reasons I've just written.

*****

I had a lot of work to do, though.

I had to go back through the original four books, make any changes I needed, and bring them back to life. I planned to start immediately, but first I had to come up with a new name for the series. I also had to decide if I was going to continue with Virginia Gaffney, or use my own name.

That was a tough decision for me. I loved the anonymity of a pen name, but I had also just spent fifteen years building internet companies based around my name, Ginny Dye. How could I walk away from the marketing potential that offered?

In the end, I couldn't.

I decided to use my name, but I was certain I wanted a new name for the series. A new name for a brand-new beginning.

But what would it be?

I truly don't remember how I discovered the word I was searching for, but I knew I had found it the moment I laid eyes on it, and then read the definition.

** Bregdan **
A Gaelic term for weaving and braiding.

This word spoke so much to me.

It's true that I love history, but it's not really the events that fascinate me so much – it's the people. History is nothing more than the story of people's lives.

History reflects the consequences of choices and actions - both good and bad. History is what has given you the world you live in today – both good and bad.

This truth is why I named this series The Bregdan Chronicles.

Finding the word – Bregdan - unleashed what I consider to be the true power of history.

It's so simple.

Within a few minutes I had written The Bregdan Principle – the true foundation of every book in this series.

The Bregdan Principle

Every *life* that has been lived until today is a part of the woven braid of life.

It takes every person's story to create

HISTORY.

Your life will help determine the course of history.

You may think you don't have much of an impact.

YOU DO.

Every

Action you take will reflect in

Someone else's *life*.

Someone else's *decisions*.

Someone else's *future*.

Both GOOD and BAD.

My great hope as you read my books is that you will acknowledge the power you have, every day, to change the world around you by your decisions and actions. Then I will know the research & writing were all worthwhile.

Back to all the work I had to do...

*****

People often ask me what I like most about being a writer. That is a very difficult question to answer...

I love the research because I love to learn, and I love to dig out the truth and details of history so I can bring it to life. I'm always surprised by what I discover, which makes me want to know more...

I love the writing because it is so ultimately fun to watch a story come to life beneath my fingertips on the keyboard. I'm so very grateful for the *gift* I have. People ask me if I'm proud to be a writer. No... I'm simply grateful to have a *gift* I have the joy of giving to others.

I love the publishing and marketing. I spent years building internet companies and learning how to market online so this is all just a natural extension of that. Marketing is like a big online game of Monopoly to me. Since I'm competitive, it's fun to win - which simply makes it fun to play!

I love communicating with my readers. I see each Blog as a chance to be a voice in your life. I long to bring hope, belief, persistence and determination with every newsletter. I love responding to readers who write back after they read my Blog. I spend a lot of time communicating with people on Facebook. What fun! Many are shocked that it's actually me responding, but it's such a privilege to communicate with the people who have turned The Bregdan Chronicles into best-sellers! Each communication is an inspiration and motivation to keep going - and to continue giving the absolute best I can.

What's the most fun? I simply can't answer that because I love it all!!   I know how blessed I am to be able to do something I love with all my heart!

<u>Opal's Sweet Potato Pie</u>

Two pounds of potatoes will make two pies.
Boil the potatoes soft: peal and mash fine through a
cullender while hot; one tablespoonful of butter to be
mashed in with the potato. Take five eggs and
beat the yolks and whites separate and add one
gill of milk to sweeten to taste; squeeze the juice of one
orange and grate one half of the peel into the liquid.
One half teasponoonful of salt in the potatoes.
Have only one pie crust and that at
the bottom of the plate. Bake quickly.

Chapter Thirteen

My first mountainous job was to bring the first four books of The Richmond Chronicles back to life as The Bregdan Chronicles.

I had not looked at them for fifteen years because I was convinced that season of my life was over.   Little did I know that my passion for equality and justice would have grown exponentially in those years. Little did I know that the explosion of the internet would open doors to research that I could only have dreamed of accessing fifteen years earlier. Little did I know that current events would make the books far more relevant.

The first thing I had to do was read them. What fun! I cried, laughed, got angry, was inspired... all the things I hope my readers feel. It felt a little odd to have all those emotions from reading my own books, but in many ways it was like reading them for the first time!

Once I'd read them, and absorbed myself back into the story, it was time to edit them and make the changes I wanted. While I thought they were good, I had developed more as a writer in the fifteen years that had passed, and I knew I could make them better.

I also got to leave in the parts that my previous editor had thought were too intense.

Hurrah for control!

While I was rewriting, I created new covers – figuring out how to use the software to do that. The first ones were okay, but it wasn't until I finished Book # 5 (*The Last Long Night)* that I discovered the amazing graphic artist that redid those first covers, and has done every cover since then. I love Iqra!

She was a young single woman when we started working together. I've enjoyed pictures of her wedding to the love of her life, and the birth of her two children. I don't know if I'll ever make it to Pakistan, but I know I have a little sister there that means the world to me.

I figured out how to format the books for the size I wanted, uploaded them to both Kindle and Create Space, and then hit Publish. It was October 2012.

Just like that, the books I thought were dead forever had come back to life!

Of course, I still had no idea of how to market them, but I knew I would figure it out.

Before I could do that, though, I had some other things to take care of. I had closed my companies, but there were loose strings that needed tying in order to finalize everything. The work would take several months. It was all-consuming enough that I didn't think much about what the books were doing on Amazon.

I finally decided in January of 2013 that I should take a look.

As a businesswoman, I know the power of numbers. Feelings and emotions can lie. Numbers never do. I know the power of keeping track of what's happening. I can't get a clear picture of whether something is working if I don't have numbers.

The funny thing is, that while I hated working with all the numbers for my other businesses, I absolutely loved (and still love) charting the progress (or challenges) of my publishing business. I don't see the numbers as dollar signs – I see them as evidence of the number of lives I'm touching with what I write.

Anyway, I have kept daily numbers of sales since January 2013. It's fun to go back and see that the first month resulted in me selling 342 books – with a grand total of $472 in income.

Okay, not enough to make a living.

February 2013 – while I was still working on closing out things from my businesses – created 604 books sold, for a total of $755.10 income. Not life changing, but sales had doubled, and I still hadn't done anything. Interesting.

Sales more than tripled in March of 2013, and tripled again in April. Without me doing anything.

The numbers certainly got my attention. Imagine what could happen if I actually did some marketing.

It was time, and I was ready.

*** I should write a disclaimer here for new authors. It won't be as easy for you in the beginning as it was for me. First, I started out with four books in a series. Not many new authors have that luxury. Second, and most importantly, I launched my series at the very beginning of the Kindle entry into publishing. If Amazon sees your books will sell, they do a lot of the marketing for you. I've been very fortunate to have ridden that wave! I'm not trying to-discourage new writers – I'm telling you that you'll have to do more initial marketing because the competition is far greater now. I believe people who market wisely can have great success!

Thus began my adventure of book marketing – a series of trial and errors that cost me a lot of money, but ultimately resulted in my claiming bestseller status on Amazon for every book I've published in The Bregdan Chronicles. I am grateful for all my amazing readers!

*****

The first thing I had to do, though, was write the fifth book in the series, *The Last Long Night*. It had bothered me that I'd never finished the Civil War before the series went out of print. At that time, I would have told you the series would end with *The Last Long Night*. I didn't know what would come after that, but I figured I would write about different things. I had started the series with the determination to tell the truth about The Civil War. I needed to finish it.

What surprised me was how terrified I was to tackle it. I'm not sure why I was surprised. I mean, come on, it had been fifteen years since I'd written a novel. *Fifteen years*. Could I still do it? Would I be able to enter the storyline again? Would I be able to connect with the characters?

The questions spun through my mind as I dug into the research. The research effort was illuminating. I did what I always do; find every book I can find on the subjects I know I'll be dealing with. What stunned me was the changes the internet brought.

First, I went into Amazon and searched a topic in the book listings. I laughed with delight at what was available – books I probably would never have gotten from my library. I clicked buttons, and within a few days research books arrived on my front porch. Yes!

Fifteen years earlier, it would have taken me days to find out how long the canal from Richmond, VA to Lynchburg was. I laughed when I Googled it and had the answer in seconds. I was able to access records and archives anywhere in the country. I could have three or four screens open at one time; comparing and analyzing the material I was reading. Little details I had once searched days for were available in seconds.

There really is no word to adequately describe the feelings of delight and awe I had, nor the gratitude that swelled inside me, when I realized my quest for the truth had had gotten much easier and more complete.

I remember the day I finished the bulk of my research, though I continue to research things the entire time I'm writing every single book. I completed the outline for *The Last Long Night* and knew it was time to start writing.

Just like I had eighteen years earlier, I found myself staring at a blank screen for hours at a time. My heart clenched as my fears that I couldn't write novels again after fifteen years seemed to be coming to life in stark reality. Thankfully, it didn't take as long to find my answer as it did in the beginning.

The voice I had heard so clearly in my office all those years before resonated through my mind and heart again. *If you write it, it will come.*

I smiled, closed my eyes for several moments, opened them, and began to write.

*****

While I was writing, I was also delving into the marketing world. Facebook had only been open to the public for a few years and I really had no clue how to use it. Time to start learning.

I listened to a multitude of webinars. The funny thing about webinars is that they teach you enough to know you don't begin to know what you need to know to do anything - unless you spend money on their courses. I wasn't interested in doing that so I kept listening to webinars and eventually pieced together enough bits of information to give me a clear path forward. Or at least a clear path to begin...

I started by creating Facebook pages that would connect me with the people who would enjoy reading my books. I created beautiful images with powerful quotes I thought readers would enjoy. I thought it was a pretty cool page but, of course, no one found it. Well, a few people did, and some of them even commented on several of the posts.

As small as the number of comments was, I recognized an opportunity to develop relationships so I responded to every single comment. People were floored that they were hearing from the *author* of the books, but I was having a blast. What total fun to be able to "talk" to the people reading my books. *That* had certainly not been possible when I started my career twenty years earlier. I made a commitment to do that forever. My commitment remains... I respond to Facebook posts and as many emails as I possibly can. It's one of my greatest joys.

Some of these people responding on Facebook started buying my books. I knew I needed to expand how to reach them, so I kept learning – reading every Blog and internet article I could find about marketing through Facebook.

*****

In the midst of this, I was bringing *The Last Long Night* to life, remembering how much I love to write novels. Every day was both a joy and a challenge.

I'll tell you here that I always write an outline. For every single book. But...

The *final* book never resembles the outline!

Somewhere along the way, every book takes on a life of its own and starts going in directions I never envisioned. I smile, type and hang on for the ride. Many times, I end up doing more research to gain the knowledge I need for the new direction I'm taking. It's all part of the fun of each book.

16 years after I released *Dark Chaos (Magnolia Dreams)*, I released *The Last Long Night* in July 2013.

My overall feeling was one of vast relief. The last year of the war was brutal to write about, even though my commitment is to infuse hope into every situation, no matter how challenging. Researching and writing this book wore me out. By the time I was done, I was sure that if I had to read about one more stupid person, making one more stupid decision that would end in tens of thousands of men being slaughtered, I was going to rip my hair out.

No one was happier than I was when Lee and Grant finally signed the surrender, and the war wound to a close.

I had no clue what I was going to do next, but I did know I had much to learn about marketing books so I turned all my attention there for a while.

*****

One year before I started playing around with Facebook marketing, they added in the opportunity to Boost Posts on a page – choosing an audience you wanted to reach. Quite simply, it was revolutionary.

By July 2013, I was able to make a living from my writing – modest, but I was thrilled. I also kept searching for ways to expand my reach.

I will never forget the comment I received sometime in December of 2013 from a reader that stated her most favorite book used to be *Gone With The Wind* – until she read The Bregdan Chronicles. I thought about that a little bit and then decided to test a theory whirling around in my brain.

The second week of January 2014 I created a cheesy looking post (yes, it really was cheesy!) that basically said, If you love *Gone With The Wind*, you'll love The Bregdan Chronicles. I had a picture of *Gone With The Wind* and *Storm Clouds Rolling In*, and a big heart in the middle. No one would have called it professional looking, but I was just beginning to learn! I posted it on my page, boosted the post to Facebook people interested in historical fiction, and then left the next morning to fly to California to visit a friend.

That night, after my arrival in California, I opened my laptop, logged into Kindle to see how sales were going that day, and let out a shriek that had my friends running to make sure a serial killer had not just attacked me with a knife. I thanked them later for running toward me, instead of away as fast as they could!

They found me staring at the screen, babbling what they insisted were nonsensical words.

I don't remember it that way. I'm pretty sure I was sputtering. "Look at this... Look at this... Look at this..." I was so excited, it probably sounded like a foreign language I've never learned!

I'm pretty sure the most copies of *Storm Clouds Rolling In* I had sold in one day was about 25 up to that point. Imagine my shock when I was staring at 500 – **yes, 500** – copies of *Storm Clouds Rolling In* sold in one day!

All because of a cheesy looking ad about *Gone With The Wind*?

That was the day things blasted into orbit.

I've known from the beginning that if I could get people to read #1 (*Storm Clouds Rolling In*) that a large percentage of them would want to read the rest of the series. I was right, and now my whole focus in marketing is to sell #1.

From that day forward, it's been fun. I market *Storm Clouds Rolling In*, communicate with my readers, and write as many new books as I can. I've created lots of ads, making them more professional along the way, and the Bregdan Chronicles Family has continued to grow.

As my schedule intensified, I knew there was no way I could schedule all the posts I've created for the Facebook pages I have with close to 100,000 followers. I've heard from tens of thousands of you that love the quotes and images I share on Facebook. When I realized I needed help, Priya came into my life.

Priya has been beyond a godsend. A young Hindu woman from India, she is professional, committed, and excellent at what she does. I'm so grateful to have her part of my team, and also feel she is part of my family.

I talk with many writers, artists and other professionals who hate the marketing end of their business. They believe that marketing their work somehow diminishes the creative part of their life. I watch as many talented people fail at creating a living doing what they love because they're not willing to do the part they don't find fun.

I'm lucky. I *love* marketing. It truly is nothing more than a game for me. I've always been an athlete and I've always been competitive. I see business the same way I see a tennis match or a softball game. It's a game. One I'm determined to win. Even though I recognize the value of money, that is not my motivating factor.

What *is* my motivating factor? The answer is simple.

If people don't read my books; what is the purpose of writing them?

If people don't read my books; why bother to use my *Gift*?

If people don't read my books, how can I change lives? How can I share hope? How can I challenge women to be all they can be?

The answer is obvious, so I've done what most authors refuse to do. I've marketed, and The Bregdan Chronicles Family has grown.

It's because of my readers that I have the privilege of doing what I love more than anything. Thank you!

*****

Once I had all my books in E-book and Print format, I explored what it would take to turn them into audio books. I was thrilled to discover ACX, another division of Amazon. I learned I could hire a narrator/producer who would create them for 50% of the profits. I also had the option of paying someone upfront, based on the length of the book, but the price was prohibitive for me.

Thus began my adventure of finding the perfect narrator. I lost track of the number of audition tapes I listened to, growing more discouraged that I would ever find the right person to bring The Bregdan Chronicles to life.

Until...

Until Christine Cunningham Smith (Chris) entered my life. As soon as I heard her audition recording, I was smiling from ear to ear. My subsequent communications with her convinced me she was the one!

My "listeners" wrote glowing reviews and waited eagerly for each new book.

It took her a couple years to catch up with me. She was recording as fast as she could, but I continued to write. It took her five to six months for each recording. It's not just a matter of reading the books out loud. The technical aspects of the job are daunting.

Chris was amazing. She had been a stage actor for years before she added narrating to her list of accomplishments. Not only were her characters done well – she *sang* the spirituals! My mouth dropped open the first time I listened. What a treasure she was!

I was working on *Glimmers of Change* before she caught up with me – finishing *Carried Forward By Hope*.

We loved working together – becoming good friends during the process. I regret I never had the opportunity to meet her face-to-face.

One of Chris' goals was to narrate every single one of The Bregdan Chronicles. She loved the books so much and wanted to be part of them from start to finish.

I was shattered when I received a message from her daughter during the summer of 2016. Chris had passed away very unexpectedly, leaving behind a grieving, disbelieving family.

My grief joined theirs.

I had lost my narrator – much more importantly, I had lost a friend.

It took me several months before I could even fathom finding someone to replace her. The insistent barrage of emails from my listeners convinced me I had to try. Chris passed away during the recording of *Always Forward*, which meant I had to find someone to start over.

I listened to many auditions but none of them met my expectations. I felt sorry for the narrators as I listened because I couldn't imagine anyone ever replacing Chris. And, really, who would want to try?

Finally, in December of 2016, I received a letter from a reader who wanted to submit an audition. She'd read every book twice, was in love with The Bregdan Chronicles, and wanted to try her hand at narration.

I wasn't enthusiastic, but I was impressed with her love of the series, and decided to give her a try.

Wow! I listened to the audition recording and knew I had found my narrator.

Enter Tiffany Dougherty...

She has been a true gift, and a delight to work with. Besides being a great narrator, she is the principal of an elementary school in Colorado, a wife, and the mother of beautiful daughters. My great hope is that she'll stay healthy for a long time, and that she'll remain in love with The Bregdan Chronicles!

I wish I could be there in her studio when she has to record this section about herself!

*****

While building my publishing company I'm reminded almost every day of an experience I had with my grandfather many years ago when I was young. He and I were visiting an old family homestead. It's possible that it was a remnant of the Gaffney family, but I don't remember that. There was only the crumbling foundation of a home... and an old rusty water pump to the side. My grandfather rolled up his sleeves on that hot summer day, walked over to the pump, knocked off some corrosion and cobwebs, and began to pump. I watched dubiously, wisely deciding to stay in the shade of the nearby oak tree.

I was young, but not too young to believe he was nuts to think he could get anything to come out of that rusty old pump. He saw my expression, smiled, winked, and kept pumping. Hard. Many minutes passed. The only water being produced was the sweat pouring down his face as he stood in the hot sun and pumped that rusty handle.

He kept pumping... The sweat now had his shirt plastered to his body and he was breathing hard.

He kept pumping... I was getting thirsty just watching him. But something else was happening. Watching him pump so hard, with such a fierce look of determination, had turned my skepticism into hope. Maybe he wasn't crazy. Maybe there was water somewhere deep beneath the earth that he was going to magically make appear. Just maybe something would come out that would quench my thirst. *He* certainly seemed to think so.

He kept pumping... "It's going to come out any minute now, Ginny Girl. You watch. It's coming!"

Just then I heard a faint gurgling sound come from that rusty old pump. I leapt forward from the shade of my oak tree and knelt down in the hot sun beside where he stood. "Come on pump! Come on!"

My grandfather laughed and pumped even harder, his whole body drenched in sweat.

The gurgling got louder, but there was still nothing coming out of that rusty old contraption.

"Come on, pump! Come on!" I yelled. Somehow my grandfather's belief had become my own.

Several more minutes passed. Sweat poured from my grandfather, and glistened on my own face, as I stared with hope at the old pump; flies and bumblebees buzzing through the summer air.

And then it happened... The gurgling exploded from the pump... in one small drop of water.

One small drop?? All that work for one small drop?

I was dismayed. My grandfather laughed and kept pumping - even harder, if it were possible. "It's coming, Ginny Girl! That little drop was just the beginning. You keep watching!"

Doubtful this old pump could quench my burning thirst; I nevertheless remained at my post and willed the pump to release more water.

Another drop. Then a bigger drop.

Then a series of drops that turned into a tiny stream.

"It's coming!" I screamed, dancing in excitement. "It's coming! Let's have a drink!" It didn't matter to me that it was faintly rust colored. It was *water*.

"Not yet," my Grandfather panted. "It's not time to stop pumping yet, or we'll lose the momentum. Run to the car and get some cups."

I was too young to understand momentum. I wasn't too young to understand that the stream was getting bigger. And, I wasn't too young to understand that my Grandfather kept pumping just as hard. It took only moments to run to the car and return with 2 cups. I continued to dance with excitement, swirling with the butterflies that had been drawn by all the commotion. It only took a few minutes more before suddenly the stream of water turned from a rather rusty looking trickle into a gushing torrent of cold clear water, splashing onto the dry ground and quickly forming a small lake.

"Now?" I screamed. "Now?" I was quite certain I couldn't wait one more second. "Now," my grandfather replied as he reached eagerly for the cups and filled them to the brim. He kept pumping, though not nearly as hard, as we satisfied our thirst. I laughed as he put his whole head under the cold waterfall and washed off the sweat, and then removed his shirt and used it as a washcloth to cool his body before putting it back on.

Then he turned to me with the look that said he had something to tell me. "Ginny Girl, just because you can't see something doesn't mean it's not there. You've just got to believe it's there and keep pumping until it works its way up to you. Most people would have given up, thinking it was too hard. I knew there was water there. I was   just   going   to   pump   until   it   came   up!"

*****

The lesson stuck...The water in the old well is just like success in your life. So many people will step up to the pump, and pump for a few minutes. When they don't see results they walk away. Some people will pump a little longer before they walk away - convinced their efforts are futile. There are even those that will pump until they hear the gurgle, or even witness the small rusty-colored stream, and then walk away - exhausted by their efforts and convinced it's all in vain.

And then there are those people... The ones that simply won't quit pumping until a torrent of rushing water is creating all they dream of for their life. They refuse to give up hope. They decide to believe it's possible, and they let hope and belief carry them until they see the results of their efforts.

Which are you?

I have a favorite definition of hope.

Hope is the bird that sings to the dawn while it is still dark.

You can *choose* to sing before the light starts flooding into your life – believing it will come. You can grab the handle and PUMP, long before you see any results.

Remember, the Choices You Make Today Will Determine the Rest of Your Life!

*****

With *The Last Long Night* behind me, I didn't know what I would do next. My research for the book I'd just finished had piqued my interest in knowing more about Reconstruction, but I had no idea whether the Reconstruction years could carry a book. Just writing that makes me laugh!

You see, when I started writing these books I would have told you I knew something about the Civil War. Most of what I thought I knew turned out to be completely wrong, but I at least *thought* I knew something in the beginning. I already knew I was completely ignorant about the Reconstruction years. My memory of history couldn't pull up anything except a vague mention of carpetbaggers. Hardly enough to base more books on.

Yet, something compelled me to spend a few days doing some digging into those years. What I discovered amazed me, astonished me, and ignited a deep excitement; an excitement to learn the history I was so clueless about, and an equal excitement to write about it.

What I wasn't anticipating was that the next book, *Carried Forward By Hope*, would take me back to the day in the Gaffney archives at Limestone College when I closed the book on my family history because I was unwilling to learn the truth.

I didn't know my world was about to be turned upside down...

Potato Chips

Peel the potatoes and wash them clean, then peel them
again with a sharp knife; if possible, make only one peel
of the whole potato; throw them into salt and water;
when you think you have enough for a dish, take them
out and lay on a cloth to dry; have some fat boiling in a
stewpan and throw them in; when a fine brown and crisp,
them them out with a slice, lay them on a sieve;
when all done, dish them up on a napkin.
You must not put too many in the fat at a time,
or they will not crisp.

Chapter Fourteen

Writing #6, *Carried Forward By Hope,* was an adventure. It was an adventure in writing, but mostly it was an adventure in learning.

My commitment, to that point, was that each book would cover a year. I had no clue that once I started into Reconstruction I would never again make it through twelve months in a book.

There was just too much rich fodder. There was too much going on in our country. There were too many experiences that demanded to be written about. And, of course, I had a growing number of characters who demanded to be included in each book. They have a habit of pouting if they aren't front and center at some point!

It took *Carried Forward By Hope* and #7, *Glimmers of Change,* before I fully acknowledged that I would write the story until I hit over five hundred pages, stop, and then roll into the next book – no matter where I was when I stopped! I create a good ending, and my thoughts surge ahead to the following book.

I've already told you I start with an outline, but none of my books resemble it at the end. *Carried Forward By Hope* was no exception.

I *started* with an outline, but somewhere along the way, just like always, it took on a life of its own. If you were to go back to my outline, after reading the book, you would cock your head with complete confusion. Don't worry – I do too!

Different things happen than the ones I envisioned.

Characters do things I didn't anticipate – but always end up agreeing with.

New characters pop in that I didn't plan for.

I love it because it keeps things fun for me; and reminds me I only have just so much control!

People also ask how I develop my characters. They assume I sat down before starting the series and very carefully drafted them out. They assume I've done the same thing with all the new characters who are now part of the Bregdan Family.

Ummm... no.

My characters come to life as I'm writing the books. I had no idea what Carrie would look like until I started writing. Or Robert. Or Rose. Or Moses. Or... you get the idea.

I didn't really have a clear picture of what kind of people they would be, or how they would react to things as the books developed. It just kinda happened...

Weird?

Possibly, but it's how I write. It works for me.

I have my amazing editor, Stephanie, to thank for putting together a massive character book. I never forget who the characters are as people from one book to the next, but I've been known to switch eye colors, or have them born in different places in different books. Stephanie saved me by creating a profile for every single character; even the horses! I'm so grateful to be able to open a Word document and be reminded that Jeremy has blue eyes, not brown; or that Captain Jones' sister's name is Susan, not Katherine! Yes – those were mistakes I made!

*****

How exactly did my life turn upside down? In hindsight, perhaps it didn't turn upside down, after all. Maybe it just finally came full-circle, and I was able to realize and understand the true depth of my passion for this series.

It all happened because of some research for *Carried Forward By Hope*. A part of my reading had me delving into information on the Ku Klux Klan. I was appalled by what I was learning, and dug a little deeper and further forward than I usually do.

I remember the moment I stiffened in my chair. The moment my mind started racing. The moment I struggled to catch my breath. It was also the moment I turned away from researching for the book, and began to research my own family heritage.

To understand what brought me to this moment, I must share a little history with you that occurs past where I currently am with The Bregdan Chronicles. The time is coming when I will cover all this in depth within my books, but I'm just going to give you a thumbnail version now.

When Reconstruction ended in the South, it wasn't because there had been a great victory and resolution from the Civil War that had created equality between the whites and blacks in the South. It was more that the government finally threw up their hands and acknowledged defeat – they were never going to get the

South to treat blacks with equality and justice. There were many other things going on in the country that demanded the government's attention, so they decided to declare an end to Reconstruction, and basically told the South the "black issue" was theirs to deal with. That single act was what created the world we're in now. Quite simply; they never finished the job that so desperately needed finishing.

The Southern states had already been doing everything they could to disenfranchise blacks and return them to the subservient life they believed they should live. Yet, in spite of all they did, blacks still made great strides during Reconstruction. They took many political offices, started schools, and claimed leadership positions.

When Reconstruction ended and the federal troops were withdrawn, all the Southern states, but especially South Carolina, were determined to take back white control. The white aristocracy, appalled by what they had viewed during Reconstruction, would stop at nothing to gain complete political dominance once again.

Reconstruction "ended" in 1877. There was a major election in South Carolina the following year. A plan went into action that involved killing both white and black Republican leaders, as well as terrorizing black voters so they wouldn't vote in the 1878 election.

The white aristocracy was all for the plan, but not about to do the actual work. They would have to depend on the Ku Klux Klan for the murders and terrorizing. The problem with that reality was the fact that "employing" the KKK was quite expensive – their services did not come for free. The politicians and leaders turned to the people of South Carolina to fund the campaign.

Unfortunately, it was terrifyingly effective.

How did all this impact me? Reading this triggered memories I had been pushing aside for almost twenty years.

Let me go back to the day I was sitting in the Gaffney Family Archives at Limestone College. I learned how Captain Michael had died in 1854, leaving his entire estate to my Great-great-great-great-great Grandma Polly, with the direction that when she died all the estate would be divided up among their children.

That's not quite what happened.

Please don't forget Captain Michael Gaffney was a very wealthy man.

In a nutshell... my Grandma Polly, when she died in the mid 1870's, donated her entire estate to the Ku Klux Klan.

That is what I read when I turned the page in Limestone College years earlier. The day I stood up and walked out; not able to absorb that reality as my heritage.

My Grandma Polly helped fund the reign of terror that returned power to the white aristocracy of South Carolina, setting up an ongoing reign of terror for the state's black population.

When I put together all the pieces in my office doing research for *Carried Forward By Hope*, I was beyond horrified and mortified. I put my head down on my desk and cried. Yes, I realized, even at the time, that I wasn't responsible for what my ancestors had done more than a century earlier.

I didn't feel responsible for what they had done; but I felt completely responsible for *redeeming* it. I had thought during all the years since I'd discovered Captain

Michael was a slave owner that I was redeeming those actions. That was bad enough, but *this...*

Funding the KKK to unleash a reign of terror against South Carolina that killed thousands?

I literally groaned as I felt the weight of the responsibility settle into my heart and mind.

After only a minute or so, though, I heard the strong gentle voice that I know so well.

It's not your responsibility, Ginny.

I held my breath, waiting for the rest of what surely must be coming.

It's your privilege.

I stiffened as the voice rang through my entire being over and over, and then gradually relaxed.

It's your privilege.

The truth of what I was hearing melted away the horror and shame. There is no denying the horror of what was done, but I didn't carry the weight of a responsibility any longer.

I carried the joy of *privilege.*

The incredible privilege of being the one who would be the voice of so many who can no longer speak.

The incredible privilege of being the one who would bring light to the darkness and reveal what had been done.

I truly believe there can be no freedom without the truth.

I believe there will never be racial equality and healing in the United States until the truth allows us to rectify all the wrongs that have been done; until white people understand just why our country is still not a place of equality for all races.

I've heard so many people protest that they didn't have anything to do with what their white ancestors did. It's not their responsibility to fix it.

No, it's not.

But it is their *privilege* to fix it.

Until we live in a country that recognizes all people as equal, we have not fulfilled the dream that launched America.

As an author, I have the privilege of being a voice for change and truth.

Awesome!

*****

People often ask me why I don't write non-fiction. They point at the mountains of research I do and insist it would be better used in non-fiction. I couldn't disagree more. Here's why...

When people sit down to read non-fiction, they know they're about to learn something. There's a funny thing about human nature; when people believe they're about to learn something they put up walls. They go into it with the weight of their own perspectives and experiences shadowing whatever they are about to learn. They filter the facts through their own colored lenses – of every color and type.

Now, think about fiction. When you sit down to read fiction, you don't put up walls. You don't prepare to read it through your own biased perspective.

It's fiction.

You're simply reading for enjoyment. You want a great story. You want characters you feel you know and can relate to. You want to be entertained or inspired in some way. Your mind and heart are open.

That is why I write fiction.

I take all the knowledge I've gained and weave it into what I hope is a really great story with characters you love.

And along the way... I wallop you between the eyes with truth.

I'm honest enough to admit it!

I write fiction because it gives me the ability to swing the hammer of truth. The best part is that you never even see it coming. You have no defenses set in place, so the words simply cut through all the static and go straight into your heart.

That's why I receive letters and comments on an almost daily basis that share how my books have changed people's understanding of racism. How my books have opened their eyes to what has really happened in our country. How my books have helped them understand the current political atmosphere. How my books have challenged them to become a voice of reason and change.

I read them and cheer. I do a happy dance around my office!

I thank God I have the *privilege* of redeeming what happened so many years ago.

Accepting the truth about my family heritage has given me such a deep understanding of why I'm so passionate about what I do. I'm not writing just to tell a story. I'm not writing for the money.

I write to make a difference.

*****

I'm writing this book in 2018. I have gotten so many emails asking what my position is on the removal of the Confederate statues. As I thought about it, I realized that besides the reality I would be skewered by people no matter what my opinion; the wrong question was being asked. In my mind, the question that should be asked is "What has led up to the demand for the removal of the Confederate statues?"

THAT is the question I have spent so many hours thinking about... And here is my answer...

The Nazi and KKK violence in Charlottesville, Virginia in 2017... the rise of the KKK in recent years... the rise of Hate Groups across the board...violence against Blacks... violence against Muslims... violence against Women... Violence against Jews...Violence against Latinos... Violence against Native Americans...and, yes, violence against white men.

As I've read and watched, I've come to a much deeper understanding.

WE ARE ALL RESPONSIBLE FOR WHAT HAPPENED IN CHARLOTTESVILLE, VIRGINIA.

Charlottesville was not a random happening. It's part of a pattern. A mosque being blown up no longer surprises anyone. A synagogue being burned has almost become commonplace. Women being raped is accepted as simply a part of our culture.

We rant against White Hate groups (as we should), but we also must acknowledge the Black Separatist groups that are labeled as a hate group.

Hate is hate.

Whites hate blacks... blacks hate whites... Latinos hate Asians... Asians hate Latinos...

Straight people hate gay people... gay people hate straight people... men hate women... women hate men...

People are choosing to hate. It seems like everyone has to have someone to hate.

You may be shaking your head and saying this has absolutely nothing to do with you... *you* are not racist... *you* don't hate... but I would respectfully differ with you.

WE ARE ALL RESPONSIBLE FOR WHAT HAPPENED IN CHARLOTTESVILLE.

We are all responsible because as a society we have allowed racism to take over America. We may not be the ones lifting the torch... we may not be the one running over a crowd of defenseless people with their car... we may not be the one putting up hate graffiti... but I believe we are all responsible - including me.

If you truly are appalled with what happened in Charlottesville... if you truly want to stop the racist violence exploding in our country... then you need to step up and take *action* to change it. If you don't, you're as much a part of the problem as the 22-year-old who plowed his car into protesters.

I'm not talking about just posting a meme against hatred on Facebook - though that certainly has its place.

I'm not talking about just signing an online petition and going about your day - though I would certainly encourage you to sign all that you can.

It's about taking ACTION. I believe the best way I can contribute to what is going on in America, besides write my books, is to share with you very specific actions you can take if you truly want things to be different. And then I want you to share them with as many people as you can.

I'm taking the opportunity to share these in this book because they will be read and hopefully acted upon for a very long time.

AT THE INDIVIDUAL LEVEL

1. Listen to, validate, and ally with people who report personal and systemic racism. Most people who report racism or hatred say that those they report it to don't take claims of racism seriously. It's time to stop defending the idea of a post-racial society, and recognize instead that we live in a racist one. Listen to and trust those who report racism, because anti-racism begins with basic respect for all people.

2. Have hard conversations with yourself about the racism that lives within you. When you find yourself making an assumption about people, places, or things, challenge yourself by asking whether you know the assumption to be true, or if it's something you've simply been taught to believe by a racist society. Consider facts and evidence, especially those found in academic books and articles about race and racism, rather than hearsay and racist rhetoric.

3. Be mindful of the commonalities that humans share, and practice empathy. Don't fixate on difference, though it's important to be aware of it and the implications of it, particularly as it regards power and privilege.

Remember that if any kind of injustice is allowed to thrive in our society, all forms can. We owe it to each other to fight for an equal and just society for all.

AT THE COMMUNITY LEVEL

4. If you see something, say something. Step in when you see racism occurring, and disrupt it in a safe way. Have hard conversations with others when you hear or see racism, whether explicit or implicit. Challenge racist assumptions by asking about supporting facts and evidence (in general, they don't exist). Have conversations about what led you and/or others to have racist beliefs.

5. Cross the racial divide (and others) by offering friendly greetings to people, regardless of race, gender, age, sexuality, ability, class, or housing status. Think about who you make eye contact with, nod to, or say "Hello" to while you're out in the world.

If you notice a pattern of preference and exclusion, be bold and shake it up. Respectful, friendly, everyday communication is the essence of community.

6. Learn about the racism that occurs where you live, and do something about it by participating in and supporting anti-racist community events, protests, rallies, and programs.

For example, you could:

- Support voter registration and polling in neighborhoods where people of color live, because they have historically been marginalized from the political process. Just because things have gotten "better", they are still far from being right.

- Donate time and/or money to community organizations that serve youth of color or a different sexual orientation.

- Mentor kids on being anti-racist citizens who fight for justice.

- Support post-prison programs, because the inflated incarceration rates of black and Latino people lead to their long-term economic and political disenfranchisement.

- Support community organizations that serve those bearing the mental, physical, and economic costs of racism.

- Communicate with your local and state government officials and institutions about how they can help end racism in the communities they represent.

AT THE NATIONAL LEVEL

7. Combat racism through national-level political channels. For example, you could:

- Write senators and members of congress to demand an end to racist practices in law enforcement, the judiciary, education, and the media.

- Advocate for national legislation that would criminalize racist police practices and institute ways to monitor police behavior, like the Mike Brown Law that has mandated body cameras for police officers.
- Join the movement for reparations for the descendants of African slaves and other historically oppressed populations within the U.S., because theft of land, labor, and denial of resources is the foundation of American racism, and it is on this foundation that contemporary inequalities thrive.

8. Advocate for Affirmative Action practices in education and employment. Countless studies have found that, qualifications being equal, people of color are rejected for employment and admission to educational institutions at far greater rates than white people.

Affirmative Action initiatives help mediate this problem of racist exclusion.

9. Vote for candidates who make ending racism a priority; vote for candidates of color. In today's federal government, people of color remain disturbingly underrepresented. For a racially just democracy to exist, we must achieve accurate representation, and the governing of representatives must actually represent the experiences and concerns of our diverse populace.

Keep in mind that you don't have to do all of these things in your fight against racism. What's important is that we all do SOMETHING.

There are more... (I have done a lot of research with the hopes you will find one or more actions YOU can take to truly make a difference).

10. Learn to recognize and understand your own privilege.

One of the first steps to eliminating racial discrimination is learning to recognize and understand your own privilege. Racial privilege plays out across social, political, economic, and cultural environments. Checking your privilege and using your privilege to dismantle systemic racism are two ways to begin this complex process.

However, race is only one aspect of privilege. Religion, gender, sexuality, ability-status, socio-economic status, language, and citizenship status can all affect your level of privilege. Using the *privileges* that you have to collectively empower others requires first being aware of those privileges and acknowledging their implications.

11. Examine your own biases and consider where they may have originated.

There are questions each person should ask themselves. What messages did you receive as a kid about people who are different from you? What was the racial and/or ethnic make-up of your neighborhood, school, or religious community? Why do you think that was the case? These experiences produce and reinforce bias, stereotypes, and prejudice, which can lead to discrimination. Examining our own biases can help us work to ensure equality for all.

12. Validate the experiences and feelings of people of color.

Another way to address bias and recognize privilege is to support the experiences of other people and engage in tough conversations about race and injustice. We cannot be afraid to discuss oppression and discrimination for fear of "getting it wrong." As advocates, we learn about domestic violence by listening to survivors of domestic violence. Similarly, the best way to understand racial injustice is by listening to people of color.

13. Challenge the "colorblind" ideology.

It is a pervasive myth that we live in a "post-racial" society where people "don't see color." Perpetuating a "colorblind" ideology actually contributes to racism.

When Dr. Martin Luther King, Jr. described his hope for living in a colorblind world, he didn't mean we should ignore race. It is impossible to eliminate racism without first acknowledging race. Being "colorblind" ignores a significant part of a person's identity and dismisses the real injustices that many people face as a result of race. We must see color in order to work together for equity and equality.

14. Call out racist "jokes" or statements.

Let people know racist comments are not okay. If you are not comfortable or don't feel safe being confrontational, try to break down their thought process and ask questions. For example, *"That joke doesn't make sense to me, could you explain it?"* Or *"You may be kidding, but this is what it means when you say that type of thing."* Don't be afraid to engage in conversations with loved ones, coworkers, and friends. Micro aggressions, which can appear in the form of racist jokes or statements, perpetuate and normalize biases and prejudices. Remember that not saying anything – or laughing along – implies that you agree.

15. Be thoughtful with your finances.

Take a stand with your wallet. Know the practices of companies that you invest in and the charities that you donate to. Make an effort to shop at small, local businesses and give your money back to the people living in the community. Your state or territory may have a directory of local, minority-owned businesses in your area.

16. Adopt an intersectional approach in all aspects of your life.

Remember that all forms of oppression are connected. You cannot fight against one form of injustice and not fight against others.

*****

Do you want America to be different than it is now? Then TAKE ACTION.

Do something today to make a difference. Choose at least one of these actions and then DO IT.

If you want to make a difference on social media platforms, share your experience. Tell people what you did. Challenge them to do something of their own.

Become a loud voice in creating the kind of country you truly want to live in.

I believe members of The Bregdan Chronicles Family are people who care - now I'm challenging all of you to take ACTION!

<u>Mulligatawny Soup</u>. (Serves 3-4)

½ oz. butter   1tbsp olive oil

4 chicken thigh fillets, cut into bite size chunks or 2 chicken breast

fillets, cut into bite size chunks or about 8ozs leftover chicken

1 onion, chopped   1 clove garlic, chopped

1 medium sized carrot, diced   1 medium sized potato, diced

1 small turnip, diced (optional)   1 tbsp. mild madras curry powder

1¾ pints chicken stock   2 large tomatoes, chopped

2-4 cloves (according to personal preference)

6 black peppercorns, crushed lightly

4ozs rice   2ozs red lentils

handful chopped coriander (reserve some for garnish) – or parsley

Salt & freshly ground black pepper

For Garnish: 1tbsp per bowl sour cream 1tsp per bowl mango chutney

chopped fresh coriander reserved or parsley

grind of black pepper or light dusting of cayenne pepper/chili powder

Mulligatawny Soup

Melt the butter and oil together in a large saucepan.

Turn up the heat and fry the diced raw chicken quickly turning

frequently until it has browned. This should take about 2

minutes. Remove from the pan and set aside.

(Cooked leftover chicken should be added about

10 minutes before the serving which should be just long enough

for it to be thoroughly heated through.) Stir the curry powder

into the remaining oil and cook briefly. Add the onion, garlic,

carrot, potato and turnip (if using) to the oil remaining

in the pan. Stir well and turn down the heat. Cover and

cook very gently for about 10 minutes. Add the stock

and stir well. Add the cloves, crushed peppercorns

and chopped tomatoes. Bring to the boil and reduce the heat,

cover, and simmer gently for 20 minutes.

<u>Mulligatawny Soup</u> ~

Return the cooked chicken to the pan along
with most of the chopped coriander, including the stalky pieces
(use chopped leaves for the garnish). Add the rice and
lentils and simmer gently until they are just cooked,
adding a little extra water only if needed.
(If leftover cooked chicken is being used
in place of fresh meat, this should be added about
10 minutes before the end of cooking time.)
Remove the cloves before serving if you can find them.
Taste & adjust seasoning.
Add a dollop of sour cream, a spoonful of mango chutney and a
scattering of chopped coriander or parsley, before serving.

Chapter Fifteen

Once I released *Carried Forward By Hope*, it was time to turn my attention to #7, *Glimmers of Change*. The research both horrified and fascinated me.

You know, it's hard to write a book where I can't reveal spoiler plot lines from the series that spawned the book you are reading now. I can tell you, though, that much of the research time was spent with tears in my eyes as I peeled back the layers of the events that transpired in the United States after the war ended.

I realized with startlingly clarity, that the war hadn't really ended. It had simply taken another form. The South didn't cease to fight; they just altered their methods.

The soldiers who fought the Civil War, on both sides, returned home to destroyed houses and families. They returned home carrying the wounds and memories of a horrific war. Many returned home with missing limbs, and a psyche that would never heal from their experiences. It changed them, and it changed America.

Yes, America had changed. The price to hold it together as the *United* States of America produced scars and ramifications we're still dealing with today.

Women changed. Hundreds of thousands of them had to handle everything while their husbands were off at war – or continue to handle them when their husbands never returned. They found jobs and a new independence.

Their new independence ignited a growing passion within many women to vote. The battle for Women's Suffrage began before the war, but the reality of the war brought it renewed vigor. Women were no longer willing to accept the dominance of men because they had learned what they were capable of.

As *Glimmers of Change* revealed, the end of the war also highlighted the determination of too many white Americans, in both the South *and* the North, to make sure blacks would never have equality. It didn't matter that Constitutional Amendments had guaranteed them that very thing. America was a big country and it wasn't possible to control all of it.

Black Americans, and the whites who fought for their equality alongside them, were facing a massive battle – one that left many casualties along the way.

Every word I read, and every new thing I discovered, only made me more determined to speak the truth.

Loudly.

*****

Writing *Glimmers of Change* also tossed me deeper into the world of homeopathic medicine, and the battles that were fought with traditional medicine. It also taught me, yet again, the power of the Internet.

Without destroying a plot line (since it's on the Amazon book description), I can reveal that a cholera epidemic was sweeping through America during this book. Traditional medicine had no treatment, meaning most patients who contracted the disease died.

Homeopathy, on the other hand, had a very effective remedy. I was determined to tell this story, but I was also determined to be accurate in my writing. That meant I had to discover just what homeopathic remedy was used to cure people. Well, that was easier said than done.

I searched for two days to find the information I needed but it remained elusive.

There were moments I told myself that if *I* couldn't find it, my readers would never know if I was right or wrong with what I wrote down, but I don't write that way. I have far too much respect for truth and for all of you. I had to know it was completely accurate or it wasn't going in my book.

Finally, and I can't begin to tell you how I did it, I stumbled into the online medical archives for Harvard University. Really, I have no idea how I found it, but suddenly I was there. I'm not sure I could get back there again.

I danced around my office – yes, I do a lot of that – when I discovered the old pamphlet, created in 1866, that gave the very homeopathic cure that was used for the cholera epidemic.

Since I had stopped writing for almost three days in order to find the exact information I needed, I was more than excited to return to writing.

*****

Another question I'm often asked is what characters are fictional, and who is real?

That's a great question.

I've also been asked if I would go through my books (in the Kindle version, where it's possible) and provide facts and footnotes on historic figures.

Ummm... No.

I write fiction. Remember? If I wanted to write non-fiction I would definitely do that, but all it would do in the case of writing The Bregdan Chronicles would be to slow me down greatly. It would do more than that, though; it would steal much of the joy I have from writing, and I'm not willing to have that happen

Here's a good way to answer the first question, though.

I can tell you that Carrie and her family, Moses and Rose, Matthew and Janie, Jeremy... all the characters you love so much are completely fictional, though of course they're based on real people from a real time in history.

Once you move beyond the fictional Bregdan Family, I can pretty much guarantee you the people in the books are real. Politicians. Military Leaders. Women leaders.

The very best thing you can do if you want to know if they're real, is to Google them and then learn all you can. I love how many people I hear from who do just that. They research people in the books. They research events. They research places. They write me and tell me how astonished they are at the accuracy of what I include in the books.

You can't go to Virginia and find Cromwell Plantation, though you can visit many other beautiful plantations that were the inspiration for Cromwell. You can visit the site of Chimborazo Hospital. You can visit the Richmond Capitol. You can visit the battlefields that surround the city, and visit the gravesites of many of the leaders.

I wonder if Richmond has figured out yet that many of their visitors are coming to experience what they read about in The Bregdan Chronicles!

I do thousands of hours of research to make certain my historical fiction is authentic, but I encourage you to dig deeper if you want to know more.

I am completely anal about the historical accuracy of my books. It drives me crazy when writers call something "historical fiction" and then don't do their research. All they do is fill people full of beliefs and perceptions that are flawed or completely untrue. I believe it does such a disservice to those writers who are committed to historical accuracy intertwined with a great story.

*****

After I finished *Glimmers of Change*, I headed down to the Oregon Coast for 12 days of vacation and research for book #8 in The Bregdan Chronicles. There are many beautiful places in the world, but nothing holds my heart like the Oregon Coast. That's where I am at this very moment while I finalize the editing of the book you're reading.

I love every single thing about the Oregon Coast. The craggy bluffs. The imposing rocks with the surf exploding as it crashes into them. The glorious sunsets. The almost private beaches (at least where I was!). The sun. The violent storms. The constant song of the surf. The eagles. The hawks. The playful seals. Hours of roaming the beaches with my dog. Amazing food. The list goes on and on...

I first discovered the Oregon Coast thirty years ago when I moved there to lead wilderness horseback trips in the coastal mountains. Yeah... there are a lot of stories from that, but right now I'm telling you about the *"Sand Message Miracle"!*

The **"Sand Message Miracle"**... *That's what I'm calling it.*

Two days before I left to come back home, my heart full of gratitude as I walked along the beach, I decided to write a huge message in the sand. I found the perfect "writing stick" and began to write a message I could send to all my Bregdan Chronicles readers who have made my life so amazing. I would write it, go back up on the bluff and take the picture from above.

I had no idea I was being watched...

I was almost done with my message when I heard a voice drift down from above. *"Hey, Ginny..."*

At least I thought that was what I heard, but I immediately knew I couldn't have been correct. I don't *know* anyone who lives in that area. I looked toward the sound of the voice and saw a woman standing on the deck of a nearby house, waving her arm wildly.

I smiled and waved back, wondering who in the world she was. The woman continued to wave her arms. It was difficult to hear over the sound of the waves and wind, but I was mystified by the words that floated down to me. "Picture... putting on... Facebook."

Huh?

Was this mystery woman one of my readers? Had I actually rented a house two doors down from someone who knew The Bregdan Chronicles? I was so eager to get back to my computer and unlock the mystery!

I finished my sand message, and then hurried back to my house on the bluffs. This is what I found on my Facebook page...

I laughed, and then clicked on the name of the person who had sent it to me. Gazing back at me from her Facebook page was Cindy Cunningham. I smiled back at her friendly smile, but two things continued to mystify me. The first was that this blond woman did not at all resemble the wildly-waving brunette who had hollered at me. There must be two women... The second thing that caught my attention were the children surrounding Cindy in her Facebook banner. I could have sworn they were Ugandan...

One thing most of you don't know about me is that in 2008, when I was operating one of my Internet companies, I brought over a choir of 20 Ugandan AIDS orphans. They toured the country for 6 months, and then took back a *lot* of money to build another school and more housing for orphans. Since then, I've paid for many of them to go to college and I still communicate on Facebook with many of them. That experience would be a book in itself, but there isn't sufficient room here. Remember... this is the story of the *"Sand Message Miracle"*! It is, however, a vital part of that story.

I took a shower to wash off the sand, walked up the street and knocked on the door of the mystery women. Cindy opened the door, laughed when she saw me, and welcomed me in. Then I met her best friend, Janet Matyas (the waving brunette). In moments, I knew I had found Kindred Spirits!

Both Cindy and I were blown-away when we learned of our Ugandan connection. Cindy Cunningham is the founder of The Village of Hope in Uganda, Africa. (www.VillageofHopeUganda.com) You should definitely check it out! The work she does there is spectacular. As she told me her story, my mouth hung open and my heart expanded. I also knew instantly why I was there...

"You have to write your story, Cindy!"

I saw the hesitation spring to her eyes. I also saw Janet begin to nod vigorously as she said, "I told you so, Cindy!" We talked for a long time about writing, the power of her story, and the legacy she will leave.

Oh yeah... you don't know that Cindy has suffered two bouts of brain tumors since she began Village of Hope in 2008. This trip to the Oregon Coast was her first trip in 18 months because of the seizures which occurred after her treatments. It was hard for me to wrap my brain around that information as I stared into her laughing face and vibrant eyes... Janet travels with her because it's not safe for her to travel alone, and because they have such a grand time together.

I was so thrilled when Cindy woke early the next morning and began to WRITE! As far as I know, she isn't done with it yet but you can be sure I'll share it when she is.

Then she went down on the beach. Later that next morning when I looked over the edge of the bluff, I began to laugh...

Cindy was hard at work with her own writing stick – creating her own message...

Village of Hope Uganda!

I ran down to the beach, and we spent more time talking about our passions and visions - forging a stronger bond of Kindred Spirits. My heart swelled with wonder and gratitude as we talked. Who would have thought that writing a message in the sand on a mostly deserted Oregon beach would create a new friendship?

That afternoon, knowing I was leaving the next day, I returned to the beach to write one final message - one Cindy could print and put above her computer...

I made sure this one was pointed right at her and Janet's house!

*****

While I was at the Oregon beach, I read a review:

The author has a very strong political agenda and it shows more and more with each book.

This one had me really scratching my head. Strong political agenda? In The Bregdan Chronicles? I pondered this review for a long time.

Do I have a political agenda? No.

Do I have an agenda? You bet I do!

I think my "agenda" was best communicated by another review I received:

Ginny Dye has used historical fiction set in well-known historical facts to ask her readers to examine their beliefs and look for the truth in formulating those beliefs. She used slavery as her heroine's challenge, but I believe Dye meant to challenge us to soul search all our beliefs.

YES! This, more than anything else, is the reason I write. I believe so many people formulate their opinions and beliefs based on what they're told by people they perceive to be authority figures, without carefully deciding for *themselves* what they really believe. I yearn to challenge people to think deeply... to explore the facts... to let history reveal the truth about today...

It's disturbingly easy for people to adopt the beliefs of other people, even when there is no true basis for it. I believe many of the things wrong in today's world would be resolved if people would step back and ask, *Why?*

Why do I believe that?

Why should I believe what that person or institution is saying?

Why should my actions be determined by what other people communicate?

Why should I believe something just because it's always been done that way, or because it's always been taught that way?

WHY?

WHY?

I've had people tell me that it's a lot of work. You bet it is! But I know that personally, I would rather be a leader, not a sheep who falls in with the herd, only following the sheep ahead with no thought as to where that sheep is headed.

What about you?

Do I have more of an agenda? You bet! I want people to learn to love history.

I want people to understand how the life we live today is determined by what has gone before.

I want people to realize that by knowing history they can have an amazing and powerful understanding of human nature.

I want everyone (especially women) to understand how strong they are, and how powerful and impactful they can be - regardless of what society tells them.

But a political agenda? No. I vote because so many women fought so hard for my right to do that, and I refuse to not have a voice in this country I love so much. Do I believe politics alone hold the answers to our problems? NO. NO. NO!!! I hope that was emphatic enough.

People hold the answers to our problems. *People* who demand truth and knowledge. *People* who learn from the past so that we don't continue to make the same mistakes. *People* who know that faith can truly change things. *People* who know that love can conquer all. *People* who are willing to stand up and take action for what they believe in.

My hope and prayer is that as hundreds of thousands, and then millions, of people read The Bregdan Chronicles and are challenged to soul search their beliefs - and then choose to live their lives with courage, compassion and love - that the world will become a better place.

Nothing will make this author happier!

*****

On the flip side of that, I've gotten a few posts and emails from people who are upset about the "liberal leanings" of the last few books, and have been told more than a few times that *I should just focus on history, and leave the politics out of it.*

Hmmm...

I've pondered how to respond to this. As always, I'm just going to dive in headlong!

First, it is impossible to write an accurate historical novel and not bring politics into it – at least not if you're trying to truly reveal what created the reality of the time you're writing about.

So much of history is created by politics.

Think about it... what are politics? In its most basic form, politics are nothing more than the decisions made by the people who are in charge of a country (city or region) at the time.

The formation of our country happened because of political decisions.

The Civil War happened because of political decisions.

Reconstruction happened because of political decisions.

Racism happened because of political decisions.

Poverty happened because of political decisions.

And on into the current times...

What is going on right now is mostly due to decisions made by politicians.

It is simply not possible to reveal what happened back in the 1800's without talking about politics.

I do realize the people writing these comments are upset by what they perceive as liberal leanings.

Do I have my own political beliefs? Absolutely.

Do I bring them into The Bregdan Chronicles as a personal agenda?

Absolutely NOT.

I will admit it's tempting at times, but I am an historical novelist – not a politician.

I will not, however, shy away from the reality of the times that created the America of the 1800's. This particular part of history (especially Reconstruction) was mandated by the Republican Party (which in the 1860's was the LIBERAL party of America).

The birth and growth of the KKK (and all the other White Supremacist groups of the time) was all spawned and encouraged by the Democratic Party (the CONSERVATIVE party of America at that time).

If someone has a hard time with that – and with my commitment to communicating the truth of the times in my books – I would suggest the problem lies not with me, but with the discomfort of the reader being presented with truth they would rather not accept.

You know, it amazes even me that I know so much about politics now. I truly hated anything to do with politics for decades - far longer than I'm comfortable admitting. I voted in presidential elections, but it's appalling how little I knew about the issues, nor the person I was voting for. I voted along party lines and thought I'd done my duty. I apologize to all the women who made it possible for me to vote!

Then I started writing The Bregdan Chronicles. I quickly learned that every political decision has ramifications throughout all of history. I realized I didn't have the luxury of ignorance, and I certainly didn't have the luxury of not using my knowledge and voice.

I committed myself to learning the truth...

If someone wants to challenge me on the historical accuracy of something, have at it. I do intense research, but I don't consider myself infallible.

Just don't write me and say I'm wrong simply because you disagree with me. Give me facts. Give me historical proof. Give me reasons for your position. Then we can have a conversation.

If you're uncomfortable simply because you don't like what you're learning, do your own research. I encourage everyone to do that. If you find out what I am writing is true, then I suggest it's time to examine your own belief systems.

So many people believe things because they saw something on Social Media, or heard it on the news, or heard it from their pulpit.

It takes effort and hard work to search for the truth. I've decided the effort is worth it. I want to do what it takes to know the truth – and then to live my life based on that truth. It's not easy, but our world would be such a different place if everyone chose to live that way!

*****

Sometimes my research makes me throw out everything I've done and start from scratch. Thankfully that has only happened with one book, but it happened twice!

Once *Glimmers of Change* had been released to such great acclaim, I turned my attention to Book #8, *Shifted By The Winds*. It sent me in so many fascinating directions, but it also forced me to start the book three different times.

Just like with all my books, I did hundreds of hours of research before I created my "pseudo-outline" and started writing. I was fifty pages into the book when a piece of history caused me to bring everything to a screeching halt.

I remember the moment. I was doing Facebook marketing, popped over to look at my personal profile, and just stared at the post that met my eyes. It revealed a part of American history I knew nothing about. Quite frankly, I didn't believe it, but I couldn't ignore it without doing some research.

I stopped writing and started digging. I was amazed and flabbergasted by what I discovered. I also immediately knew it was a story that had to be told. I deleted the fifty pages I had written, did two more weeks of intensive research, rewrote the outline, and started fresh.

This time I got one hundred pages into the book before I came to another screeching halt. I was doing some other in-depth research into an aspect of what had made me rewrite everything in the beginning. I turned a page, stopped, took a deep breath, shook my head, and then spent two more weeks doing extensive research.

I was more surprised than anyone when Carrie ended up being a descendent of Lord Cromwell of England. Not an actual blood relative (she is fictitious, you know!), but I had no idea when I named her Carrie Cromwell in the first book more than twenty years ago that her name would introduce an entirely new story line into the series – at the exact same moment I was covering the issue that made Lord Cromwell so infamous.

All I could do was roll with what I was learning...

I deleted the hundred pages I had written, did more research, rewrote the outline, and started fresh. *Again.*

It was all worth it, but I'll admit I'm glad that it's the only book (so far) that I've had to do that with. Somehow, I managed to meet the deadline I had set for *Shifted By The Winds*.

Amazing!

*****

Historical fiction can be challenging – not so much for me, but for the reader. There are times when a reader, discomfited by what they're reading, will decide it simply can't be true.

Shortly after releasing *Shifted By The Winds*, I received a review that said too much of the book was unbelievable. They decried my lack of research in several areas.

The reality is, while I found much of what I learned very difficult to believe too, every major event was true. Without ruining future reading for anyone:

- Moyamensing   Real & true

- Lord Oliver Cromwell   Real & true

- Events in Ireland   Real & true

- Irish Slavery   Real & true

- Intro of Black Slavery   Real & true

- Scottish vessel   Real & true

- Cholera remedy   Real & true

- American Medical Association   Real & true

- Irrepressibles   Real & true

- KKK   Real & true

- Homeopathy   Real & true

- Barber Surgeons   Real & true

Do you get the idea? Anything I write that is historical will always be true - backed my hundreds of hours of endless research. You can count on that!

*****

Deadlines. People ask me how I set them, since I'm also my publisher. Easy. I figure out a date I know I can make it happen by, and then I tell you when it's going to be.

Before I tell you how I set them now, I have to share some humorous history with you. I also had deadlines when I worked with a publishing company. The whole issue became somewhat of a joke – with the editorial staff waiting to see what would happen to me with each book.

I never missed a deadline, but it was certainly challenging at times.

During one book, I was attacked by a swarm of yellow jackets that had landed on my dog. My attempts to help him ended up with both hands so terribly swollen from bee stings that I couldn't write for more than a week.

Another time, I was helping a friend bring his herd of cows in from the pasture. It took me a while to recover from being body slammed against the fence by a two thousand pound bull!

Another time I was racing a horse down an Oregon beach for the owner who was filming it. I was having a fabulous time until something (that I never saw) scared the horse. The end result was him body slamming a tall sandbank. He crashed sideways, trapping me beneath him before he rolled and stood back up. The saddle barely missed my throat, but I was still a mess when I showed up at my publishing house the next day. I could barely walk, and it took weeks for the bruises to fade.

But... I met my deadline.

It is crucially important for me to set release dates. If I didn't, I might never get a book finished.

I always take at least a month off between books in order to allow my thoughts to clear, and also to recuperate from the push of a final manuscript. I pour all of myself into whatever I'm writing. My mind. My heart. My soul. My emotions. When I'm finished, I'm usually exhausted.

Add in the publishing, marketing, and then signing and mailing the 100 copies of books I give away with each book release... I'm pretty much toast when I'm done.

I relax. I spend time with the people I had to push aside when I was in "book mode". And I play. A lot. I love to hike. And bike. And swim. And paddle board. And kayak. Basically, anything that is outdoors.

The problem is that when I'm in play mode, it's hard to settle back into *book* mode. As much as I love research and writing, it definitely cuts down on my play time.

So, I set deadlines because I would never disappoint my readers.

Now, there have been times I thought I would have a book finished sooner than it actually happened. The book following this one is an example. I thought I would have *Misty Shadows of Hope* to you this summer (Summer 2018). That was before I got sick again. I wrote all of you, letting you know what was going on, and you encouraged me to take care of myself.

That's exactly what I've done – with a heart full of gratitude. I was determined to take the summer off from research and intense writing, but I also can't live without creating *something*, so I wrote this book.

Amazon has created a program that helps me meet my commitments. They call it their Pre-Release Order program. The way it works is that I determine a date for a release, let you know about it, and allow you to pre-order the book. It's delivered to you via Kindle on the day I release it. Print readers have to wait until the release date to order, but there is nothing I can do to control that – at least at this point in time. I'm hoping the future will change that.

The kicker is that if I don't have the book ready on the Pre-Order Release Date, Amazon becomes very unhappy. My penalty is not being able to do a Pre-Release for my next book. Besides the fact that I would never want to disappoint my readers, Amazon has created a consequence I'm not willing to live with.

Hence, deadlines work for me.

Once I have one, I'll move heaven and earth to make it happen.

And then I'll play for a month!

*****

I received another Amazon review while I was writing *Glimmers of Change* that I'm going to share with you now. Part of it said...

Also, they're constantly crying – tears brimming, swelling up and trickling down the cheek - just about every second page they seem to cry. After 5 books, I have the distinct impression that Carrie, Rose, and Aunt Abby went through extremely difficult times which would have made them very resilient and tough indeed. I cannot imagine that they have such loose waterworks. I found this quite irritating.

I thought about this review for a long time - not because I was offended or hurt - but because it goes so deeply to the core of people's perceptions.

Let me start by telling you a story. You already know my childhood was very difficult. I was five when my father left. Though I don't remember most of my childhood, I do remember that day clearly. I walked around our front yard crying. I believed that if I cried, my father would know how much I was hurting, and he wouldn't leave. He left anyway. I made a few decisions that day.

- Don't ever show your feelings because they don't matter.

- Don't ever cry because no one cares.

Those decisions carried me through for quite a while. It was eight years before I shed another tear. Everyone simply saw me as the class clown - cheerful and happy-go-lucky. No one knew I was dying inside.

The day I understood the power of God (at age 14) is the day I cried again. I decided God must be pretty powerful if I cried about it!

However, another seven years would pass before I cried again.

I was convinced tears were a sign of weakness. I thought they did nothing but make you vulnerable. I thought they were simply not a part of my being a strong and powerful girl or woman. I felt sorry for those women who cried so easily and showed their emotions. Surely, there had to be something wrong with them!

To say I've changed and grown would be putting it mildly. I'm not afraid to cry now, and I don't see it as a sign of weakness. When I had an opportunity to put these thoughts into *Glimmers of Change*, I took it. Here is the passage...

*****

Carrie frowned when tears filled her eyes. "Don't you get tired of me crying?"

"Why would I get tired of you crying?" Abby asked in astonishment.

"I'm supposed to be a strong, independent woman," Carrie responded. "Shouldn't that bring with it a certain toughness that would preclude crying so much?"

"Do you think it should?" Abby asked carefully.

Carrie laughed suddenly. "I feel like it's five years ago, and I'm eighteen again. You always just asked me questions back then, too."

Abby smiled, but her gaze was steady. "I really want to know. Do you think being strong and independent means you shouldn't cry? Do you want to be tough?"

Carrie considered the question. Finally, she shook her head. "I know tough women," she said. "I don't really want to be like them."

"Do you think the tough women you know don't have feelings?"

Carrie thought carefully, sensing this was an important discussion. "I think everyone has feelings," she finally said. "I think they've just learned how to not show them."

"Why do you suppose that is?"

Carrie shook her head, suddenly impatient with the questions. "Does it matter?"

Abby narrowed her eyes. "I think it does."

Now it was Carrie's turn to ask the questions. "Why?"

Abby chuckled. "Turning the tables on me, are you?" Her expression turned serious. "I *do* think it matters. I've watched so many women become tough and hard. At first, I thought it was a necessary part of being strong and independent, or just an expected result of going through horrible times, but the more time I spent with those women, the more I realized I didn't want to live that way. I didn't want to shut down my emotions, and I didn't want to carry the guilt that tears are a sign of weakness."

"So, you don't think they are?" Carrie was suddenly relieved.

"I think they're a sign of strength," Abby declared, laughing at Carrie's astonished expression. "Women have always cried more easily than men. I prefer to think it's because we are more tender. Being strong and independent doesn't change that tenderness, unless we let it. I want to live my life freely as a *woman* – not try to become a man in order to make my life easier. I believe that is the whole point of fighting for women's rights. It's not just about getting the vote," she said, and then paused, staring out over the countryside. "It's about the right to live as a woman the way I want to live."

Carrie stared at her. "You've thought about this a great deal," she realized.

"I have," Abby agreed. "I love the fact that your heart feels deeply enough to shed tears. You and Rose have both kept that ability, even after all the horror you went through in the war. So many others have shut down their emotions because they believe it will protect them from pain."

"But it doesn't," Carrie murmured.

"No, it doesn't," Abby said softly. "You are getting ready to live your dream, but it is also going to carry pain. You're going to miss Robert every day. You're going to miss Rose and Moses. You're going to miss the plantation. You're going to miss the freedom to run Granite down the roads. You're going to miss riding into Richmond to visit your father and me."

Carrie blinked tears again, but this time she didn't brush them away. "I will miss it all," she said softly.

"It's okay to feel it," Abby said. "I already know you'll push through the pain to make the most of this new time in your life. There is no need to harden yourself. You may cry yourself to sleep a lot, but that's okay – even for a woman *doctor*."

*****

My hope as you read The Bregdan Chronicles is that you will choose to live your life authentically. Too much of society tries to make people conform; to be a certain way so they can fit in and be considered normal.

Normal?

Yuck!

I long to be authentic and real. If I feel like crying, I'm going to cry. If I feel like laughing, I'm going to laugh. Loudly. If I want to dance, I'm going to dance – no matter where I am. If I'm feeling deeply philosophical, I'm going to share that part of myself and challenge people to think.

I invite you to join me in living your authentic self – on your own authentic journey.

*****

Part of my authentic journey involved selling my home at the end of *Shifted By The Winds*. It was time for another change. Since I wasn't sure where I wanted to be I decided to roam the country for a while...

Black Eyed Peas

Put black eyed peas in a large pot and cover with about 4 inches of water. Soak the peas overnight, then drain.

Put the black eyed peas in large pot, cover with 4 inches of water. Soak overnight and drain. Rinse the peas. Heat the oil in a large pot over medium-high heat. Sear pork shoulder meat that has been cubed until the pork is browned on all sides.

Add a little chopped onion (garlic too if you have it) and cook, stirring, until the onion and garlic are lightly browned.

Add some salt, black pepper. Cook until the entire mixture is coated. Pour in water bring the mixture to a boil, reduce the heat, simmer covered, for about 30 minutes. When the pork begins to fall apart, add the soaked peas to the pot and simmer until the peas are very soft, about 1 to 1 1/2 hours. Taste. Add hot-pepper vinegar, if desired.

Chapter Sixteen

I was living on the Florida coast when I wrote Book #9, *Always Forward*.

After years of living in Bellingham, WA, I sold my house and decided to set out on a new adventure. Part of it led me to a wonderful home perched on the dunes above the beach in St. Augustine. The house I leased for eight months was perfect. My office was located in what I called the "Crow's Nest". You had to walk outside, and then take a set of stairs up to another part of the house that was three stories up. From there, I could see far out to sea, and miles up and down the beach. I loved it!

I will admit it was difficult to write at times, though. The glistening water beckoned me to come play. I would always run outside and watch as the kite surfers ripped past my house – soaring above the waves and doing flips before they landed. One day I will join them. Perhaps not the flipping, but certainly the soaring!

I also ran outside when a motorized paraglider sailed past my house. Jealous? With every particle of my being! That's on my list, too. Within the next few years I will disappear to the mountains above Salt Lake City, Utah so I can become certified in paragliding, and then I will strap a motor on my back and take off across parts of the country. The underside of my paraglider will read, *DiscoverTheBregdanChronicles.com*. How's that for creating the perfect business write-off? Advertising while you have fun!

People will at least know the writer is cool!

*****

St. Augustine also presented me with a challenge I'd never considered. I wrote this short piece about it.

Is it possible for me to make friends with the wind? I didn't really know, but I was hoping the answer was YES. Only time would l tell...

There are many things I love about living on the beach in St. Augustine. The wind is not one of them. I was grateful when the cloying heat retreated before the winter months, but was a little alarmed about how much the wind started blowing. 15 mph... 20 mph... 30 mph... as the days of high winds rolled on, I kept checking the weather to find out when this was going to pass. Surely there was just some kind of disturbance out to sea that was causing it. My heart sank as I saw high winds forecast for the 10-day forecast – *every* day that I checked it.

Surely, it isn't going to be like that all winter!

During a fabulous Thanksgiving celebration with friends, I asked my hostess (who has lived here for 20+ years) if the wind always blows in St. Augustine. Her reply? "Well, it doesn't blow hard here in town, but there is always a stiff wind on the beach."

I stared at her in dismay. "Always?" I echoed in disbelief.

"Does it bother you?" she asked with a smile.

"Yes!"

So why does it bother me so much? I'm trying to figure that out. When I'm sitting here in my 3rd floor office overlooking the beach, it is completely disquieting to have the wind howling, and the windows quivering in their frames. There seems to never be a moment of peace and quiet – something I crave.

Another thing is that I love biking on the beach. Having a 30 mph wind at your back is exhilarating as you fly down the hard-packed sand, but at some point you have to turn around to come home. Riding *into* a 30 mph wind is not quite so much fun!

Ditto with a paddle board out in the waves... I haven't been biking or paddle boarding since the wind started blowing so hard.

Walking is not quite so daunting, though walking into a 30 mph wind isn't really all that much fun either. I still do my 6 miles a day, but I can't even take my dog. I put on sunglasses and a scarf to protect my nose and eyes from the biting sand, but I can't offer him the same protection.

Yesterday a short squall came through. I watched in disbelief as 40 pound chairs were picked up and thrown around. Seriously?

But the biggest issue is never having a moment of quiet and calm.

So what do I do? As I sat outside this morning, watching the beautiful moon glisten on the water, being buffeted by winds... Sigh... I realized I have to make friends with the wind. I can grumble... I can moan and complain... I can sigh... or I can simply accept the wind is going to BLOW. Since I'm not really into being a victim and martyr, the only other choice is to make friends with the wind.

I've started by trying to focus on all the good things about the wind. I had to stretch to identify them....

The wind keeps any mosquitoes away (that's actually a BIG one here in Florida).

The wind makes the sea oats dance and sway – creating beautiful patterns on the dunes.

The wind makes a cool rustling sound through the palm trees.

The wind keeps it from feeling as hot as it really is, and it dries my sweat as I'm power-walking on the beach.

I'm not the only one who doesn't like the wind, so the beaches here aren't as crowded as other places (that's a BIG one, too!).

I was entering into the spirit of finding good things about the wind, but the next one was a little more difficult to embrace…

The wind forces me into a place of conscious gratitude as I try to come up with the good things about the wind. (Okay, I suppose this is another BIG one!)

The wind is great for kite flying (It's time to haul out my stunt kite)!

The wind brings out the kite surfers. That's a BIG one, too, because I love watching them soar through the air over the water – the brilliantly colored kites pulling them along. I so want to do it!

So see… there are good things about the wind. Since it is evidently not going to quit blowing for a very long time, I have the opportunity to practice conscious gratitude *a lot*! I'm going to choose to be grateful for that.

After writing all the good things about the wind; somewhere along the way, I have truly made friends with the wind. I feel cozy in my office as the wind buffets the windows, and blows the sand so hard I can't see down the beach. I know I'm safe. I sip my hot chocolate or tea, and I smile because I have the privilege of enjoying the wind.

So here comes the question…

Come on – you knew it was coming!

What do you need to *make friends with*? What do you need to choose *Conscious Gratitude* about? We all have things in our life that we simply have no control over. You and I both know the wind is not really a big deal in the scope of life. There are things in life we can't control that are much bigger... The loss of a loved one. A painful divorce. A major natural catastrophe that rips our world away. I'm sure you can add to my list.

Lack of control is lack of control. It's easy to allow it to consume us, to swallow us, and to steal our joy and peace. But... that is something you *can* control.

We can control how we respond to it... how it impacts our life... how we choose to deal with it.

I'll keep on making friends with the wind – and whatever else comes my way! I encourage you to look at the things in your life that you need to make friends with – and begin to do it today!

*****

Somewhere in the midst of writing *Always Forward* I made a trip to the North Carolina mountains but was forced to leave early by the threat of heavy snow. On the drive back to Florida, I listened to NPR. I'm usually more of a "drive in silence" kind of person because it gives me time to think, but once I turned on the radio I couldn't bring myself to turn it off.

I was both sickened and fascinated by what was being played out in American politics in the months before the 2016 elections. I was also mesmerized by the reality of how many similarities there were with what I was writing about in 1867. I am well aware that history repeats itself, but this was more than a little surreal.

Driving home, I knew *Always Forward* would be one of the most important books I would ever write. It also was one of the most emotional.

I can't talk about what happened without revealing a plot line, but I can tell you that what happened was *not* in the outline. You might think I'm crazy if I tell you that I watched with horror and sadness as my fingers created a scenario I had not envisioned when I started *Always Forward*.

I've had countless readers write me to say how hard they cried when they read it.

I get it. I cried the same buckets of tears along with you.

I also got so angry at the state of our country that made what happened necessary. While I would love for every single character to have a happy ending in The Bregdan Chronicles, that's not real life. It also doesn't reflect what was going on in America in the Reconstruction years.

Writing *Always Forward* made me more determined than ever to continue on with the series; to write about the circumstances and situations that have brought us 150 years into the future – only to acknowledge we haven't learned what we should have learned.

It drove home to me; at an even deeper level than I had experienced before, just how important The Bregdan Chronicles are. It enhanced my commitment to write the *whole* story, no matter what.

*****

I loved my time in Florida, but it was also lonely. I had left behind a lot of close friends in Washington, and I was feeling the loss. Writing a book doesn't leave you much time for meeting new friends in a place where you don't know a soul. I have no problem talking to people, but to do that, I had to find time to do more than sit in my office and write.

An idea one afternoon had me writing a new Blog. I offered to meet some of my readers for dinner in St. Augustine. I knew I had readers in Florida. I hoped a few of them would want to have dinner with me. For at least one night, I wouldn't be lonely.

Wow!

Fifteen amazing people showed up for the first dinner in St. Augustine.

We laughed. We talked. I made them tell me about themselves and discovered that each person was fascinating and delightful. They asked me questions, and we talked about how the first eight books of The Bregdan Chronicles had impacted them. Tears filled my eyes so many times as they shared how the books had changed them, helped them, and given them hope. Hours passed quickly as the sun set in a blaze over the glistening intracoastal waterway.

It was so much fun to meet my readers face-to-face. In just one evening they went from being my readers, to being my *friends*. I knew I wanted more of that.

I love connecting with people via Facebook and email but sharing a meal with them was so special.

That was the beginning of what I now call The Bregdan Gatherings. When I finished *Always Forward*, I had three more. I met readers one more time in St. Augustine, but I also drove south to Vero Beach, and then across the state to Anna Maria Island (where I also had the best shrimp and grits I've ever eaten!).

Each experience was memorable and so very precious to me.

I have done quite a bit of speaking, and I enjoy it, but Bregdan Gatherings are not about me orating to a large crowd. It's about meeting the people who make my life possible. I can only do that with small groups, so I limit the number of readers who can come to twenty. I also promise to stay until everyone is ready to leave. Most of the Bregdan Gatherings last four to five hours. I love every minute of them!

When I was involved in the traditional publishing world I did several book promo and signing tours. I didn't hate them, but I can't say I enjoyed them. I didn't have a chance to truly meet anyone – people just passed in front of me long enough for me to sign books. I know it was unfulfilling to me; certainly, it was unfulfilling to them.

I tried to meet the expectations of my publisher, but there were times I revolted. One such time was at a major bookseller's convention where I was signing my teen novels. No way was I going to just smile at the hordes of teenagers standing in line. Despite directions to the contrary, I took time to speak to each reader for at least a minute or two. I'm sure it was still disappointing to the kids, but at least they knew I cared enough to look them in the eye and connect with them.

I don't do book signing tours now because I don't see the point. I don't know why anyone would be excited just to see me and have me scribble my name in front of a book. The Bregdan Gatherings are different.

I love it that everyone is excited for all of us to get together for a long afternoon or evening.

I've done a Bregdan Gathering in Chattanooga, TN, when I was visiting my sister, one in Vancouver, WA (on the Oregon border with Portland), and also two in Bellingham. I intend to do more.

I've learned things along the way:

- Only do them on Saturdays because I don't want work to interfere with anyone's ability to attend.
- Only do them in restaurants that offer a private dining room because that gives everyone the best experience.

The second one is usually the kicker. It can be extremely difficult to find a restaurant with a private dining room for 21 people that doesn't have crazy stipulations on it. I can't tell you the number of hours that have been spent in the attempt to find the perfect venue in the cities I have had Bregdan Gatherings. I've loved meeting everyone, but making it happen was certainly not easy. There has been only one perfect venue.

Bellingham, Washington.

I have much more to tell you in this book, but for now just know that I returned to Bellingham after roaming the country for a few years. It's where my heart is, and where it will always be. I'm jumping ahead a little, but this is the time to tell you I've decided to hold at least two Bregdan Gatherings a year in Bellingham.

My first one was Spring 2017. There is a fabulous restaurant on the waterfront that has the perfect private room. I was astonished when people flew in from different parts of the country to join me and the people who drove in from cities in Washington and Oregon. They came from Louisiana, Missouri, and Kansas.

They came to meet me, but they also enjoyed being in an absolutely beautiful city on the Puget Sound waterfront. They extended their stays a couple days and made the most of it.

I repeated it in November 2017 and once again had people come in from all over. I had an equally wonderful time.

After thinking about this a lot, I've decided to not attempt to come to all the readers who beg me to visit their city or area. I love to travel, but if I did Bregdan Gatherings everywhere I've been requested to, I would never have time to write another book.

I'm going to plan in advance, and invite as many of you as possible to come meet me in Bellingham twice a year – in May and November. Just so you can plan, I'm committing to the first Saturday in November and May, each year for as long as I'm able to do it. We'll all have something to look forward to!

I already know there are many of my readers who will never be able to make it to Washington to join me. I'm truly sorry for that, but I hope my choosing to keep my focus on writing will make it an easier pill to swallow.

*** If you're reading this book 15 – 20 years after I published it, just go to my Blog to see if I'm still doing Bregdan Gatherings. While you're there, make sure to sign up for my newsletter so you won't miss one! Go to www.AVoiceInTheWorldBlog.com.

I'll do the Bregdan Gatherings for as long as I'm able, and for as long as people want to come!

*****

On another note, during the writing of *Always Forward* I got a letter from a reader saying she enjoyed the storyline in *Storm Clouds Rolling In*, but that when she realized there was no vivid sex, she didn't want to keep reading. She asked me, *Where is the Sex*?

I laughed so hard I thought I would fall off my office chair. I'm not even close to being a prude, but I also believe most books written today don't portray life as it's truly lived. Okay, be honest, how many of you have wild, raucous sex several times a day? Once a day? Once a week? Once a month? Hmmm... If at least 90% of you couldn't say yes to that question - which I already know you didn't - then why write historical fiction that doesn't portray real life?

It irritates me that so many writers say they are writing "Historical Romance", when all they are really doing is throwing a little history into the middle of a lot of hot sex. I totally get that there are people who love those books, and I respect their preferences, but it's not the kind of writing I do.

Romance is entwined in The Bregdan Chronicles because that's life. Most of us fall in love at some point. A majority of us marry, have babies, and deal with grief when we lose someone. My passion is to communicate life the way it's lived.

Other writers can focus on wild, raucous sex!

*****

I received another interesting question from a reader while I was writing *Always Forward*.

Ginny, I want to thank you so much for the Bregdan Chronicles. They are eye opening, so well researched, thought provoking, your characters are strong, interesting and intriguing and I cannot wait for the upcoming books. The series has been very thought provoking for me. I know you are busy and may not have time to respond, but would be interested in your thoughts.

Our country is made up of immigrants. Native Americans are the true natives of our country. Most people came for a better life, to escape a horrific life and/or to live in a land of potential opportunity. Your books made me realize that the slaves were brought to this country against their will to be sold like an animal and many, if not most, were treated as such. I know that this is part of their history, as is the history of other cultures where genocide or persecution occurred. Many ethnic groups left their countries and were sequestered in communities and were looked down upon by those living in the U.S. at the time. **Help me understand why some cultures cannot move beyond their history, learn from it and try to work**

for a peaceful existence. **What are your thoughts?**
Your books have opened floodgates in my head and helped me to learn and understand. Thank you again for your beautiful and thought provoking books. I look forward to many more.

*****

This was my response...
I love it when reader's questions join me during my long morning walks. I have pondered this question for many miles as I moved down the beach. Here are my thoughts...

I do not know of *any cultures* that cannot move beyond their history, learn from it, and try to work for a peaceful existence. History has taught me that over, and over, and over.

Though that was my initial response, it took many miles before I had pondered and analyzed why I feel this so strongly. I certainly know of many *people* who cannot (for whatever reason) move beyond their history, learn from it, and try to work for a peaceful existence. They choose to remain stuck in the pain of their past, and in the injustices that created challenges that no one would *want* to have to work through. They seem to thrive on not taking responsibility for their current actions by blaming it on their past.

However, in *every* culture, there are so many people who choose to be more than their past. They choose to acknowledge and learn from the injustices – and then to move forward to make their life (and the lives of everyone they touch) better than what was before. They choose to change the reality of their past. They choose to be more than what others believe they can be – opening the door of possibility for everyone who follows. I've had the joy of knowing them, of writing their stories, of sharing their purpose with the world.

I applaud those people with all my heart! These people have done so much to change the world and make it a better place. People from every nation, every race, every ethnic group, every gender, every religion, every sexual identity, every... EVERYTHING. They are simply people who look beyond what is... They look to what can be – and then they make it happen!

I also wish every culture would acknowledge the struggles of the *people* around them, and reach out a hand to make things better for every human being on this planet. It's so heartbreakingly easy to judge. It's so easy to think that for whatever reason you are *better than*. It's so heartbreakingly easy to criticize anything different than you because for some reason you think it makes you better. Heartbreaking, because I believe it makes every person who makes that choice, *less than*.

All of us have both the privilege, and the responsibility, of offering a hand up to anyone wanting to change their life. We have the privilege, and the responsibility, of working to undo the injustices that have made life so much more difficult than it should be for entire cultures. We are not cultures...

We are PEOPLE. All of us. Just *PEOPLE*.

It is really so very simple. If you looked at every human being on the earth and simply saw another human being with the same desires, wants and hopes as you – and then tried to help anyone you can create the best life possible – what an amazing world we would live in.

So, of course, my challenge to you today is to look at every person through the eyes of possibility. *What could be possible* if you reached out? *What could be possible* if you looked beyond whatever exterior package there is, and simply saw another human being who is absolutely no different than you? *What could be possible* if you gave someone an opportunity to be more than what history or circumstances has given them to overcome?

What could be possible?

*****

Something else happened while I was working on *Always Forward...* I wrote this Blog in 2016, a few months after I released it. I share it because it put my life on a completely different course.

A little magnet has been on my printer for almost 10 years... staring at me... challenging me... mostly being ignored because I got so used to seeing it.

Until a couple months ago.

Suddenly, the ignored little magnet was shouting my name... demanding I pay attention...making me question decisions and life choices. I tried to ignore it because I had so many things on my mind, but it simply refused to be dismissed. There were times I wanted to rip it off my printer and toss it in the trash, but I couldn't. It demanded to be heard... demanded to be examined... demanded to be acted on...

What does the little magnet say?

Destined to be an Old Woman with No Regrets

If you had asked me a few months ago if that was true for my life I would have said, "Yes." I'm doing what I love more than anything in the world (writing books) successfully, I have amazing relationships, I have more adventures than just about anyone I know, and I have the freedom to make choices I want to make.

I mean, come on, wanting anything more than that seems more than a little greedy, and it also made me very uncomfortable, because suddenly I was examining some of my choices and realizing that pesky magnet was no longer completely true – I wasn't going to be an Old Woman with No Regrets.

Sigh...

I finally quit ignoring it, and I spent many long hours examining what things in my life would cause me to grow old with regrets. I had to face them with unflinching honesty because, *more than anything else*, I truly want to live with NO REGRETS.

Once I had identified them, I realized I was faced with choices and actions I didn't necessarily want to make because I knew they would not be well received.

I continued to struggle.

No Regrets... No Regrets...

The day finally came when I knew that no matter what the cost, I was ready to make the choices and take the actions that would free my mind and soul to truly live with no regrets. I never want to look back on my life and wish I had done something different... wish I had done the thing I feared... wish I had done the thing people thought I shouldn't (or couldn't) do...

I have made those choices, and am in the midst of taking the actions. I can truly say I feel free to live the life I am meant to live, and that I am looking solidly into a future with *no regrets*. It hasn't been easy, and there have been pain and tears along the way, but my heart is at peace.

While my choices and actions are important to me, I wonder how *you* would answer that question?

Are YOU Destined to Grow Old with No Regrets?

I challenge you to take a good, long look at your life. Will you wish you had done something differently? Will you wish you had done the thing you feared? Will you wish you had done the thing people thought you shouldn't, or couldn't do?

I invite you to join me on the Path to *no regrets*.

The path isn'tt easy. There will probably be some pain, tears, and fears. There will be people who completely believe you are making wrong decisions because they will probably be so different from the choices you've made before. Here's the thing, though...

It is YOUR life.

YOU are the only one who will look back on your life and wonder if you lived it with NO REGRETS.

Join me... I can promise you it's worth it!

******

Two and a half years later, I can tell you I am SO glad I chose to live as a woman with no regrets! I strive to be that person every single day - making choices that will ensure every day is a celebration of life!

You know, I love writing The Bregdan Chronicles, but I equally love writing my newsletters because it means I can show up in my reader's lives on a regular basis, and I can say anything I want to. The Bregdan Chronicles are historical fiction. While I can share many things through my books, when I write a newsletter I have no limits. I can share my journey through life. I can share stories to motivate and inspire you. I can answer your questions.

I have the joy of hearing from thousands of you – developing friendships along the way. It's remarkable.

Twenty years ago, when I started my career, that was not an option. The internet has opened up so many opportunities to communicate. I love it!

If you haven't already, you can sign up for my newsletter by going to www.BregdanChronicles.net. I'll look forward to having you there!

*****

When I released *Always Forward*, I started wondering what the next book would be about. It was another Facebook post that grabbed my attention...

Greens

About a peck of greens are enough for a mess for a family of six, such as dandelions, cowslips, burdock, chicory, and other greens. All greens should be carefully examined, then be washed through several waters until they are free from sand. The addition of a handful of salt to each pan of washing water will free them of insects and worms. Let the greens stand in the last salted washing water for 30 minutes. To boil the greens, put them into a large pot half full of boiling water, with a handful of salt and boil steadily until stalks are tender. This could be be 5 minutes or 25 minutes. Remember that the long boiling wasters the tender substances of the leaves, diminishes the nourishment of the dish so it is best to cut away any tough stalks before cooking. As soon as they are tender, drain them in a colander, chop a little, return to fire with salt, pepper, butter, a little vinegar. Serve hot.

Chapter Seventeen

Book #10, Walking Into The Unknown was an adventure back into my own heritage. It all started with a random Facebook post talking about the Navajo Concentration Camp in the 1860's.

Huh?

I had absolutely no idea what they were talking about, so of course I had to dive into research to find out. Once again, what I discovered appalled me. I also immediately knew it was an important story that needed to be told, and since a vital part of it was happening during the year I was writing about, well...

All of this was important, but it wasn't the entire reason I chose to write about the internment of the Navajo. The real reason was that it was a tribute to my great-grandmother, and all the ancestors who came before her.

I told you before that my great-grandmother on my mother's side was full-blood Cherokee, and that my grandmother was shunned by the Gaffney family because she was a half-breed.

Not that you would ever get my mother to admit it. She was as unexcited about being part Cherokee as she was about admitting Captain Michael was a slave owner. She denied it till the day she died. I thought, and still thought, she was being ridiculous.

It's a heritage I'm proud of.

The only reason I know it is because of my grandmother. For whatever reason, Nina (my grandmother) decided I would be the keeper of the family history. I didn't realize until decades later that I was the only one she ever told the stories to – or ever showed the pictures to. I'm so grateful she did.

I told you in the beginning of this book how terribly the Gaffney family treated Nina. Though she chose to cover up her past, she obviously wanted to make sure the story didn't die with her. I wish I had been wise enough in my teens to ask her all the questions that clog my mind now, but that door of opportunity has closed.

I've done much to learn about my Cherokee heritage in the last several years, however. When I left the beach house in St. Augustine, Florida, I moved to the Pisgah Mountains around Asheville, North Carolina. I grew up in Charlotte, North Carolina, and have spent a lot of time in the North Carolina mountains, but I was never before on a quest for information.

While I was there, I spent time in the city of Cherokee. I explored the Cherokee museum and bought an entire library of books, but the most important thing I did was what I did repeatedly, that brought me close to my roots.

I drove to the top of Pisgah Mountain many times. I hiked the trails and found an overlook that took my breath away every time I went there. I had a favorite tree that I rested against as I gazed out over the mountains and valleys my ancestors called home. My heart felt completely at peace there.

As I listened to the wind sigh through the trees and watched the hawks soar overhead, I could easily imagine the agonizing pain my ancestors felt when they were wrenched from their homeland and forced onto the Trail of Tears. To have left such beauty for the stark flatness of the Oklahoma Territory... to have watched thousands die around them during the journey... to know they would never see their home again... to know future generations would have no memories. My heart aches just to write this.

As I sat there for hours, I could feel my ancestors around me. I felt their heartbeat... the gratitude for all life gave them in the mountains... the joy they lived their lives with... the challenges of a hard life. And I felt their grief.

I will tell their story one day.

*****

In the meantime, I had the privilege and responsibility of sharing the plight of the Navajo Indian tribe when they were ripped from their homeland. As I researched and wrote, I cried. I gritted my teeth. I was both angry and heartbroken.

It also gave me a clear picture into more of the reality of how America was formed.

I love my country with a passion, but I am ashamed of so much that has happened here. I am ashamed of the vast numbers of people who were mistreated and murdered so that the "white conquerors" could take what they believed was theirs to take.

None of us who live today can go back in time and undo the damage and harm that was done. But we *can* work to make things right now.

Whether it is African Americans... Or the Irish... Or the Native Americans... Or women... Or whites who struggle in poverty... Or people of a different sexual orientation...

So much that has been done in the past is so terribly wrong. It is all our responsibility to make things better – to make them right. We can turn our backs on the past and pretend it didn't exist – which is what too many politicians and leaders want us to do – or we can face it, embrace it, and determine to create our country in a different way moving forward.

Once you know, you can never claim ignorance.

Once you know, you can never say there is nothing you can do about it, or that it's not your problem to fix.

I believe if you're an American, it *is* your responsibility to make things better for everyone. I hope to instill that reality into every single person who reads my books.

*****

Another thing happened while I was writing Walking Into The Unknown. This was the story I wrote about it:

When I returned from wandering around the country for fourteen months I was approached by a very special young woman who asked me to be her mentor because, in her words, I am the most passionate, purposeful person she knows, and she is searching for her purpose. It was easy to say yes because Jody (not her real name) was already special to me.

I'll never forget our first conversation after becoming her mentor. We talked about a lot of things before I brought the subject of "Purpose" up to her.

Her eyes clouded as she shook her head. "There is part of me that wants to have a true purpose, and then there is another part of me that just wants to live my life for myself. In many ways, I believe that is what my life is meant to be."

"Can you elaborate on that?" I asked, truly wanting to understand her thought process.

"Well, I just have so many things to work on in myself," Jody answered. "I'm a single, disabled mom with a young son who needs me." She shook her head again, obviously struggling with her frustration. "But every book I read... every podcast I listen to... says I need a purpose much larger than myself that will change the world." Her eyes filled with tears as she took a deep breath.

I reached out and took her hand. "So let's just work on you for a while," I said gently. "Perhaps Purpose will come knocking on your door – and perhaps not – but we won't worry about that now."

Jody and I have been meeting for the last 2 months. I've thought so often about what she said during our first time together. And I've thought back over all the books I've read... all the personal development gurus I've heard speak... and all the audios I've listened to over the years. They do indeed impart the message that every single person needs to find their BIG purpose that will allow them to find their worth, and impact the world.

The more I considered it, the more I had a question exploding in my mind...

What if they're wrong?

What if they're setting people up for frustration?

What if they're fueling a feeling of failure because people have yet to find that *huge* Purpose, and so they spend their life and energy wondering what's wrong with them?

Oh, I believe each of us has a purpose, but what is the definition of HUGE and Life Changing?

What if Jody's purpose for this lifetime is to be the best mom she can be – loving and giving, and healing from the tough things life has thrown her way so her son doesn't carry on those scars and pain?

I'd say that is pretty huge purpose!

My purpose is to be an author who hopefully writes life changing books. Does that make me any more special than anyone else? I don't believe so. I'm simply using the *gift* I was given the best I can. I get more public recognition and I know lots of people think it's a big deal, but it really isn't. It's simply what I do.

Is my purpose more important than the person who picks up garbage every day, and then goes home to be with their children?

No.

If you disagree with me, wait and see how you feel after a garbage strike, when the streets are reeking with the smell of uncollected garbage. I believe you will change your mind quickly!

The truth is that EVERY single person has a purpose that is needed by the world. Garbage collector, scientist, waitress, financial planner, cashier, store manager...

We tend to attribute value based upon income or recognition, but I believe that's so wrong. We are all dependent upon each other. The financial planner can't spend any of their large salary if there is no one to take their money at the store, or serve them food at a restaurant. Unfortunately, too many times they look down on the very people who make their world go around.

Unfortunately, they erroneously think their Purpose is more important.

I've heard so many conversations that go like this:

"Why are you a waitress? Don't you know you're meant for so much more than that? You need to discover your Purpose."

"Don't you know that every person has the ability to be wealthy? Why are you selling yourself short? You need to find your Purpose. Once you've found it, you'll have all the money you dream of."

"You're satisfied with working at Walmart, and then going home to be with your family? What's wrong with you? Find your purpose, and life will hold so much more."

Are they right?

I don't believe so. I will also admit there were times when I was the one saying those things. Knowing that makes me so sad.

Here's the truth...

If the waitress is happy being a waitress, then she has found her purpose for this season of her life – perhaps her entire life. She may or may not be meant to do something differently in the future, but that's up to her to decide.

Every person is not going to be wealthy, in spite of the wonderful appeal of the promise. Think about it. If every person was wealthy, who would do the work to make the people wealthy? It's a matter of numbers and reality, but so many people wallow in discontent because they're scrambling for *their* way to the wealth they've been promised.

If the person working at Walmart and going home to their family is happy, who are we to tell her she hasn't yet discovered her purpose?

Here's what I believe now...

I believe every person has a purpose they can be proud of if they choose to live their life with passion and love.

How differently people would feel about themselves if everyone was honored and appreciated for what they do – no matter how anyone else defines it.

Here's another thought I've had since I started meeting with Jody – one that I shared with her yesterday...

Your purpose right now might not be your purpose in the future. Jody's purpose right now might be to be the best mom she can be to her son. What happens when he is twelve? Or eighteen? Or twenty-five? Her purpose could definitely change. Her desires could change as she changes as a person.

I believe all of us go through seasons of our life – with our purpose changing as the seasons of our life change.

I know that has been true for me.

As I've pondered this, I believe it boils down to something very simple: BE A BRIGHT LIGHT IN THE WORLD.

It doesn't matter what you do... It doesn't matter how much money you make... It doesn't matter how much recognition you gain...

At the end of the day, all I want to know is if I was a bright light to someone. Did I make someone else feel special? Did I do what I had to do with excellence and passion? Did I look for a way to make the world a better place?

If I can answer YES to that question, then I know I have fulfilled my PURPOSE for today.

*****

As soon as I finished *Walking Into The Unknown*, I walked into my own period of darkness.

After being healthy for ten years, having beaten back the Epstein-Barr Virus in my body, I was eager to tackle the exciting season of my life that had opened up when I determined to Be An Old Woman With No Regrets.

I was on the verge of turning 60 in a few months. I was so excited to share that milestone with special friends that would come in from all over the country.

On March 22, 2017, I hiked ten miles on my mountain with my dog. Okay, it's not really "my" mountain, but it is as far as I'm concerned. I've hiked my mountain thousands of times. I've discovered all the trails... all the outlooks... all the hidden places.

Back to March 22. I was in great physical shape and brimming with energy.

There was nothing about that amazing day to prepare me for the next day.

I woke feeling lethargic. I attributed it to hiking too far, or perhaps eating something that had created a problem. I decided to relax that morning and then get moving in the afternoon. I didn't get moving in the afternoon.

Or the next day... or the following day.

I spent most of the next two months in bed. Fever. Fatigue. Aches. Useless brain cells. The inability to form words. I knew the symptoms all too well. For absolutely no reason that I could determine, the Epstein-Barr Virus had once again taken hold of my life.

Thus began a pattern... After two months, I was finally able to get out of bed for more than a few minutes at a time, but I didn't regain my energy. Every day I felt like I was moving through sluggish molasses. I did things, but I also slept ten to fourteen hours a day.

This was not how I had envisioned turning 60.

I was discouraged and totally burnt out. When it came time to finalize plans for my "60th Bash", I knew I didn't want it. I wanted to spend the day just with my family. That was all I had energy for. I didn't have enough energy to even care that something I had looked forward to for so long wasn't going to happen. It was a relief.

I also had another book to write.

I had promised *Looking To The Future* by September 2017. I wasn't going to disappoint my readers. My days became a litany of writing and sleeping. It was all I could do.

In spite of everything, I loved writing *Looking To The Future*. Part of the description of the book says: *When everyone really just wants a simple, clear future, each person finds they have to make the choice every single day to Look To The Future.*

I was having to make that very same choice, every day, while I was writing that book. I felt like I was walking into the unknown, but I was also determined to look to the future – a different one where I was healthy and vibrant again.

It was also such a joy to write, even with all I discovered about what was going on with far too many women in America. When I first read a tidbit of research about the main topic of *Looking to the Future,* I was sure it couldn't be correct.

Of course, my research proved I was wrong. It was all too achingly correct, and it sent me into a world I knew absolutely nothing about. I devoured all the materials I could find, wanting to make sure I portrayed it accurately.

*****

Book #11, *Looking To The Future* also took me deeper into the world of medicine. I've been asked by many readers to write a book on herbal medicine. While I'm honored to be asked, I'm not even close to qualified enough to do that. Yes, I've done a tremendous amount of research, but the books I use as resources prove another one is not needed – at least not one written by me.

I am, however, passionate about taking the mystery out of herbal medicine and homeopathy. There are certainly times when traditional Western medicine is the right solution, but there are far too many times when traditional medicine does a tremendous disservice to the patients that so desperately need their help.

I choose to live my life holistically, researching and discovering every natural supplement and remedy I can. I was flabbergasted when the Epstein-Barr Virus took control of me again because I thought I was doing everything I could to live in maximum health. Obviously, I had more to learn.

The last sixteen months have been a journey of fatigue, frustration, learning and finally... victory!

Without going into a long, boring story, I struggled with my health from March 2017 through June 2018. I turned the corner when I discovered an amazing Homeopathic Remedy for Epstein-Barr Virus, and also discovered the need for NAD. NAD (or nicotinamide adenine dinucleotide) is a vital resource found in all living cells that diminishes greatly in our body between ages forty to sixty. I learned about it during a conversation with a doctor in Mexico.

I had already started feeling better from the homeopathic remedy, but when I added NAD into the mix, everything turned around. I'm back to walking 3-5 miles a day, swimming, deep-water running, and working. I love to exercise and workout (though I prefer to call it "playout"), so I am beyond happy!

One of the things I hate the most when the Epstein-Barr Virus strikes me is that I quit caring about anything. I don't have enough energy to care, but I have enough energy to know I don't care. Since I'm basically passionate about everything, that reality is the most disturbing part of being sick.

I'm going to continue to do all I can to remain healthy and vibrant. My goal is to live to be 107 – writing books until the day I die. I love what I do. When I can no longer do it, or do it well, I'm ready to go.

I have readers that assure me bad health is just part of aging. I could not disagree more. I believe bad health is almost always the result of choices we make. Please note that I said *almost always*. I am aware there are circumstances beyond our control that can ruin our health, but I believe the vast number of illnesses are the result of our lifestyle. Which means we can change our health by changing our lifestyles.

Think about this...
Staying healthy is hard.
Being sick is hard.
It's up to you to choose.

I'll choose the hard work it takes to stay healthy any day!

*****

I released *Looking To The Future* in September 2017, as promised, but the effort cost me. I spent another two months in bed before I could muster enough brain cells to turn my attention to #13, *Horizons Unfolding*.

Writing these books have led me down so many roads I never could have envisioned. I knew a tiny amount about child labor in America, but nothing could have prepared me for what I discovered as I did the research for *Horizons Unfolding*. I found myself buying book after book to teach me everything I needed to know to do the subject justice.

The research also revealed that ultimately, it was women who changed things in our country for child laborers. Women who made sure children would get an education, rather than just be buried in the bowels of American factories because of corporate greed.

The vast majority of my readers love the Bregdan Women (Carrie, Rose, Aunt Abby, Janie and the rest). But then there are those who write me to tell me they are completely unrealistic, not gritty enough, and not human enough. I'm sure there are those who think the same thing about the men, but my focus today will be on the women.

Hmmm... I've told you already that I'm not bothered or offended by negative comments or reviews. I learned a long time ago that *no* writer writes for everyone. No one can write for everyone's style or taste. I'm good with that, knowing that *my* audience is growing on a daily basis.

I appreciate the negative comments because they give me a lot to think about, and they provide the springboard for discussions of why I write the way I do. That is certainly happening today...

I've thought so much about the Bregdan Women.

First... I have created the Bregdan Women to be the type of woman I long to be. I want to live my life as a free-spirited, independent woman with a heart full of compassion and love for others. I want to always strive to be learning and growing, constantly thinking and living outside the box so that I can make my world a better place.

Second...I believe *most* women want to live that way. We really don't have a desire to live life as self-centered, selfish individuals who thrive on flaunting our human weaknesses. Somewhere along the way, I think too many authors have decided readers want to read about these kinds of people because it appeals to their lesser nature, or because it makes them feel better because at least they're not *that* bad. While there may be some truth to that, my exploding number of readers tells me the Bregdan Women are supporting who they long to be, and to become.

How I write about women (and people in general) is a huge responsibility to me. Only a tiny, tiny percent of the population writes books, yet we have such a massive impact on how society perceives the world, and how individuals perceive how they should live their lives. That is not something to take lightly; rather, it is a huge responsibility that should be handled with great care.

My passion is to empower women (and all people) to live their best lives. To live lives full of love, compassion, and the power to make a difference with every breath and with every decision. I choose to do that through historical fiction - by bringing to life the women who have helped make our world a better place.

The world we live in - well, the better part of it - has been created by women just like the Bregdan Women. It has NOT been created by self-centered hard individuals.

Brave, caring, compassionate women helped create this country.

Brave, caring, compassionate women led the way in the Abolition movement to free the slaves.

Brave, caring, compassionate women opened the way for women's right to vote.

Brave, caring, compassionate women rebuilt a country after millions of its men had been killed or wounded (in more than one war).

Brave, caring, compassionate women are still working in every facet of life - all over the world - to make the world a better place.

Brave, caring, compassionate women are struggling for a girl's right to education in Afghanistan, Pakistan, and other countries all over the world.

Brave, caring, compassionate women are fighting to bring equality to all people.

I could fill pages of all the things brave, caring, compassionate women are doing, but I think you get the idea.

I want you to think about the women in *your* life. How many of them wake up every day and decide they're going to be self-centered, egotistical women out only for themselves? How many of them flaunt their weaknesses and seem to thrive on them? Oh, *all* of us struggle with our weaknesses and with the things we don't like about ourselves, but do most of the women you know seem to want to hold onto them and thrive off them?

I don't believe so.

Every woman I know *wants* to be a better person. They *want* to live their lives with courage, compassion and love. They *want* to know their life matters, and that because they have lived the world is a better place. They *want* the truth of The Bregdan Principle to resonate through their lives.

That is the woman I write for! I long to empower every woman to be the person they truly want to be. I want every reader to be inspired by Carrie, Rose, Aunt Abby, Janie, Marietta, June, Annie, Opal, and all the rest...

They are women, just like all the women alive today, who simply want to be the best woman they can be. I know writing about them inspires me every single day to be the best woman *I* can be!

*****

I wrote a Blog one day that requested my readers send me their thoughts on what being a Bregdan Woman is all about, and how the Bregdan Women have inspired them. I can only share a tiny amount of them, but I've kept every single one.

*****

I relate to Rose as a BREGDAN woman. Rose values education and she has worked so hard and so long, and it was exciting to read that she finally got her college degree. I was born the third child of a middle-class working family. While I had two older brothers, I was the oldest daughter and was expected to watch the other four younger children and help around the house. I LOVED to read and wherever I went I had my "nose in a book" as my mother used to say.

Reading took me away from all of the "chores" I had to help with. I also LOVED school and learning any new thing. I tried never to miss a day of school. I remember when I was getting ready to enter high school and wanting to take the "college path" classes that my parents told me they could not afford to send me to college and that I would be better off taking business classes, becoming a secretary and getting married. I was so shocked that I sat down in the chair in our living room and felt like I had the life knocked out of me.

I put my head down and started to cry but all the while I was telling myself that I WOULD go to COLLEGE and that I would GRADUATE and I would do it if it took me all of my life. I was so naive that I had no idea at the time that I could have gone to a school counselor and asked for help with student loans. My parents had told me NO and until I was no longer with them, I had to listen to what they said.

The BREGDAN woman that I am, I did take business classes and I took accounting. I also took typing and shorthand, and I got married very young.

The knowledge from these classes are what allowed me to put myself thru college five years after I graduated from high school. It took me eight years to get my bachelor's degree and I worked and paid for it as I went along. I always had two jobs and went to school. I valued education and could not understand those students who did not show up to class. Of course, since I was paying for my classes, I wanted to get my money's worth! At age 40, I decided that I wanted to get my Master's degree, so again I went back to school and in three years, obtained that degree.

Like Rose, I never quit and I kept moving forward and even though it took longer than most people, I knew I was going to get the education that I wanted. Rose is such an amazing woman and I am excited to continue reading about what she accomplishes back in Virginia. I am still reading and as long as I am able will continue to learn new things because a BREGDAN woman never gives up, she stays strong, and she is educated.

*****

I am a Bredgan Woman but I didn't get there on my own! For the first 16 years of marriage I was a stay-at-home Mom and mother of 5 children. I took a job as a nursing assistant to help supplement our income as my husband was laid off from his job and was attempting to start his own business.

A year later I was encouraged to further my education in nursing, however we didn't have the financial stability to take out a loan for my schooling. I was very disappointed but had told God if that door was not open I would accept that meant He had other plans. He is an on time God!

Several days later at my work I was told they had a grant program. I signed up and little did I know that soon my life would change drastically. The first day of school, my husband was diagnosed with kidney failure. I was ready to quit school but he encouraged me to press on.

I juggled school and worked weekends as my husband could no longer work. I received my LPN license a year later. Hubby was becoming sicker and needed a kidney transplant. My supervisor said I needed to go back to school for my RN degree. She told me that if anything happens to your husband you won't make it on an LPN salary. Again, God provided the finances.

My dreams of long ago were becoming reality. It was very hard work, as again I juggled school during the day, tending to a sick husband on dialysis and kids in the evening, sleeping 4 hours and going to work 8 hours. Only with the strength of God did I become that Bredgan Woman.

You see, to me a Bredgan woman pursues her passion in life. With a support system to lift her up and encourage her she can accomplish that which she feels she is called to do. She doesn't quit in the face of adversity. She may doubt her decisions but the strong survive. It may mean a change of plans or putting them on hold for a spell, but she will move forward, never looking back. She is always looking for an opportunity to add experience or skills to accomplish her goal.

Not only did I become a Registered Nurse; I became a Master of Dental Science, and then a Director of Nursing, adding to that, a Medical Records Director. I had a goal to advance the quality of life and the care of the elderly. I love how you created many Bredgan Women in your series. It is these Bredgan Women that draws me again and again to continue following them on their journeys through life. I can't wait to see what's in store for each of them in the future. Life is not about the destiny, it's about the journey.

*****

I have been thinking about your questions for the last two days because I wanted to give a thoughtful response, and because your books really do provide lessons which I have taken to heart.

What does it mean to YOU to be a Bregdan Woman?

It means to me that I need to strive to achieve the dreams I have, no matter how big or how small. My dreams may change over the years or they may be completely new and different, but they are mine and I have a right to have them whether other people like them or not. It does not mean you can be rude about your desires, but it does mean that it is okay to be who you are and do what you dream. It also means to me that there is room in your heart for fear and doubt, but you cannot let it take over too much space.

How would you define a Bregdan Woman?

I would define a Bregdan Woman as one that is comfortable with who she is and shares herself with others in whatever capacity she can. I have pressured myself for a long time to be more outgoing, and little by little I am learning to let go of that and be who I am and give what I can. Strength is not defined in a strictly physical capacity, but in the everyday mental battles we all wage.

What characteristics does a Bregdan Woman have?

Kindness, forgiveness, compassion, strength of heart, and willingness to change. I am sure there are many more

Why do you love the Bregdan Women?

They give me the courage to change how I operate with the people around me, to accept whole people with faults and all, and inspire me to dream and be patient with my life as not all dreams need to be carried out today.

I think while your books are very eye-opening (for past events which also mirror current ones), they are also very inspiring.

*****

A reader wrote this poem for her daughter, telling her they were both Bregdan Women...

My strength comes from someplace within
Maybe an ancestor I never knew
Who gave me my strength to follow through
Darkest days of life
I stand tall, hold my head high, take the challenge
My strength comes from someplace within
Maybe an ancestor I never knew
It is passed on to you
The strength to follow through
To stand tall, hold your head high take the challenge
That comes to you.

*****

One more...

When I think of the Bregdan woman I imagine her as a Wagon wheel.   The spokes are all her wonderful characteristics.

One is her quest for knowledge which increases her capability to understand and analyze the situations she encounters.

Another spoke is her self-confidence to be HERSELF, even if it is not conforming to the acceptance of society.

The third spoke would be her Tenacity to keep working hard to achieve her goal.

The fourth spoke would be her love, caring and kindness to her family, friends, and fellow humans.

One of the other spokes would be the relationships and special bond with her other female comrades. This Special sisterhood (old Sarah, Rose, Abby etc.) gives her more confidence and additional strength, especially when the challenges of life become too difficult to handle alone. Every action will have a reaction, whether it is good or bad.

All these spokes go into the hub of the wheel. As the wheel turns the spokes move around, mixing all these wonderful traits into the hub.

I believe the Bregdan woman is the Hub or center.

*****

I loved every single response!

I can't finish this book without telling you about one of the most amazing women I've ever known – a true Bregdan Woman. I wrote this about her years ago...

<u>BETH TIELKE</u>

O'Neill, Nebraska is a small town on the wind-swept plains. The residents are good, honest and hard-working. One, however, stands out...

Beth Tielke is/was a role-model and mentor to me, refining my meaning of the word success. When I met the 72-year-old mother of 7, and grandmother of 40 (last count) in 2000, I immediately fell in love with her, and knew I wanted to be like her. Though we lived more than a thousand miles apart I was fortunate to develop a very close relationship with her.

Early on, she claimed me as her eighth child. She was an adopted mother to me in every sense of the word. I was lucky enough to have a mother by birth, and a mother by choice.

Beth worked hard for many years on her family's dairy farm, battling cold and heat alongside her husband, Bill. She raised her 7 children; then aware there was not enough money to send them to college, she plunged into the business world – owning a store, several restaurants, and a sandwich business – learning as she went. Several of the businesses are still running, only now her children operate them.

At 72, Beth had earned the right to sit back and enjoy life. Did she? Well, she enjoyed life immensely, but she certainly didn't sit *back*. This dynamo of a woman traded in her brick-and-mortar businesses for 3 different home-based businesses. The phone never stopped ringing, and her home was full of friends, clients and family – that is when she wasn't roaming all over Nebraska spreading love to as many people as she could!

All of these things are wonderful, but they are not what makes Beth Tielke such an amazing person to me. To understand that you have to know about Share Our Dream.

Beth is only happy when she's giving –when she is making a difference in someone's life. She understands that in order for a gift to make a difference it doesn't have to be large – it just has to be given from the heart, to the right person, in the right way.

Share Our Dream is about spreading a little bit of sunshine to as many people as she can. It's about allowing other people to give small gifts – all they are able – so they can know the joy of giving.

It's about an elderly woman who just lost her husband, crying with joy when she received a Share Our Dream card with a certificate for a piece of pie from a local restaurant.

It's about a little boy who realized someone cared when he got a certificate for a free ice cream cone from the local ice cream parlor.

It's about local businesses giving coupons for a cookie a week for Beth to give away to someone who needs a little drop of sunshine.

It's about a local florist donating one arrangement a month to bring joy to someone's life.

It's about a local resident with very little money who has committed to providing a coupon for one ice cream cone a week – making a difference with what little she has.

It's about helping a 14-year-old pianist pay to have his first CD cut, then using a portion of the proceeds to give more gifts.

It's about the Share Our Dream website where local people had the joy of reading the stories of their lives, and of their friends and neighbors.

The stories go on and on.... Since Beth started Share Our Dream (paying for most of the costs from her own pocket) over 1600 people have benefited in some way.

It's about neighbors and friends feeling special and helping others feel special.

It's about teaching all of us how to live. It's about realizing success is not just about what we have, it's more about what we can give. It's about realizing that while we may not be able to "Out give the Universe," it certainly is fun to try.

One of my goals in life is to be like Beth Tielke as I grow older – trying as hard as I can to emulate her *right now*.

Beth passed away when I was writing *Shifted By The Winds* – never slowing down until cancer claimed her very quickly at the age of 83. I keep a picture of her on my desk, but her true self is imprinted on my heart, and deeply engraved in my mind. I miss her every single day, but I am so very grateful I had her in my life for as long as I did.

I flew to Nebraska to be with her for part of her final weeks when I was working on *Shifted By The Winds.* I would sit with her during the day, and then go back to my hotel to write at night. One of the last things I did was to read *Shifted By The Winds* out loud to her. When I caught up with where I was, she would impatiently wait for me to write more pages so I could come and read them. She boasted to everyone who walked into her hospital room that her daughter was an *author.* We didn't finish the book together, but I can feel her cheering me on every single day.

She was a true BREGDAN WOMAN!

She taught me so much about the joy of selfless giving.

All of us have the ability to make a difference – no matter how much money we do, or do NOT, have. Giving comes from the heart. All it takes is creativity and sensitivity to those around you.

*****

There's another Bregdan Woman you should know about... I have many readers who meet the definition of *Golden Agers.* In my opinion, that means you have moved into the Golden years that give you the freedom to live your life with the wisdom of all the years that have gone before. Unfortunately, I've heard from many of you who believe it means the best years of your life are behind you. You believe you don't have anything else to look forward to.

I couldn't disagree more. I've always believed it, but when I met Ilona I believed it even more.

There are some people you meet that your soul instantly connects with.

That was my experience today when I walked into the home of a good friend to meet her "adopted mom". I was immediately drawn to the woman who rose from her chair with a welcoming smile and outstretched arms.

Vibrant... alive... radiant... and 87 years young.

Yep. 87 years.

She traveled from southern California to visit my friend Meredith. I had been invited to meet her before, but something always conflicted.

She left for the airport at noon that day. I arrived at 10:45. Within one hour I had been blown away, and my heart had been captured.

I was also inspired...

As we shared stories I learned of her childhood years in Holland during the Nazi Occupation of World War II. To show solidarity with her Jewish friends banished to a ghetto, she (along with a dozen friends) arrived at school with large yellow stars pinned to their clothing. They were expelled for their efforts to show justice and challenge a system they innately knew was completely wrong.

She spent over 50 years as a psychotherapist - touching thousands of lives with her unique brand of compassion, joy and gratitude. She touched me in just the hour we had together!

I have not met many women in their 80's that made me think, *I want to be just like her when I'm that age.* There are not that many that compel me to want to emulate them...

Ilona did.

She spoke a little of her childhood, but followed it with a brilliant smile as she said that *she had no need to live in the past because her NOW is so spectacular. At 87...*

After fifty years of being a psychotherapist, she finally retired at age eighty. Well... retired from *that* profession.

I will never forget the look on her face when she said, "When I retired, I didn't just want to dabble in a hobby. I was determined to create a new career because I have so many years left!"

Her new career? She is a professional artist. I should add she is fabulous! Her realistic art makes me feel I am right there in the beautiful scenery she depicts. Some of her art now hangs on my wall. And then add in her modern art. WOW! I was astounded when I realized just how talented this vibrant 87 year old is.

The purpose of telling you about Ilona is simply to inspire you to live your best life as long as you have life in you. I see so many older people who have simply given up – they're passing their days without a purpose... without goals... without dreams...

They wonder why their life is empty and boring. The answer is simple - they quit dreaming.

Sure, you might not be a fabulous painter, but I firmly believe that if you're still breathing, you should still be dreaming, and you should still live every day with a purpose that is bigger than you.

It's what gives you the joy of living.

It's what keeps you from living in the past, because the NOW is so amazing.

It's what keeps you vibrant and alive.

And... it's never too late (or early) to start. You might be a thirty year old who has given up on your dreams and you don't think you will ever have an amazing life. You might be a 70 year old who has decided the best part of your life is over, and now it's just time to exist until you die. Or an 80 year old... or a 90 year old...

I want to be just like Ilona who said *she had no need to live in the past because her NOW is so spectacular.*

What about YOU?

*****

I hear from a huge number of women who say my books and Blogs have empowered them to become Bregdan Women, and then they ask if there is more – more to keep them moving forward to their goal of becoming, and staying, Bregdan Women.

Remember me telling you about the 800+ stories written over the years for Someone Believes In You? I decided to do something more with them.

I created *The Bregdan Woman Journal!*

This is the description you'll find on Amazon. I'm going to share them with you here because I am 100% convinced of their power to change lives!

My shelves are full of Journals I have kept over the years. I treasure them for the memories, but mostly I treasure them because writing down my thoughts, hopes, fears, accomplishments and failures, helped me become the woman I am today.

A BREGDAN WOMAN.

I strive every day to become more of the woman I desire to be. So many of you have asked me for help in becoming the woman you truly want to be. This is the best gift I could possibly give you…

The **BREGDAN WOMAN Journal** is like none you have ever seen. First, it needs to be big enough to really allow you to journal your life – so it's 500+ pages!

Each 8 1/2 X 11 page is lined and ready for you.

You have 16 different covers to choose from. They are all right here on the Series page.

But that is just the beginning... It doesn't matter what day of the year you start your journal – it will be with you for 365 days – until you're ready for your next one.

A Journal becomes even more of a treasure when it becomes even more than a Journal. *The Bregdan Woman Journals are so much more than a Journal.*

You'll find **Bregdan Woman Stories** - amazing people who will make you realize you can do ANYTHING with your life. (52 stories for every week of the year)

Every single day you'll get a **Bregdan Woman Quote**.

You'll be challenged with 100+ **Bregdan Woman Actions** for how you can make a difference with your life.

And every day you'll have a place to write down your feelings, thoughts, challenges, hurts, disappointments, successes, celebrations, relationships, actions, experiences, adventures – all the things your life is made of.

It will empower you to move beyond your fears and doubts – becoming a BREGDAN WOMAN who can live the life you dream of.

The Bregdan Woman Journals will become irreplaceable treasures as you look back on your life!

A few of the cover options:

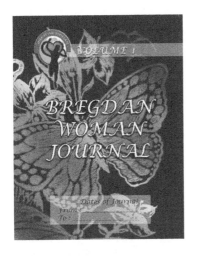

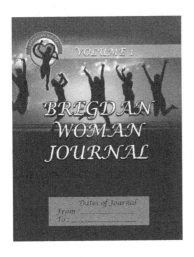

Cinnamon Rolls

Mix in salt and baking powder. Add in ½ cup sugar, buttermilk, whole milk, melted butter, vanilla extract, and eggs. Gradually mix in the flour a little at a time, using just enough so that the dough pulls from the sides of the bowl. It will be slightly sticky but shouldn't stick to a clean fingertip. Once dough has formed place the ball of dough into a large, lightly greased bowl. Cover.

Let sit until the dough is double. Gently punch the dough down a few times to release the air. Sprinkle a work surface lightly with flour and turn dough onto floured surface.

Knead the dough gently a couple of times and then pat the dough into a rectangle that is about ¼ inch thick. Brush the dough with half of the melted butter.

In a small bowl mix, together brown sugar & cinnamon. Sprinkle on half the brown sugar mixture. Brush again with butter and finish with remaining brown sugar mixture. Starting from the

Cinnamon Rolls

end furthest from you, begin tightly rolling up the dough.
Place the roll seam-side down, and carefully slice
the roll into 12 pieces. Place the rolls in a greased baking pan with sides
touching. Cover and let rise. Bake in medium oven until sides of
cinnamon rolls are lightly golden. When cinnamon rolls come
out of the oven, let cool and then. spread on a thinned sugar
and water glaze.

DOUGH MIXTURE: ½ cup sugar

⅛ cup buttermilk or whole milk (room temperature)

8 tablespoons butter, melted 1 tablespoon vanilla 2 eggs, slightly beaten

1 teaspoon salt   1 teaspoon baking powder

4 cups flour, sifted (may need more or less)

FILLING MIXTURE

1 cup brown sugar. 1 tablespoon cinnamon. ½ cup butter, melted

Chapter Eighteen

Now that all my beloved readers have enabled me to make more money than I could have envisioned, the question becomes, *What do I do with it?*

Part of that answer was driven home to me on top of a lighthouse in Denmark. I wrote this story the same night I had the experience.

*****

Yesterday I stood on the top of the Rubjerg Knude Lighthouse perched on the limestone cliffs of Lokken, Denmark, gazing down at a churning, roaring ocean that glimmered emerald green far below me. Frothy white icing danced on the waves moments before they exploded against the rocks, but it was when I looked down and around that I truly comprehended the force of nature – the force of the power that creates and changes.

Climbing up and over the sand dunes surrounding the lighthouse was quite a challenge as we leaned into the 30 – 45 mph winds howling from the North. A beige curtain shimmered across the dunes as the wind picked up the fine particles of sand, turning them into miniscule missiles that battered our faces and worked their way into our hair, noses, mouth and ears. We leaned into the wind and trudged upward, keeping our eyes on the lighthouse that pulled us forward.

The same lighthouse, now barren of a flashing beam, once warned boats to stay far away from the rocky shoals. Its proud stone tower now called us forth – challenging us to brave the high winds and biting sands to scale its heights.

After the required exclamations and picture taking, my soul told me I was there for another purpose. I pulled my hood over my head to shelter it from the worst of the winds, and then leaned in to the call.

I watched, mesmerized, as the wind picked up the dune, reshaping it before my very eyes as the ocean roared below.

And I heard the still voice I recognize so well...

The world changes at this same pace every single day – every single moment. The force of my power will never leave things the same – never leave things to rot in stagnation and mediocrity. Some change is wrought by human choices and decisions; many good, many bad.

Change... always change.

Power that shifts... moves... sculpts... realigns... calls to attention... demands action.

This very same lighthouse that used to stand proudly on the cliffs, its light burning for miles, was once buried beneath the dunes that swept in on sand deposited from around the world – flying thousands of miles, carried on the wind. No match for its power, humans retreated, giving up the lighthouse, the church, and much of the village surrounding it.

And then, hundreds of years later, the very same wind moved the dunes it had so ruthlessly deposited. The dune, shifted by the power of the wind, simply departed, leaving the lighthouse to stand proudly on the cliffs once again. Yet not the same...

The lighthouse once stood 600 feet from the chalky limestone cliffs. The roaring waves of the ocean have carved those cliffs. It has claimed them for its own, crumbling them with its mighty onslaught. Today, the lighthouse stands a mere fifteen to twenty feet from the edge of the cliffs – cliffs that are being devoured every year.

In just a few years, the lighthouse will be no more. It will either be crumbled into the sea, claimed by the same force devouring the cliffs, or humans will move it to retain the history. But no matter...

Change... always change.

Power that shifts... moves... sculpts... realigns... calls to attention... demands action.

At first, I thought the message was only about the force of change in my own life. The winds have blown so powerfully in the last year – sculpting... shifting... changing. Nothing ever remains the same. As much as I love the reality of change, it can also be challenging and painful as you lean into the powerful wind blowing biting sand into your face.

I laughed as I stood tall on the lighthouse, and then threw my arms wide to embrace the change and express utter gratitude for the biting sands that had deposited me at a new place in my life.

And then... I saw more.

The voice spoke again...

As I watched the wind roar over the dunes, as the colors were muted by the veil of beige sand, I saw more. I realized each grain of sand represented a life – a person struggling to find their way in the world as they are picked up by the winds of change.

And then I saw what I believe I was brought there to see... to understand.

I saw each grain of sand as just one of the people who will soon comprise Millions For Positive Change.

Millions of people determined to take action each day to make the world a better place – to pour love and kindness into the world around them.

Millions of people shifting the world with the power of their actions.

Change... always change.

Power that shifts... moves... sculpts... realigns... calls to attention... demands action.

A simple call to action.

A simple action.

Millions of tiny grains of sand have reshaped the reality of the limestone cliffs in Denmark.

Millions For Positive Change... millions of people will reshape the reality of our world.

They will shift people's perceptions all around the planet.

They will move barriers that keep people in poverty and misery.

They will sculpt people's minds and beliefs about how the world can really be.

They will realign the paradigms that hold people back.

They will call to attention the possibility of change.

And they will demand action – from themselves, and from everyone around them – knowing that tiny actions performed by MILLIONS truly will make our world a better place.

I left the lighthouse a different person. Just as the mighty winds of change during this last year have sculpted a new reality in my own life, the same mighty wind continues to roar in my life – demanding me to take action, to move forward, to bring Millions For Positive Change to reality.

I'm leaning in.

I'm throwing my arms wide to embrace the change – and I am expressing utter gratitude for the biting sands that have deposited me at a new place in my life.

*****

What is Millions For Positive Change?

It is the charitable division of Bregdan Publishing.

This is the place I will pour my money in the future - inspiring millions of acts of giving all around the world. Every time you buy a book, I put a % of it into my dream. I will never keep a penny that is generated within Millions For Positive Change, and I will never ask anyone for money. It will all go back to mobilize more people to make a difference.

I will use a combination of a Blog and every aspect of Social Media to reach millions around the world in every country – giving them the World Changer Series of books I began writing more than a decade ago.

The Blog will be a regular source of ongoing inspiration and stories – compelling people to make a difference in their everyday lives. The Social Media posts will serve the same purpose.

I ask people all the time if they want to know their life is serving a purpose – that it makes a difference in the world. I've never had anyone tell me no, but almost everyone responds with, "Yes, but I don't know what to do, and I don't have a lot of money."

From that ongoing statement, I began to create the World Changer Series – providing more than 1000 ideas of how to make a difference with your life. Many people have helped me along the way. The books are ready – now I am going to use Social Media to inspire and mobilize millions to use them!

World Changer Series - The E-books will always be FREE downloads from the Blog site. If people want them through Amazon Kindle or Print, then 100% of profits will go to projects, and the price will be kept as low as possible. I simply want these books to be in people's hands.

The series includes:
*   101 Ways You Can Change The World
*   101 Ways Women Can Change The World
*   101 Ways Youth Can Change The World
*   101 Ways Your Church Can Change The World
*   101 Ways Your School Can Change The World
*   101 Ways to Help Planet Earth
*   101 Ways to Help Animals
*   101 Ways Your Business Can Change The World

I envision the Blog and Social Media pages being done in every language (or at least a whole lot!) so we can mobilize people all over the world.

After 10 years of dreaming, I have now entered the season of *doing*. It will be fun to see how this develops across the world!

Thank you to all my readers who are making this possible. I'll keep writing books so that I can keep reaching more and more people to create a Tidal Wave of Goodness in the world!

Join us on Facebook by going to www.MillionsForPositiveChange.com. That's where you will find every book, and also connect with others around the world who are committed to making a difference. It really is the beginning of a work in progress, but I wanted all my readers to know about it first because it's YOU that has made it possible!

*****

I've learned about giving back in so many fascinating ways. About thirty years ago, while living in Southern California, I had a very interesting experience - one that totally freaked me out at first....

I had a fire pit on my back patio, but no money for wood, so when I saw an ad in a local newspaper for free firewood, I called immediately. A gentleman answered the phone. I told him I was responding to his ad, and then there was a long pause. Just as I was wondering if we had lost the connection he said, "You know, I like your voice. You can have my wood." I should have realized then that I was walking into an odd situation, but I was too excited about getting the wood to heed any internal cautions. I just jumped in my truck and started driving!

I noticed two things right away. One, I was in a *very* upscale, expensive community full of million dollar homes (and that was more than thirty years ago!). Two, the long driveway was lined with thousands of black plastic flower pots full of plants - some that looked rather pathetic. Okay, so it was a little odd, but I was still just fixated on my wood, and now my curiosity was aroused even more.

I drove up, knocked on the door, and was met by a silver-haired, distinguished looking couple. I felt relieved... until I looked over their shoulder. Their elegant home was FULL of stuff. I mean FULL. There was a small aisle through the middle of the room, and just enough area around the sofa and chairs to sit down. Now, before you think hoarding, you have to realize I was looking at antiques, fabulous statues, and amazing art.

Turns out I was looking at the results of their worldwide travel before retirement. *Both* of them were retired UCLA professors. I could feel myself relaxing more. They might be odd, but surely they weren't dangerous. *Until...*

"How much do you think we spent on groceries this year?"

I stared at David (the husband) when he asked me the question out of the blue. "Excuse me?"

Instead of answering right away, he stared at me hard for several long moments, and then said, "I like you."

At this point, I was back to being nervous. "Ummm... thank you," I murmured, wondering if now would be a good time to make an exit.

He looked at me hard for another few moments, glanced at his wife, and then looked back at me. "We *really* like you."

I didn't know how to respond, but I was seriously doubting this was a good thing, and I was plotting how fast I could escape through the mountains of priceless antiques. In the midst of my thoughts, he repeated his earlier question...

"So, Ginny, how much do you think we spent on groceries this year?"

What kind of question was *that*? By then, I was afraid if I didn't answer correctly, they might not like me as much, and I might not ever get out of the house. My mind raced as I thought of potential answers. If they were asking me, it was probably because it was a low amount. It was June, so I was working with six months. I'd gotten a glimpse of their backyard when I came in the house, and knew they didn't have a garden - just an empty swimming pool - and none of the millions of black flower pots seemed to hold produce (just flowers). As they stared at me, my brain raced with numbers. They waited patiently for an answer.

"Uhhhh.. $1200?" I ventured. It seemed like a pretty low amount to me. I mean, who can eat off $200 a month?

Both of them threw back their heads, and broke into laughter. I was simply relieved they weren't angry so I joined in the laughter. Until David said...

"Yes, we *really* like you."

Were they going to lock me in a closet and never let me go? I was strong and athletic, so I was fairly confident I could overpower two old people, but still...

Sarah (the wife), prompted by a nod from her husband, picked up a tiny, little spiral notebook sitting on a table in the only clear space in sight, and handed it to me. I just looked at it.

Lettuce	$1.00
Milk	$2.39
Chicken	$5.28
Total:	**$8.67**

"What is this?" I finally asked.

David laughed heartily. "This is what we spent on groceries so far this year."

I glanced back at the list, and then looked at them. They both seemed to be in good health - actually, excellent health, with eyes that gleamed with life. My curiosity grew, especially since I was struggling to make ends meet. "How?"

Sarah jumped up. "We want to show you something." She began to walk toward the kitchen.

Go deeper into the bowels of the house? What if I never came out? Would anyone ever find me? I scolded myself for being ridiculous (I was young and reckless), and followed them. Mary walked over to their refrigerator and opened it. I gaped as I peered at shelves *stuffed* with every food you could imagine.

That did it... I was in the home of thieves. That's probably where the plants came from... and the antiques... and...

What was I going to do? How could I turn in two silver-haired UCLA professors?

They laughed at the expression on my face, and then Sarah grabbed my hand and pulled me into another room. There was another refrigerator, and a freezer. I knew what to expect when she opened the doors, but I still couldn't help being shocked by the amount of food stuffed into both of them.

David finally took pity on me. "We are bin rats, Ginny."

I could tell by the tone of his voice that he was trying to make me feel better, but his words were pinging around in a brain emptied by shock. What was a *bin rat*? I searched for words, because I was still certain I didn't want to offend these people. What would happen if they stopped liking me? "Excuse me?" I finally managed.

"I think we've scared her, David," Sarah said gently, and then led me over to the dining room table to explain.

My two silver-haired college professors were self-acclaimed dumpster divers. Every night they made the round of every grocery store dumpster they could find. They loaded up all the food they could - making several trips a night - and then brought it home. That's when the real work started. They sorted through the food, and then distributed it to homeless shelters and Food Banks in the Los Angeles area. The food stuffed into their refrigerators and freezers was headed to a shelter that afternoon. They had delayed their delivery because David *liked* my voice and wanted me to have the firewood. Once they decided they *really* liked me, they decided to trust me with their secret.

The black pots lining the driveway were castoffs from local nurseries. Sarah carted them home, nursed them back to health, and then gave them away.

What a relief to realize I wasn't trapped with thieves. I was being welcomed by *angels* - two amazing human beings who weren't content to just see a problem, they were determined to be part of the solution.

It got better... I was working with high school students at the time. One of them, a young man named Stephen, was living with me. He came from a 2 bedroom home housing 14 people. He had never had a room... never had a bed... and he didn't eat enough. Until he moved in with me. But the other thirteen people...

I told David and Sarah about his family. When I left that day my truck was loaded with free firewood and... a case of orange juice, a garbage bag full of loaves of bread, and boxes full of canned vegetables, fresh produce, whole chickens, packs of hamburger, and more. I took them straight to Steven's family. Their delight and gratitude almost matched mine.

Every week, for the remaining eighteen months I lived there, I spent a day with David and Sarah - ending each day with a trip to Stephen's home with all the groceries they needed. When I had to move, David took over making the delivery trips.

I truly believe David and Sarah were angels on earth.

After many moves, I lost touch with them, but the extraordinary beauty of two people who put their beliefs into action has never lost its impact on me.

I ask myself every day what actions I'm going to take to support my beliefs. I'm going to ask you the same questions.

Do you believe that people in America shouldn't be hungry? ***What are you going to do about it?***

Do you believe people in your neighborhood shouldn't be lonely? ***What are you going to do about it?***

Do you believe America shouldn't be dirty? **What are you going to do about it?**

Do you believe...?

Get the idea?

Your beliefs have no value - unless you take *action* to change the things you believe should be better. Ask yourself the question; *What am I going to do about it?*

*****

If you're thinking that what I'm suggesting is not as simple as it sounds, I have one more story to share before I answer the question still burning in your mind...

HEADING WEST

Many years ago a movement swept through America. The call went out to all who had the courage and vision to "Head West." What a picture was drawn for them... *The West is where you want to be. There is land for everyone - for the taking!*

Beautiful. Fertile. Opportunity for everyone. Don't miss your opportunity to be one of the first to stake your claim!

The call went out and hordes signed up to join the wagon trains pulling out of Independence, Missouri. As the pioneers bought supplies and lined up their wagons, their eyes shone with the excitement of what would be waiting at the end of the trail. I think it fair to say not one of them had a real understanding of what lay between Missouri and the far west they envisioned in their dreams.

Can't you hear the conversation...?

"Why, honey," one confident husband says to his rather nervous wife, "there isn't going to be anything to this. We've got a nice, sturdy wagon. We're all together, and we have plenty of food. We're just going to roll along the trail for a while and soon we'll have everything we've dreamed of. Just think of it!"

I don't know how long before the starry looks faded from their eyes – somewhere between broken wagon wheels and Indian attacks. Maybe it was the weevils in the flour, or the snowstorm that left them stranded in the mountains for months. Perhaps it was losing a child to illness because there weren't enough medical supplies, or simply the fatigue that came from fighting dust, heat and long days of the grueling cruelness of the trail.

Every pioneer who started down the trail, if they didn't die, had one of three things happen. Some gave up and turned back. Others decided they couldn't take any more and simply built a house where they stopped. Then there were the others... the ones who made it all the way to the West.

Yes, somewhere along the way the starry look faded from their eyes. . . *faded*. . . to be replaced by determination. Broken wagon wheels; Indian attacks; weevils; snowstorms; death; fatigue; choking dust and long days. They all became daily obstacles to be endured and overcome, but at some point each person who made it simply decided nothing was going to stop them. They had left behind their former lives to go someplace new.

They were going...

*****

What about you? Do you have a dream? Do you have something you've started, but then turned back because it seemed too hard? Or maybe you're still on the trail, wondering which obstacle will be the one to destroy what you've worked so hard for.

Maybe you're looking at the trail, thinking, "No way. Not me. That looks too hard." Yet your heart yearns to go where the trail will take you.

You have a choice to make every single day. You can stay right where you are, or you can go on an adventure to accomplish what you dream of accomplishing. Not going may seem safer, but the truth is that not going will only assure you stay right where you are in your life.

What do you want? Where do you want to go? The only way to get there is to start your journey – then determine to not let anything stop you. You can do it! You can turn your life into one grand adventure after another!

Chapter Nineteen

It's time to answer the questions still burning in your mind. There are two questions that I get almost daily.

Ginny, will The Bregdan Chronicles ever be a movie or a television series?

Ginny, how long will this series last?

These are good questions.

I have been approached a few times about The Bregdan Chronicles being either a movie or a television series. After careful consideration, and quite a bit of going back and forth, I have decided the answer is *No, I'm not willing to do that.*

I've had producers argue that I can make a lot of money from putting them on the screen, but writing these books has never been about money for me so that argument doesn't work.

My main reason for not being willing was best voiced by one of my readers at a Bregdan Gathering in Florida, after he asked me if I would ever consider putting them on the screen. My response was to ask him whether he thought I should.

He paused for several moments, obviously gathering his thoughts, and then said, "I believe putting them on the screen would dilute their power. When I'm reading, I have the privilege of knowing what everyone is thinking; not just the person speaking. I'm let into the inner workings of everyone's minds. But, it's more than that.

When I'm reading, I find myself stopping and thinking about what I've just read. Sometimes it will be thirty minutes before I keep reading because I'm pondering what has already been said. Putting it on the screen would take away that ability."

Well said!

I could not agree more. By now, you know all the reasons I write these books. You understand my passion and see the bigger picture. I know what happens when books get put on the screen.

Facts are changed. Situations are diminished or left out because there isn't enough time. Neither of those scenarios are acceptable to me.

Might the person come along that I would trust to bring the books to life on screen? I don't really believe so, but I'm keeping an open mind to the possibility.

One of the things I've learned in life is never to say never! Though my answer right now is a resounding no, it's not completely inconceivable that I would change my mind.

In the end, all I want is for The Bregdan Chronicles to affect change, inspire people, and teach truth.

I suppose the very best answer to this question is... Time will tell.

*****

Ginny, how long will The Bregdan Chronicles last?

That's a question I'm more than *willing* to answer, but the truth is that I don't *have* an answer.

If you had asked me twenty years ago, the answer would have been that the series would end when the war did. We all know that didn't happen...

A few years ago, I would have told you the series would cease at the end of Reconstruction. I suppose that is still a possibility, but I already want to tell the story of the early 1900's, and also the story of the Civil Rights Movement – with future generations of the Bregdan Family.

I mean, how can I not let Carrie, Rose, Janie and the other women have the joy and satisfaction of casting their first vote in 1919?

How can I bear to not follow Hope, John, Felicia and Amber, little Robert, and the twins as they live their lives through the turbulent years ahead of them?

How can I not communicate the sheer courage it took to fight back in the 1950's and 1960's – with both blacks and whites banding together to start the true course to equality in America?

I've had people write to ask me if I'll just keep The Bregdan Chronicles going – one year at a time – to present times. Hmmm... since I'm not twenty, simply living long enough to do that is probably an impossibility; not to mention that a year gets added to "present times" every single year!

I love writing series because I love *reading* series. When I fall in love with characters, I'm always so sad when a book ends. I don't want them to leave my life and I have so many questions about what comes next for them.

I'm as much in love with the Bregdan Family as all of you are. I don't want to say good-bye to any of them. I'm always going to want to know what happens in their lives as the years unfold.

At some point, they'll have to end, but I honestly can't tell you when that will come. It's going to have to remain a surprise to all of us!

I'm going to keep writing as long as I can write well and give excellence to my readers. I hope I'll know when that is no longer happening. I have favorite authors that I've been reading for years. It always makes me sad when they continue to write, but the books are no longer the quality they were before. Whether it's because their brains are older and tired, or because they simply no longer have the passion they once had, I don't know. What I do know is that I want to quit writing the moment I can no longer do it with passion, or when I can no longer do it with excellence.

My goal is to live and write until I'm 107. I can only hope that is God's idea, too!

Do I want to write about other things? You bet I do! I want to write a series about the Cherokee Trail of Tears. I want to write about German Internment camps during World War I. I already have the beginning of an outline for a series based around the Japanese Internment Camps during World War II.

I want to write suspense novels. I want to write more teen novels, and more children's stories.

Basically, I just want to write.

It's who I am.

I turned my back on my *Gift* for a very long time. I think often of the day I decided I would never write again. It's hard to remember that intense fear because of the overwhelming joy that comes from using my *Gift* every single day.

*****

I am down on the Oregon Coast as I write these last pages. This morning I got up early and took a long walk with my dog as soon as it was light enough to see – rejoicing in the empty beach. As I walked and gazed out at the crashing waves, I relived all I've written about.

I laughed as I thought about all the twisted roads that have led me to this day.

My eyes filled with tears of gratitude as I pondered all the pain and confusion I have walked through to get me to this day.

My heart swelled with awe as I thought about the sheer joy and privilege of living the life I live now.

There are decades more of writing ahead of me. I have no way of knowing the twisted roads, challenges and obstacles that await. I do know, however, that walking into the darkness is always worth it as long as I look to the future!

Thank you for sharing this journey with me!

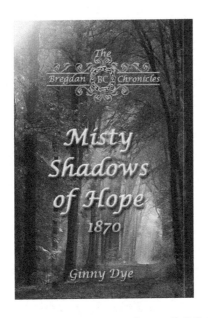

Coming December 2018

Would you be so kind as to leave a Review on Amazon?

Go to www.Amazon.com

Put The Twisted Road Of One Writer, Ginny Dye into the Search Box.

Leave a Review.

I love hearing from my readers!

Thank you!

The Bregdan Chronicles

Storm Clouds Rolling In
1860 – 1861

On To Richmond
1861 – 1862

Spring Will Come
1862 – 1863

Dark Chaos
1863 – 1864

The Long Last Night
1864 – 1865

Carried Forward By Hope
April – December 1865

Glimmers of Change
December – August 1866

Shifted By The Winds
August – December 1866

Always Forward
January – October 1867

Walking Into The Unknown
October 1867 – October 1868

Looking To The Future
October 1868 – June 1869

Horizons Unfolding
November 1869 – March 1870

**Many more coming... Go to
DiscoverTheBregdanChronicles.com to see how
many are available now!**

Other Books by Ginny Dye

Pepper Crest High Series - Teen Fiction
Time For A Second Change
It's Really A Matter of Trust
A Lost & Found Friend
Time For A Change of Heart

Fly To Your Dreams Series – Allegorical Fantasy
Dream Dragon
Born To Fly
Little Heart
The Miracle of Chinese Bamboo

All titles by Ginny Dye
www.BregdanPublishing.com

Join my Email List so you can:

- Receive notice of all new books
- Be a part of my Launch Celebrations. I give away lots of Free gifts!
- Read my weekly BLOG while you're waiting for a new book.
- Be part of The Bregdan Chronicles Family!
- Learn about all the other books I write.

Just go to www.BregdanChronicles.net and fill out the form.